LAKE ISLE

LAKE ISLE

A HENRI CASTANG MYSTERY

NICOLAS FREELING

OPEN ROAD

INTEGRATED MEDIA

NEW YORK

ISBN: 978-1-5040-9224-1

This edition published in 2024 by Open Road Integrated Media, Inc.
180 Maiden Lane
New York, NY 10038
www.openroadmedia.com

LAKE ISLE

CHAPTER ONE

Henri Castang, an officer of police in the criminal brigade of a large city in the provinces, loitered through a Paris street, his hands in his pockets. He was a smallish, closely-knit man and did not slouch: he strolled. He was on his way towards work, a bit before time.

Going down a steepish hill, he had Paris at his feet. He had been a boy here, a student here, and since then ten years away from here had given him objectivity. An image came into his mind.

It is like a stained-glass window, he thought. An old one, medieval even; much broken and patched, and suffering like most old things from a lot of restoring in bad taste. Filthy too, etched and scored by the acids of pollution, and crusted by plain dirt, and perhaps the more brilliant for that.

He had nothing else to think about and his image pleased him. He did not want to think of what lay ahead. The long grey boulevards of Paris are lead, the lead in the window, but between these monotonous streets are irregular splinters of brilliant glass, high in colour. Seen on a sunny morning at the beginning of autumn – it was mid-September – the grimy streets had the patina of an old coin on which the ugliest, lumpiest profile has become dignified, ennobled.

Nobody could become sentimental about the Porte Saint Denis, least of all Castang. An uninteresting piece of meaningless masonry, dividing a slummy street from a slummy faubourg, at the crossing of a vulgar noisy boulevard. Still, it was an ancient highroad, full of history. Full too of horse-butchers, whores, and rotting greengrocery, and he liked it.

He went on down the hill. He was in the Rue d'Aboukir. No lead here; it is one of the most luminous splinters in the huge brilliant rose window.

It is a steep, narrow street where the traffic is always jammed. A double row of tawdry shop-fronts full of cheap textiles. Tourists do not come here, where the wholesale rag trade is crammed in greasy proximity. Darting in and out of every doorway are meagre painted shopgirls, young men too well dressed. In the windows are the sewing-machine girls, nervous and anaemic. On the pavements the elderly businessmen with diamonds and suits beautifully cut talk in mime, and the tough middle-aged businesswomen in complicated bras are giving their bra-less young ladies fierce brief lessons in sales strategy – or the sack.

In the street is Fagin, theatrical against the backdrop of gaudy fairground booths, like the coachmen in *Petrushka*, shaking a long-nailed finger at the dirty boy pushing the handcart. And the mighty army too of the old women of Paris with their bandaged poor legs and old tennis shoes slit to ease bunions, doing everything imaginable that is eccentric and dignified, humble and proud.

Castang was looking at it all, but with only one eye. The other was professionally examining the Levantine boltholes of the Rue d'Alexandrie and the Place de Caire. Somewhere along here a man was in hiding, a man whom Castang had come to Paris to arrest. A dangerous man, who carried a gun. Castang was on his way to meet someone who had found out the hiding-place. The disposition of traffic might come to have importance.

He pattered on, sweating slightly in warm humid air, his jacket buttoned because of his gun in a belt holster. Shoulder holsters sound fancier, but are mortally slow.

The Rue d'Aboukir ends abruptly. Contrasting-coloured glass: the Place des Victoires, a quiet, shabby little square with a discoloured periwigged Louis on a horse. Here policemen hold discreet rendezvous with pigeons; a colleague was waiting for him, a bony man with dust-coloured hair, eating small bits of bread with a sad head held on one side, the pigeons sneering at him. The two men shook hands limply. The Paris cop left his car where it was: in the Rue d'Aboukir a car is no use to anybody. Behind them two more plain-clothes cops strolled up the hill, all marble unconcern. When their superiors turned into a court-yard stuffed with rags they posted themselves and waited quietly. Nobody appeared to be expecting them, but the place was oddly free of people.

The two officers had not met before this morning, but understood each other: a simple sign language guided them. They crossed the court, entered a passage, found themselves with a choice of doors. The first was an office, empty but for dust and paper, the second a dank lavatory. The third, when gently tried, seemed locked. There was a brief mimed debate. There are various ways of dealing with locked doors but the shortest was the best. They examined the door frame, nodded, stepped back, lifted each a leg, and hit the wooden traverse together hard. The door broke, but gave unwillingly: it was barricaded with bales of rags. It delayed them, and the delay meant a fusillade. They couldn't help that, but were glad that baled rags will stop bullets.

Three pistols together made a tremendous noise. The Paris cop, flat on his chest, fired five times without stopping, with no particular idea of hitting anything but hoping to intimidate, to make the man duck, flinch, and give Castang behind a bale time to get over it. He was elastically built and had been a fairish performer on parallel bars: he went over feet first and found himself very close to a man with a gun, close enough to punch him in the stomach with his pistol barrel instead of shooting him. While they were both on the floor the dusty man, now dustier than ever, jumped the bale and hit the gunman under the nose with the heel of his hand. They all got up sneezing, the gunman further handicapped by tears, a smear of blood and handcuffs. Ten shots had been fired and only the rags had been hit. Castang picked up two pistols and gave the man a paper handkerchief.

A kind of nest had been made, furnished and fortified by bales. There were some empty coffee cups and beer bottles, some gnawed sausage and several newspapers. For some days it had been home.

Behind his barricades this man had built illusions of peace. He had been left quiet and had come to believe in safety. He could daydream of green fields and softly flowing water. He could gather strength, concentrate force, hope, plan. To be sure there was very little difference from a cell in the Santé prison. But Castang, sharpened by having just risked his life, saw beyond the rags.

One could dream about peace anywhere. What difference was there that counted between this dusty storeroom and a country cottage, or, come to that, a suburban living-room with a piano? Or a flat with a picture window, looking down onto Paris-by-night, high in a tower? It was the peace which counted. Home can be the framework of one's mattress.

In the yard, the two cops were saying 'Move' to a few morbid onlookers attracted by gunfire. In the building, nobody had budged, which was as planned. They took the handcuffed man by the elbows, neither gently nor roughly, and hurried him down to the car in the square. People looked with mild interest.

A change from waiting for the lights to go green at the top, but it was just another bundle of rags, more or less. There were circles under Castang's arms, from fear as much as humidity. He hitched his shirt off a sticky back, but the others were in the same state.

CHAPTER TWO

At Police Headquarters there was a long boring wait. Most police work is a problem of disposal. Arresting somebody takes a second; the paperwork following takes hours. Castang thought, now, about nothing at all.

Of everyone present the gunman was the least bored. He was a professional: he had been here before and knew all about it. He sat on a wooden chair and watched the coming and going, and fussing with papers, with no curiosity but with a kind of interest. It was a distraction: from now on he would have a lot of time on his hands, and this was as good a way of passing it as any that would be proposed. One plans little recreations in advance, rationing them to fill the hours getting something to eat or to drink, going to the lavatory under escort and cadging a cigarette on the way. Nobody worried him: he might have been on a little island surrounded by peace, with tiny waves lapping round the wooden chair.

Paris was in no hurry. This was a provincial affair, and Paris had disposal problems enough of its own. Nobody bothered about Castang's time, for he was only a provincial police officer. Nobody was even interested in the boring crimes – a matter of thirty-five robberies committed 'with offensive weapons'. All this had to be written down in lifeless formulae. Eventually, this man would be tried down where he, and Castang, came from. Paris was only acting on an interrogatory commission, issued by a provincial magistrate. In a few weeks – there was no hurry – a couple of yawning gendarmes would ferry him down like a parcel in a railway compartment.

Just as Castang and his gunman were both falling into a coma, from sitting on wooden chairs staring at their toes, a judge of instruction was found who unaccountably was not in a coma; who had even read the interrogatory commission, which nobody else had. Who was impatient with disposal problems, and even sensitive about a waste of public funds. Castang was going home, wasn't he? And this man would go too, to be judged? What did a robbery more or less in Paris matter? The judge signed a form turning him over to a different jurisdiction, and Castang had to sign several more. Accepting responsibility for a body, for its possessions, for a shopping-bag with a gun and a few other legal exhibits. Goodbye shower, not to speak of a possible pleasant meal. Police car, grim little railway-police waiting-room, snack-bar sandwich. And a few hours to spend in a train being sorry for himself.

He had to keep awake too. His gunman was overcome by apathy, and they were handcuffed together, but even if prudence was maintained he needed to stay alert.

The gunman had some money, luckily. Professional criminals take care to be provided with money when facing a longish stretch in the jug. Sufficient to the day is the evil thereof, and this is the cops' motto too. The gunman was agreeable to Castang making a small investment for him, in cigarettes, chewing gum and comics. For himself he bought a crossword-puzzle book. All he really wanted was peace, but you couldn't buy that at the bookstall.

He had time in front of him, to think. Of something professional, and not the thirty-five armed robberies, which were boring as hell. To pass a few hours in a train, without losing sight of his Siamese twin, who lacked imagination, but mustn't be allowed to get ideas contrary to the regulations of the railway company.

CHAPTER THREE

The train stood still in a station. Doors finished slamming and the sound of feet hurrying died: there was the familiar complete silence of a train about to start. Softly, another train alongside pulled away, giving one the disconcerting feeling of travelling backwards.

How had the old woman got in to see him? He had no clear idea; attempts had been made to get rid of her: he had made a few himself. Suggestions that she went to see a lawyer, or took the advice of the bank manager or the pastor, or practically anybody, had been turned firmly down. A woman of strong character. As she said herself, she had taken a long time making up her mind but once it was made up she wasn't going to be deflected from her purpose.

He had such a feeling of going backwards that he had to fix his eye on a lamp standard.

His gunman had fallen asleep, boneless and comfortable in the corner. Best thing he could do. Barricaded by Castang's legs; and the door was locked. But he couldn't go to sleep himself.

How, or why, she had made up her mind that the police could be of use to her he had not determined. No crime had been committed. Nor, she said, did she have any knowledge of a crime about to be committed, or planned, or even envisaged. She had funny feelings, and the obstinate notion that the police could be of help, if not of use.

She'd gone to the local commissaire of police, in her local small town. A man of experience, he'd been firm with her. Polite, yes. He didn't laugh, or suggest she consult a psychiatrist. But sorry, Madame; he just could not see any conceivable way he could be concerned. He would like to be of service, but with respect and apologies, his time was much taken up.

Why hadn't Castang said this too? So he had, several times. It hadn't stuck. Admitted, he wasn't doing much at that moment, so he had listened. And in the end, in spite of himself, he had become interested. It wasn't just eccentricity. What was it that had brought an old woman an hour and more in the local train, from a little town called Soulay out in a cul de sac of the province, where Castang had never even been? All the way to the city and trotting through streets to the 'Cité Administrative' to search out the Regional Service of Police Judiciaire, the group of small specialised brigades existing to combat gangsterism or the narcotics traffic. Who wouldn't as a rule be in the least interested in the imaginary terrors of old ladies leading a solitary existence. He asked her. What good, she asked, were cops who would be no more excited than they would be by a stolen bicycle?

How, in heaven's name, had she got in to see Richard? The Commissaire, head of the local PJ, didn't as a rule get his time taken up by old biddies. He was protected by filters. Sometimes, though, the very efficiency of these filters created a backlash. Richard could become irritated at what he called 'isolation by over-zealous subordinates', and instead of staying deskbound cruised about, and listened to unlikely people. Naughtier was his habit of listening for a few sentences and then deciding that an inspector could listen to the rest.

This was one reason why he could not dismiss her out of

hand. She had succeeded in catching Richard's eye. Another reason was that she was no 'old biddy'. A lady!

Not a lady in the sense of 'family', perhaps, and certainly not placed in a position by a couple of generations of prosperous bourgeois commerce. A character in her own right, a woman of education, a person with manners and elegance. He was further impressed to learn that she was a poet. A Lady Poetess. He hadn't known there were any. The name of Sabine Arthur hadn't meant anything to him.

He was relieved to find later that it meant nothing to Richard either. Typically, Richard at once rung up somebody who would know, and did. He had peculiar friends, who knew everything. Irritating the way Richard always wanted to know everything. Still, he was a divisional commissaire. Castang was a 'Principal Officer', a nobody.

Ho, yes, the friend – some pedantic professor, no doubt – knew all about Sabine. Good poet. Not well known, but commanding respect. Individual writer, didn't waste words. Difficult. Lucid though, and had written some memorable lines. She dated from a while back: the professor thought she must be getting on in years. Hadn't published anything in a stretch. Not better-known because, you know, prickly. Not a cosy sort of writer.

Castang hadn't found her really cosy either.

'Dotty?' asked Richard. 'Fairies at the bottom of the garden? Malign influence, just outside the bathroom door?'

'No, no,' replied the professor. 'Feet firmly on the ground.'

'I didn't see anything dotty,' said Castang honestly. 'Uncomfortable, yes.' He knew the professor was not talking nonsense because he himself had been oddly reminded of a picture Vera liked, by Delacroix, quite jaunty and circussy at first. A horse, in a gay blue colour, prancing. There was a tiger riding on its back, looking in some danger of falling off. It was only after looking twice that you saw a sanguinary death, not drawn but in the picture, so that the circus became, abruptly, disconcerting. He thought that Sabine was to be taken seriously.

Richard, who wore glasses for reading, suddenly put them on.

'I was struck by her myself,' he said.

She sat very straight, upright as an elderly dancer. A trim and wiry figure still muscular and vital: the lined grey face was firm, the look direct. Behind spectacles the grey eyes were bright and candid. The mouth was thinned and puckered by age but even now wide and generous. There was nothing weak or foolish.

He had been himself sufficiently struck to tell Vera, that evening. She knew all about tigers and wild horses, and things that weren't quite in the picture.

'No, you aren't talking nonsense,' she said – a strong-minded and sometimes acid woman. 'As long as you say what you see.'

But even while looking at Sabine he had tried to behave in a chill professional way. The thin figure, spare but tough in its navy blue jumper and serge trousers, was compelling. But what is written down can be looked at afterwards by another man, seen through Richard's eyes.

Name Sabine Arthur, age seventy-three. In excellent health, thank God, she added offhand. Was never ill. Never had been. Relict of Vincent Lipschitz, deceased. Profession – none. Housewife, if he liked. Forget about the poetry.

Lived on a small pension, and a small income from rents. Mr Lipschitz had been a municipal employee, which was to say curator of the local museum. The town was historic: there were Roman, Gallic, and other remnants. Much of this was of interest, and Mr Lipschitz had been an authority on the architecture, history, ethnography of this corner of the province.

Castang said he was sorry; he had never been in Soulay. Hadn't it been fortified by Vauban in the seventeenth century? There were walls, weren't there, and a citadel?

Yes it was, and there were, and all preserved, and a historic monument, and Mr Lipschitz had been justly proud of his work in averting destruction, or speculative building. The museum was in the citadel. Soulay was still a smallish town, of fifteen to twenty thousand souls, but had spilt beyond the ramparts. Had grown a lot in recent years.

She lived herself in a village, a few kilometres outside. Even there a lot of new houses had been built.

Very good, Madame. Now, at least, he had some idea. But why now, exactly, had she come to them? What was it she hoped for?

'Help,' said Sabine with simplicity.

'But your local commissaire…'

'He's a man without imagination. I don't mean to imply that he isn't competent; I've no doubt he is. But stolid. I have no tangible ground for complaint, so in his eyes there is no way of registering it.'

'So you came here, thinking that we…?'

'I think nothing, except that petty officials may be of mediocre quality.'

'I'm not trying to sound discouraging. The Police Judiciaire works in a specialised, fairly complex manner. Generally at the orders of a judge of instruction. In all logic I ought to send you back to your commissaire, but I see that would be useless.'

'I had thought the police existed also to protect people.'

So it did. He wanted to laugh. It was unanswerable.

'We'll do what we can. We may be able to help you. We have to be free to decide whether we are competent.' He was caught in two minds. However obvious that here was a sensitive and intelligent woman it was still terribly like those clouded tales that the neighbours are sneaking in at night, to pour weedkiller on the dahlias.

Her clear direct look faded and blurred.

'No doubt I've made another mistake, and you too will tell me that these are the fantasies of a silly old woman.'

He picked up his pen invitingly and waited for her. Sabine pulled herself together, settled her glasses on her nose in a nervous gesture which he would get to know, and said, 'The facts are as follows.'

She rambled. There were gaps in her memory, she sometimes said things twice, she would jump into a new set of circumstances thinking him familiar with the personages. But he couldn't see much wrong with her mind. No self-pity, no self-indulgence. A conscious, careful wish to be objective. Sadness, but unembittered. The phrase with which she finished her tale was 'Where have I gone wrong?'

'There's no way I could answer that,' said Castang. 'I've got it all down. Can I think about it?'

'Have I wasted your time?'

'No. But I don't know what I can do. I'll have to talk to my chief. You'll have an answer, though, and I promise to make it myself.'

'I think you've been very patient,' she said getting up. No umbrella, no handbag even. A light raincoat, and a scarf to tie round the short, coarse grey hair. 'And polite... why are officials in or out of uniform such mediocre persons?'

He shrugged; he hadn't that answer either.

'Here's my card. If anything becomes critical, reaching a crisis, then ring me. Meanwhile I'll do what I can.'

'Crises occur daily. If things weren't critical I would never have come. I think I have been patient. This thing has grown like cancer, imperceptibly. But I love him, you see... If I ask for help – it is for him.'

'Yes. That's the whole difficulty. It's not a police problem, and I don't know who else it concerns.'

'I realise. Thank you, Monsieur.'

'Au revoir, Madame.' They stood there bowing at each other.

CHAPTER FOUR

That evening Castang reread his notes before going to see Richard.

'What have you got to regale me with?' asked the commissaire in a slightly sick voice, like a rich man asked what colour Rolls-Royce he prefers.

'That old girl you sent me. There are a lot of half-facts. I'll leave those out, shall I?'

'Are there any facts at all?'

'There's a surprising amount of money. More than she realises. If there were a dispute about the inheritance there could be grounds for a threat – but the threat itself is a half-fact.'

'Go ahead and fill it in.'

'The lady is the widow of a man who ran the museum. Soulay; it's a cultural-affairs sort of place – there isn't much else. He was a respected local citizen. Placid existence, Legion of Honour after a worthy lifetime of preserving bits of monuments. From his father he inherited a large suburban house. It's been converted into flats, and brings the widow a rent. That's the first fact. The man retired a few years ago, and a twelve-month or so back succumbed to infirmities. Leaving her this

17

house, which might be worth a good deal nowadays. Hard to tell from what she says. She's shrewd enough, but has no idea of money. Rare, that.'

'Avoid comment.'

'Second fact: the widow is the daughter of a grain-dealer, who gambled, grew rich, grew poor again, ended with a country house, where she has always lived, and still does.

'Third, this couple was childless, and in middle age adopted an orphan of unknown parentage from the Assistance Publique. A boy of then around ten. An impulse buy, as the supermarkets call it. This child gets introduced into a cultured sensitive atmosphere, comfortable if not wealthy circumstances, and has everything lavished upon him – medical, psychological, educational; you name it. School, university, the boy grows up. He's said to be highly intelligent and sensitive, but won't work. Eventually, a bit of mild local string-pulling found him a pretty junior job in the local administration and there he has stayed.

'Fourth, he marries, the offspring of some shopkeeper in Paris, quite bourgeois. Two children of his own. This, it was hoped, would stabilise him. It has and it hasn't. It's a smallish living. The mother helps them all she can. She says it's not much. I'd call it a good deal. They have a rent-free cottage next door, which is part of the property. It's nothing much perhaps, but it's free.'

'It all sounds a bower of roses to me and where's the snag? I haven't yet understood the considerable sum of money, either.'

'It's the sort of thing nobody foresaw, a few years ago. This house is old, two or three hundred years. Bought by the grain-dealer in his days of affluence. It's not big, but has a large walled garden. It has been modernised, central heating and so on, but unchanged. The cultural affairs people have classified it: historic building in local regional style. To her it's just where she has always lived, and of course she's attached to it, and wants to end her life there. But it's worth, suddenly, a lot. Building land is scarce around there too, and dear, and there's this huge garden. Another large sum.'

'But mutually exclusive. You couldn't knock down a classified house for speculative building.'

'You wouldn't have to. One can build a wall. The proof is that an estate agent is after her. Polite and suave, but pressing. She turned it down; not interested. Now she wonders whether it was a mistake, and whether it is too late to change her mind.'

'Didn't this museum man realise all this?'

'Like I said, it's ironic. Have you been in Soulay?'

'Once or twice. Castles and ramparts.'

'Right; seventeenth century she tells me – fortified by Vauban. This man made it his life's work to preserve it, and he won. Nobody has the right to build above a certain height inside, and no horrible great blocks outside the walls. It never occurred to the man that land prices would go rocketing in neighbouring villages. Look, she's a poet, he was an archaeologist. The house was pretty, pleasant: high wall and big garden. They'd always had it, and thought nothing of it. Furthermore it's stuffed with antiques. Old furniture bought in the days when you had it for a song. The fellow scoured the countryside. Medieval fountain being used as chickens' drinking trough. Sculpture, I don't know what. The place is a goldmine,' shouted Castang, excited. Richard never got excited.

'All right, I admit the considerable sum. And the inheritance is being disputed, is it? As I gathered, she claims she's being put in fear. More half-facts, no doubt.'

'The young man – he's nearly thirty – grows increasingly domineering and even bullying. She attributes this to the daughter-in-law – they don't get on, of course. Now, she says, there's a whole campaign being mounted to drive her out, by making her life a misery with little stratagems. Now she has found out what the place is worth, and is wondering.'

'How many relations are there?'

'Look, I went into it, carefully. There are no other relations. This boy was legally adopted. It's incontestable. He is the sole heir.'

'Then all he has to do is wait. She's an old woman.'

'She's not that old, and says she's in perfect health. Certainly seems tough and spry enough. Now suppose she decided to sell. Her relations with the boy have grown worse. According to her, and this is all no more than her account, he goes about grumbling, accusing her of plots to diddle him out of the inheritance because she regrets the adoption.'

'Once one starts to imagine…'

'I gave her that for half an hour. It's what everyone tells her – she comes here to find someone who'll give these fears some weight.'

'They all do,' said Richard dryly. 'She's acquiring ammunition. If the boy is tiresome she can say "Now look, stop bullying me, because I've been to the PJ".'

'I don't think she came here with that sort of motive.'

'She may have convinced you, but have you convinced me?'

'I think,' said Castang slowly, 'that a good sign that there might be something in it is that she refuses to believe it. She sees no knavery in the boy. Turbulent and difficult, yes. Deadly suspicious, yes. She finds that natural. He was already ten when they took him: all the traumas were already built in. She is afraid that no amount of affection and stability and unselfish devotion could ever quite obliterate the terrors, and embitterment. She's had a lot of fancy psychological opinion to work on it. She's pretty objective about this. She maintains that he is basically a good and kind person with real affection for herself. To her the villain of the piece is the wife, in whom she can see little good. She feels superseded in his affections; yes, all that's textbook stuff. But she realises this, knows it, compensates for it.'

'What form do the persecutions take?'

'Petty meanness. Wheedling things out of her, and aggression. The boy walks about saying the place is his, helps himself to stuff he fancies, strips her in various ways. Rows and reproaches – she gets shouted at, accused of cheating and robbing him; even of conspiracies; her friends are accused likewise of being in league. Crude abuse and coarse language.'

Richard's face said clearly that this was all very sad, and no business for the police. Castang wondered why he should be making the effort. But he had liked Sabine, found her a gentle, humble person. The least he could do was his best.

'She feels driven to seek help because, she says, she can no longer make headway against the persecution, which has become serious. He creeps about – she says – spies on her, listens to conversations and phone calls, reads her letters, rummages in her affairs. Finally there was a threat of violence. He has hit her a couple of times, but this was a threat with a gun. I suggested that it was bluff, immature brandishing. She agreed soberly that she hadn't believed it either. A good boy, but suggestible, and the wife is a pernicious thing – blah, blah.' This was coat-trailing. Richard stepped on it.

'What blah, blah? What did he do with the gun?'

'Oh, he threatened to put a charge of shot into something valuable. Point was that it isn't his, something even that he has no conceivable claim upon. It had been in her keeping and she wanted to restore it to the owner. He got in a towering rage: she was a dupe and so on, claimed she would always league herself with anyone to do him out of his rights. It shocked her a lot. The vandalism shocked her too.'

'And you take a grave view of this drama?' Richard's turn to trail his coat.

'Drama, yes. I told her that was all it was. This young man sounds like a simulator. Still, that goes side by side with the real thing sometimes. She says she's afraid of real violence now. He may be capable of it.'

'What do you think you can do?'

'One might drop a word to the cops there – suggest they straighten the boy out a bit. He's only got to stay his own side of the fence. It might pull him up. He sounds that immature psychopath type: the imperative wish which must be satisfied, and suspicions of all being leagued against one.'

He could not have made a sillier suggestion, really. Making diagnoses of somebody on hearsay could have been calculated to rub Richard the wrong way.

'Cock,' said the Commissaire unanswerably. He lunged suddenly across the desk for his internal telephone.

'Robert, whereabouts was it they found that car abandoned?... Good, thanks,' and lapsed into meditation as though there were nobody there. Castang was used to this. He picked up a roneoed sheet, originating as it appeared from some obscure authority in the Ministry of the Interior; concerned at some length with misuses and abuses of telecommunications systems. These had been distributed all over the office, and gone at once into everybody's waste-paper basket. Richard, unaccountably, hadn't slung his yet, which seemed a good excuse for reading it.

'I've a job for you,' said Richard abruptly. 'That car may have something to do with a man who left home, and hasn't been seen. I've no details: the dossier, or what there is of it, is in Longueville. There's a story of a girlfriend here, but the thing needs stitching together. The gendarmerie has been muttering about bloodstains, alleged, in this car; query human pending a lab report. You can trot over there tomorrow.'

'Yes sir.'

'And if it doesn't take all morning you could drop over as far as Soulay, and check on this good lady of yours. Just see if it's all pure myth. No time to waste; I'll want you back here directly after lunch: we've both got to be in court for Zamansky.'

'Yes sir,' said Castang politely.

CHAPTER FIVE

Longueville was half of what its name said: long, but far from being a town. Even as a village it was an abortion; a main road that straggled on interminably, with always one more café, another filling station, another block of grimy-looking houses. He found the gendarmerie barracks, looked at the sequestered car, read a procès-verbal, heard a rambling tale of a man who said he had been fishing. He had borrowed the car, that is to say Jo lent him the car. No, Jo hadn't been with him: no, he hadn't seen Jo. This blood; well, he'd cut his thumb. Cleaning fish. No, of course not gutting fish in the car but he hadn't a handkerchief, see, and in the car was a rag used for wiping spilt petrol stains… It all sounded as fishy as the thumb, and for all anybody knew it might be true, since Jo was nowhere to be found.

Castang made the two obvious suggestions; to take a blood test of this man, to see if the stain corresponded; and to look in the river in case this other man were in it. He had plenty of time to drive the fifty kilometres further, to Soulay. Or not exactly Soulay, but the little place outside it where Sabine Lipschitz lived. He wasn't bothered about lunch: he bought a bottle of milk and Vera had made him a steak sandwich.

Saint Martin-du-Val, which was really in a valley, in pretty countryside sloping down to the river crossing which had been strategic once, was a much nicer village than Longueville, with a pleasant tiny square and an ancient lime tree in front of an unpretentious little whitewashed church. The hands of the church clock said ten to three, and had done so, probably, for a generation. At the far side of the square was a little café with two tables in front of it, called 'Aux Bons Amis'. To be avoided: the Good Friends would be tremendous gossips and, at this stage, listening to village tattle would be of no use.

In fact he had no trouble finding Sabine's house, which was instantly recognisable from her description. A high stone wall along the whole of one side of the square, with a rusty iron grille at one corner. Within could be seen a lot of overgrown trees and bits of high-pitched slate roof, with mansard attic windows, needing paint. At the other corner there was a wooden door in the wall, and that would be the cottage. Nothing wrong with the geography.

He parked and went like a good cop on a bit of a tour around. It was true – wedged into every bit of waste ground were new-looking bungalows and little villas. They were certainly doing well out of land hereabouts. Ten minutes' walk brought him back round to Sabine's corner and a road sign saying 'Soulay 3 km.' He found a bell over his head, a tingle-tangle on a rusty iron chain. There was a long pause, but then a suspicious voice said, 'Who is it, please?' He looked up startled: her face was peering short-sightedly over the wall from a vantage point. He held his face up to be recognised, with a sunny 'Bonjour Madame', like a man selling insurance. She took a moment to recognise him before the face cleared.

A key grated in the lock of the grille, which was backed with sheet metal: Sabine believed in privacy. A path wound across grass-grown gravel and grassy earth, between piles of rubbish. Crates of empty bottles stood outside a dilapidated shed; heaps of brushwood; last year's decaying leaves vaguely raked into a pile and left there; a tree-trunk rotted through the middle, lying cushioned on discoloured sawdust, waiting to be turned into firewood. All that could be seen of the garden was jungle, trees thickly swathed in ivy. The pathway led to the kitchen door at the end, and along the front, which was a row of French windows: the centre one stood open to the morning sunlight. Sabine led the way, wearing her navy-blue trousers, an old darned sweater and a kitchen apron.

The sunlight penetrated no further than a little lobby with oak panelling. A worn polished oak stairway climbed up in a spiral. The floor was fleur-de-lys red tiles and a Persian rug with its pattern effaced. The smell of a very old country house came rich and delicious to his nose: ancient earth and wood, dust and wax polish, faded flowers and dry leafmould. She directed him to follow through a further door, beyond which it was pitch dark.

'Sorry. I'll open the shutters.'

Creaks, groans, rusty screams from keys, bolts, hooks and the unoiled hinges of the tall old wooden shutters. Old women living alone always barricaded themselves. The light flooded in upon his eyes.

It was a mixture of living-room and dining-room. A big oblong table of massive wood one could scarcely see for the piles of paper and junk. A space at the far end was cleared and laid with a Chardin picture: a linen cloth, the end of a loaf, a coffee-bowl, a painted faience dish of fruit and an unopened morning paper. Beyond, next to the door leading to the kitchen, stood a beautiful great dresser-cupboard of patined oak with brass bindings, plainly very old and of considerable value.

'That's a fine piece,' said Castang with polite admiration.

'Yes,' said Sabine pleased, 'it's fifteenth century, ship's timber and one can see made by a naval carpenter. One wonders how it got here. I think it came from Flanders: I love it very much.' He turned around, staring uninhibitedly. Large straw-bottomed chairs made for solid country rears. A tall stone fireplace carved along the high chimneypiece with Roman letters and the classic text, 'The Night Cometh when no man can Work.' The corners filled with angle cupboards overflowing with heterogeneous objects. There was a television set on a trolley pushed back into the chimney embrasure, the only modern thing in the room, but its screen was thick with dust. Sabine's interest in today's world was slight and remote. She seemed to interpret his silent appreciation as tacit disapproval and dithered, thinking twice about asking him to sit down.

'Oh dear. What a mess. Somehow one never does get tidy. Please forgive me – I'm used to it, and I no longer notice how squalid it all gets. I'm comfortable, you see, like a moth in a ragbag, or whatever beast it is that chews paper up to make nests. I love paper – I'm always cutting things out which interest me. I feel ashamed of this, though – suppose we go in the other room.' Castang followed her, wanting to see all he could. Back through the lobby was a hallway, with another French window through to the patio at the back of the house. Beyond the hallway was a big salon, stiff and grey, and musty with disuse. It was too dim in there to make much out except many shelves and alcoves and vitrine cupboards stuffed with pieces of pottery and sculpture.

The hallway seemed to be used as a working room. She opened the shutter and motioned him to sit in a little Empire armchair. She sat herself on a folding canvas chair like those provided on movie sets, behind a card table littered with letters and manuscripts.

'You still work, I see,' he said politely, but fishing.

'Poetry, you mean?' unselfconscious. 'Not really, not now. I scribble at notions. And there are always letters, from huge numbers of governmental and municipal busybodies – that's not meant for you,' with a sudden gleam of humour. 'Polite of you to come. You must allow me to offer you a drink. I hope there is a drink,' vaguely. 'One never can be sure, but if there isn't I'll pop out for one. Is a glass of wine all right? No, you'd prefer a pastis. Men always like that. I'll get a glass.'

He got up; the chair was not comfortable: plainly no one ever sat in it. He roamed about policeman-like, peeped through to the patio, which was a broad glassed-in verandah looking out to the huge overgrown jungle. More sculpture here, stuff on pedestals, lots of art. He knew nothing about art and was stupe-fied by all this. A sniff through the archway to the still stale air of the salon: he could make out faded brocade chairs and curtains and another big chimneypiece, marble this one in the heavy severe style of the seventeenth century. On this stood a bas-relief of carved limestone, gothicky and ecclesiastical.

'I'm sorry to be poking inquisitively.'

'I don't mind. The police always poke about, don't they? One expects it.' Yes.

'Thanks, Madame; your good health. Now... I don't pretend I've come for a specific purpose, or with suggestions. To see how the land lies, and not to get a false impression.'

'And to see whether I was filling you up with imaginary terrors: dotty old biddy.' This directness was disconcerting. She had filled her glass with water over a thimble of pastis and was sipping away peacefully.

'Well, it isn't easy. To evaluate, I mean.'

'Mm', uninterested, taking off her glasses, rubbing them on the sleeve of her sweater, gazing blindly about.

'You are very attached to this house?'

'Yes... Very much indeed. It...' gesturing... 'encapsulates... every morsel of my existence. My father, my mother, my husband, all in turn died here. I should like to die here too. We have outlived our time, both this fabric and myself: it is time for us to go, to be transformed. You know, I would like just to lie down on the floor and go, simply and without fuss, here where I've lived. I am over seventy, you know, but sound, and it irks me to think I may live another twenty years, that I might be taken away to where competent but pitiless doctors would prolong an existence that had grown meaningless. I am not tired of life, but am bored now with the details of living. If God wishes me to live longer, what design does He have for me? It puzzles me. I have no son or daughter to prolong myself for. It seems a useless way to peter out, clinging to these shadows. Whereas if I let it all go...

'There might be a healing then, and a renewal. To renounce it all freely, simply making it over to him, since that is what he wants – perhaps that is what God wants of me. All these stupid objects; they're a burden. And this cramped stretching and reaching for what is gone and can't be recovered: it is nefarious. And so too an old acquaintance told me the other day, someone I had not seen for many years but who had known this house when it was gay and full of vitality. Whereas what is it now? A source of malice and poison... And yet,' in a sudden deep voice, 'I just don't like being conned.'

She straightened up and put her glasses back on, sipped from her drink, grinned.

'Rambling, aren't I? Tell me now though, why should your advice not be good, and why should I not take it? Perhaps, without realising, that is what I came to you for. You are a man of the world and of experience, and objective. Think. You see this now, and I see it through your eyes; it's dead, this house. There would be hope, if it passed into the hands of a man whose children might feel happiness here, that it would come to life. Nothing whimsical about that. Even if I sold, as I am being urged to do, poor Gérard might reap reward from the money. I'm told it's bound to be a large sum. There should be enough to provide for me too. Poor boy, he's so anxious, he can just never feel sufficient security. The money might heal the breach between us too…

'The trouble is,' talking to herself, 'that this all sounds convincing, and sensible, and I don't altogether believe in it. And I can't help wondering what lies behind that advice, and whether it is disinterested… Tell me now, what you think.'

She really was asking him, waiting for a sensible reply. He felt he had been got into a corner.

'Advice can be sincerely asked for,' he said, 'but it isn't ever really wanted, is it? Seldom taken in any case. I can't risk advising you: I don't know enough. If things are as you describe then so be it. But I'd say there was an essential condition for any decision; to make your mind up in serenity. If I understood your visit, you feel that is not the case. You gave me to understand that you were under pressure, that you were being persuaded, even manipulated, and that even if the end was just the means weren't. Was that right? Have you changed your mind?'

'I wish I had.'

'An estate agent wants you to sell? Who is he acting for, do you know?'

'I've no idea.'

'Whereas your son would like you to make the place over to him – is there any connection between the two?'

'Why would there be? I don't think Gérard wants to sell… Perhaps he does: I don't know.'

'Have you thought out what would become of you if you made the property over and he then sold over your head?'

'I could live, I dare say, on the rent from my flats. This house costs as much as paying for a studio, in rates and repairs. I wouldn't care. To dispossess oneself in favour of one's child cannot be bad. No family quarrels then. Nor would I stay here to be a burden and reproach. I know something of that – my own poor parents… I would disappear.'

Castang smiled politely.

'I don't think I'm going to be much help to you, Madame. Anything I can say will only confuse the issue further. I think I can tell my superior that your anxieties are resolved by your own common sense.'

'I should like that. I wish it with all my heart.'

'Is there something else?'

'I don't know,' said Sabine drearily.

He began to feel exasperation. What the hell was he doing here? It was midday. Time, just, for a quick one at the 'Bons Amis' and then make tracks.

'Emotional tangles... A decision one way or the other might get you out of a false position. The police can't help you.'

'Oh, you misunderstand – it isn't a thing for a civil court. There's no litigation.'

He was looking for a formula to take him out politely, already on his feet, when Sabine stiffened and held out a warning finger before laying it dramatically on her lips and then saying in a loud voice: 'I'm afraid I'm not really interested, Monsieur.'

It sounded false, not everyday enough. It was supposed to warn him to be ready to play a role: it would warn everyone else that a role was being played. His ears had caught a step on the gravel, and they were no sharper than the average eaves-dropper's.

It was not, though, an eavesdropping sort of step. A man's figure, tall and slim, appeared in silhouette against the light, glanced casually through the window, passed on to the lobby, stepped casually through the doorway. He paid no attention to Castang.

'I'd like to know where the woodshed key is.'

Sabine was standing flustered, looking like a child caught with its hand in the biscuit tin. A clumsiness arising from excess innocence, perhaps.

'Really Gérard, you startled me, bumping in like that. Excuse me, Monsieur Er – my son. The woodshed key? How should I know? I never go there – except of course in winter.'

'Since,' in a mildly sarcastic voice, 'I want the saw, I go, naturally, to the woodshed. I find it locked and the key unaccountably missing. It seemed the obvious thing to come and ask you, since you're always hiding things away like a jackdaw. Though what you could possibly want with it passes my understanding, except if as usual you are trying to aggravate me.'

'Good heavens, Gérard, what a way to talk. Such nonsense. And really, this is not the moment to go airing grievances. Before another person too; what will he think?'

In fact she didn't sound too displeased, Castang thought. Look, the tone was saying, you didn't believe me, but this is the way he behaves towards me.

'He doesn't seem much embarrassed,' glancing at Castang with casual negligence. No hostility; just insolence. Or call it just bad manners. 'He's probably used to little domestic scenes. What is it, life insurance or encyclopaedias? I should think we've all we need.'

'Monsieur is a furniture dealer,' said Sabine fussily, pushing with her finger at the bridge of her glasses, with the little hunch of her neck as though to settle her collar. It wasn't clever. No explanation was needed: why give one? But the young man seemed to expect her to account for things.

She was opening and shutting drawers in an aimless fashion. 'Really,' in a worried way, 'I've no idea. I can't recall seeing the woodshed key.' Castang wondered whether it was missing at all.

'Your mother has some nice things here,' he said easily, 'but she doesn't want to sell any. I won't take up any more of your time. Good day to both of you.'

'Just a moment,' said the young man, as easily. 'You're a dealer, you say. Perhaps you wouldn't mind saying who you are, and where you come from.'

'Why?'

31

'Anybody can say he's a dealer,' seeming quite happy to pick a quarrel. 'It's a good pretext for strolling into people's houses and having a peek around.'

Castang, being a cop, got accused about once a week of being a blackmailer, a pornographer, a peeping Tom, or just for a change a perjurer. This was jam. He smiled and let his driving keys twirl on his forefinger.

'I'm under no obligation to furnish you with any explanations, Mister. So I'll be off, Madame; my apologies for troubling you.'

'No no – it's I who must apologise.' Stupid Sabine, rubbing it in, fussing. 'I'll come with you to the gate, to open it.'

Yes; there, surely, was the woodshed. Nobody had passed to try the door. Castang, facing the window, would have noticed. He felt surer still that Gérard knew where the key was. A pretext… He did not look round but knew that the young man had stepped out, was leaning indolently against the shutter, studying him with much interest although it was nothing but a view of his back. Why be so suspicious of a passer-by?

The grille clanged shut; the lock snapped. Castang wound the window of the car down before slamming the door loudly. Sabine's voice, high and uneven, carried over the wall.

'Really Gérard, that was insufferable and quite uncalled for, being rude like that to a harmless stranger.'

He swung his car and headed homeward. He'd come to make a sketch, to pick up an outline. Well, he'd got one.

An interesting face, that young man. Reminiscent of some well-known illustration or popular portrait; now who?… But of course, the young Napoleon: the high stock of the uniform like a polo-necked pullover: the straight lank hair falling to the shoulders: the large eyes staring strikingly out of the thin hollow face. Mesmerically intelligent and good-looking.

This boy was neither. Eyes had an excitable hyperthyroid look. The face was not particularly bright, the mouth petulant, the jaw meagre. But there was force there. And suffering; Sabine had not exaggerated. A hungry animal with wolfish white teeth. A haggard look of tension, as though perpetually on his toes for a bomb due to go off somewhere, sometime soon, and which might be within range. It roused one's curiosity, but not much.

Twitchy, too, and uncoordinated: the kind that is always grimacing and scratching at something. He had not noticed whether the fingernails were bitten, but if they weren't something else was; Sabine for example: biting at her was a pastime, or a tic more likely.

It would have been interesting to see the wife. Interesting, that was the word. There wasn't anything he could do about any of these people, and he didn't intend to try.

CHAPTER SIX

Castang yawned and shifted his backside on the stiff, slippery railway cushions. The train was travelling fast with a steady driving rhythm, through a shower of rain that blurred upon the windows. He looked at his watch, rubbing his wrist where the handcuff bit into it. Over halfway. He looked at his prisoner, curled up and sleeping peacefully, tucked into his corner like a hermit crab, a sort of grin on his face; happy as... as a moth in a ragbag, as Sabine said. In that dusty dishevelled house she pottered around in, full of all that art she never looked at. Very like this fellow here in his storeroom full of rags, doing crossword puzzles: Sabine too cut out bits of paper and strewed them around. They made a pair, didn't they, both uneasy and alert for surprise or treachery, both of them wanting peace and not getting it. Even if the resemblance ended there, it was still striking enough. He looked at his passenger with quite a friendly eye. Shooting at me this morning, though nobody would think it to look at you now. An uncomplicated, straightforward relationship: we understand one another. Whereas Sabine... the thought of her had niggled at him then, and still niggled at him, even now. Like sticky resin

34

on one's hand; the more you try to brush it off, the worse it gets.

'We aren't any further,' he had told Richard. 'Not that it was a waste of time. And it's real enough, and not just her fantasies. Nothing of course that we could do about it even if we wanted to.'

He remembered the conversation as having been carried on in bits and pieces.

He had got back just in time to pick Richard up at the PJ office and go with him to the court. It had been an unofficial visit, and not a thing for which wearisome reports would have to get written.

Instead, a series of little sketches made standing in a lavatory doorway while Richard was scrubbing his fingernails; in the car stopped at a red light on the way over to the Palais; on a bench in a draughty corridor, outside the courtroom.

'It's a nice house all right; be really good if it was tidied up a bit. Inside and out, like the nest of one of those animals children have. A hamster, is it? They tear everything up.

'Place is full of antiques, valuable enough, too, by the look of them. Strewn about everywhere as though they'd no importance. Well of course, to her, they haven't.

'She told him I was a dealer. Plausible enough, but just the wrong thing to say. Put the boy's back up straight away. He really might be frightened of her selling the place, over his head. Certainly curious and suspicious, obsessively so. Looked at me as though I were going to take his lollipop away, just for being there. No exaggeration on her side there.

'Peculiar tactlessness she has. Gift for putting everyone's back up. One could easily sympathise with the boy, if he'd let you. This woodshed key – I'm sure he hid it. At the same time I could easily imagine her hiding it. Not out of malice, of course. Some vague idea of putting it in a safe place and then forgetting. Done so stupidly that you could believe it was malice, that she was lying, being contrariwise. They're at odds, so each little step puts them more at variance and drives them further apart. One can get a divorce for things like that, but one can't divorce Ma.'

'What's the boy like?' asked Richard.

'Quite bright perhaps, but pretty futile. Wouldn't want to say more, on that acquaintance.'

'What's it he does?'

'Administration something, in local government. She told me but she's vague herself. She hardly knows, you could guess, partly because she's not much interested and perhaps even more because she's humiliated about it. She had big ambitions and they came to nothing.'

'Reading too much into it,' said Richard.

'I don't think so; it's consequent enough. The boy had a lot of promise but didn't live up to it. The father, she told me, pulled a string to get him a job in bureaucracy, and I'd say the boy was just the type to be frustrated about that. A familiar type, no, the ones who are always getting brilliant schemes in their heads but can't carry anything out. We see plenty of them.'

'You saying this boy is a potential criminal?' asked Richard with no enthusiasm. At that rate, his voice meant, you'd need a police force the size of the Russian army.

'Not that daft,' jogging Richard's elbow as the usher appeared in the courtroom doorway.

Castang looked at his watch, such a commonplace thing as not to be worth mentioning, except that if your watch-wrist is chained to a person asleep whom you don't want to wake, it takes more trouble.

It was the very stupidity of it all which made it interesting – the ability of someone like Sabine to get into a tangle. Who could be threatening Sabine? The boy? When such a thing was directly against his own interest?

And even if the boy was annoying, driven by obscure psychological needs and torments, why had she so little common sense? She had only to say, more or less, 'This is mine and stays mine, and now leave me alone with this clearly understood: after my death you can do as you please.' Some agent had offered her a tempting buy, so that she would be hesitating between snapping it up or holding on in the belief that land prices would go higher yet.

The tragedy, as far as there was one, was her inability to do one thing or the other. He shrugged. Artists...!

It wasn't 'police work', not as the public understood that phrase anyhow. Reassuring muddled old ladies didn't sound like the criminal brigade. Not exactly the casual drawl telling the press that we've this minute put our unerring finger on ten kilos of heroin. Still, if a few more commissaires were like Richard the cops might do better.

Few were. Much more numerous were the technicians, aseptic and sterilised, talking about the 'underworld' as though it were germs. Castang, though a youngish cop with a university degree, didn't think much of his more pasteurised colleagues. He knew too that Richard was right in saying that there was small use in pontificating about crime. A cop was there to obey orders.

Castang did though talk about the subject, sometimes, with a few of his colleagues, with Vera, with a few friends, one or two of whom were in the business too, like Colette Delavigne who was a juvenile court magistrate. They had to take the 'underworld' literally. No use discussing its deprived childhood: it was motivated by nothing but money. Brutish, sometimes vicious savages like this one chained to him, distorted by greed. Nibelungs, swarming out of black smoky fissures in the earth's crust.

You couldn't talk about crime – said Vera, said Colette, said even he himself when not being too blunt and cop-like – without defining it, getting rid of the confusion, the never-drying stream of cant upon the subject. Look – he said – there is crime, which is a technical infringement of a formal code. It can be combated by technical means, a technician's mentality. And there is evil, which is an abstract idea but real, and technicians, except the gifted ones (who are rare in the ill-paid and ill-considered ranks of the police) cannot cope with an ethical abstraction.

There was even a doubled confusion. A lot of highly educated and intelligent people would say that the penal code, being based on Christian and Jewish ethics, was artificial nonsense, criminals being the faulty product of an imperfect society and evil being a superstition.

Castang didn't know a single cop who'd be starry-eyed enough to go for that one.

He did know a few who went to the other extreme, equally barbarian, which was to claim that everything which was a breach of the code must automatically be evil. This, the guillotine-and-treadmill brigade, vociferous about indulgent judges, was as bad as the other but less, perhaps, to be blamed. They'd been mugged, quite often.

Castang thought about it, a good deal, but didn't let it get him down. He paraphrased Goethe, who said that if you saw things done, persistently in the wrong way, you must not complain, but continue, in the measure of your capacities, to do things the right way. Even if this maxim was of small comfort, like most other maxims, to cops. Goethe should have been in the police!

Castang was pretty lucky in his superior. Richard could go on a lot about a disciplined body, but he gave responsibility to subordinates. This is a rare trait in bureaucrats, whose central weakness is not wanting to stick their neck out, for fear of official disapproval further up the hierarchy. Too many commissaires were just too frightened, whereas Richard would call you in and chuck a folder across the desk.

'Seems a complicated affair, this. I haven't looked at it; don't propose to, either. Do as you think best.' After getting your feet in your mouth a few times, you learned to do quite well.

Richard would stay in his provincial corner too, probably, for a long time. Higher authority deplored this state of affairs, but preferred not to do anything about it. Cops still got promoted for twenty years of imbecile subservience and craven entrenchment behind the regulations, but Castang still liked his job. And Richard was an ally, in difficult situations where a peace-loving policeman might feel uneasily exposed; to some evil-minded magistrate, to tart editorials in the local paper, or to Paris, pointing out to the Prefect that the electoral district was wobbly and don't let the cops just sit on their hands.

Why had Richard allowed time to be spent on Sabine? Castang thought he would never know. Probably just eccentricity; caprice.

The train slowed. He was home.

CHAPTER SEVEN

He shook his left wrist: his man woke, uncurled, went to rub his eye in a childish, pathetic fashion and remembered his right hand was cuffed. Castang forgot about Sabine. She had been a useful device for keeping his mind oilstoned over an hour or so, necessary because this sad burden he had been convoying had shot at him that morning. A few hours in a train had increased his apathy, but he was still a burden, now more than ever. He had to be carted over to the local stone jug, and signed for a good few times in a painstaking fashion, like a registered parcel that has come undone and may have been tampered with. Accepted, but without prejudice to possible future complaints. It means a lot of shilly-shally for the postman. The prison officer was owlishly suspicious of Johnny. Strings and seals had come apart on him before (Johnny had in fact made a clever and well-publicised break from provisional detention once before, away up in the Pas de Calais). Was this tatty package even really Johnny? Not by any chance some other individual with the same name as well as place-and-date of birth?

There was a good deal more bumbledom about Johnny's

possessions, which were few; now this money he's carrying: of suspect origin surely, and the judge will have something to say about that.

Having – at last – got all his papers rubber-stamped Castang found it was past six, and hell, he wasn't going back to any poxy office. Nothing but a sandwich for lunch, a thing that had happened too often recently. Back to wife, and uxorious flesh-pots. Stolid, perhaps, for a man who had been shot at a few hours ago, but no, not really. A travelling salesman, a professional of the road and the car, will come, statistically, face to face with some cretin opposite him who is overtaking blind. Quick reactions and a nasty squeeze gets him past with no more than an accelerated heartbeat. A moment later he puffs his breath out, feeling his lips tight and his jaw muscles rigid, gets his shirt collar unstuck off his neck, and tells himself that that was a narrow squeak, for we tend to talk in clichés when disturbed. He goes on driving, since he has work to do. He will not, perhaps, tell his wife. What would be the use of her feeling frightened each time he was on the road?

Since a car is a more dangerous weapon than a gun, and kills more people, including policemen, Castang saw no need to dramatise being shot at.

As for Vera, who had not seen him since the night before, she was glad to have her travelling salesman back. He was having supper after a beer and a shower – all three unusually welcome – when the phone rang. Punishment for not having rung the office.

'Castang,' said Richard's flat voice.

'Yes, my lord. Just this moment in. Thought you'd gone home.'

'Thoughtful of you. Paris has been on at me, being a bit officious, to tell me you were bringing that burglar down with you.'

'That's right. Got him in the cellar now. I was going to tell you but I was just rinsing off the blood.'

41

'He give you trouble?'

'Full report for you in the morning. Petty cash account and everything. Let's see; chewing gum, comic book, postage stamps, sticking plaster –'

'That will do,' said Richard.

'You want me to come in and type it all out now?'

'What are you doing?'

'Just getting into my dinner jacket – there's the banquet for the visiting team and then we've all got tickets for the Folies-Bergère after the big booze-up.'

'Come in to see me tomorrow first thing. Pack your little bag, because you'll be on the road.'

Castang made a face. Vera, listening to the spare earpiece, made a worse one.

'What is it this time?'

'Oh, nothing unduly strenuous,' with a faint sarcastic emphasis. 'A telex. Your old woman who writes poetry. I know nothing about it at all, except that she is in the past tense and the judge has decided upon an enquiry.'

'Oh,' went Castang; an 'oh' of surprise, slight shock, discouragement, and irritation, but not of boredom. He had liked Sabine, even if she were – had been – a most irritating person.

'What happened?'

'A housebreaker, I gather; vagabond of some sort. Open-and-shut affair, no doubt. The local people have had all of today to work on it and seem to be treating it as banal. The judge is being zealous, that's all. You've met her, you know what she told you, and you've been on the ground, so you're the obvious choice. I tell you now simply so that you'll be ready to leave.'

'Oh all right, all right.'

'And Castang,' said the quiet voice.

'What is it now? Help! – my bandages are slipping.'

'Yes, I know, Paris told me all the exciting news. All right

42

then; take it easy, there's a good boy. No need to get worked up, next week will do for the haircut. All right boy; good night.'

He put the phone down and said, 'I'd better go to bed,' in a resigned voice.

'What was all that about your bandages slipping?' asked literal-minded Vera, suspiciously.

'Stupid joke. Just a way of saying I was tired and fed up.'

'I see,' said Vera. What was the use of asking more and getting told lies? 'I'll pack a bag. How long for, d'you think?'

'No idea. Make it three days. Maybe I can go fishing.'

CHAPTER EIGHT

I've heard nothing more, so I still know nothing,' said Richard, turning up the corners of a pile of forms to sign his name on them. 'Routine demand for routine investigation, signed by the judge in Soulay. Makes a change from Paris – nasty dangerous place, that Paris. You can take young Lucciani.'

'Haven't you anyone else?'

'No.'

'What about technicians?'

'The local people have done all that. What more do you want – sound effects man and a continuity girl? There's nothing to it; I'm only sending you because of the coincidence. The judge doesn't know, and I see no need to run and tell him, that this woman came here with tales of persecutions. No need to frighten him with false fire. See what it's all about, that's all. Your expenses will be okayed. The state got saved money by your bringing back that hooligan. A fine one, that. Don't bother about him; he'll keep. The judge is in no hurry for him, no hurry at all. Forty robberies! Whereas this bastard in Soulay is merely wanting to make a fuss. Sleepy hollow. If he were any good he wouldn't be there.'

With young Lucciani driving, Castang could 'put his feet up'. Soulay was a sous-préfecture, and sub-prefects are small beer. A sub-prefect is a bland personage nicely dressed, like a hotel manager, with an agreeable smile for important guests, who does nothing much, and is really only there to terrorise page-boys. If there is a flood he is in charge; not that he will do much then, except send messages to the government asking to be declared a disaster-area. Noisy ones, to draw attention to his energy. And momentarily to increase his importance. A sub-prefecture is generally a town of perhaps ten thousand souls, where everybody knows everyone, and everything. Within this wooden O he is a strutting personage, and the local bigwigs compete for invitations to his bridge parties. Among these turkey-cocks is the local judge of instruction, and between the career official and the career magistrate is a bond of sympathy: both would like to wipe the dust of Soulay off their feet. In order to bring this about they both dread and secretly hope for a scandal. To attract the attention of Paris is important, but to gain the good opinion of Paris may prove ticklish; hence the dread. It is an instance of the weakness of centralised bureaucracies.

There was of course nothing even remotely political about the death of an ex-poetess. But Castang had needed no explanations to know that he was going to have trouble with this judge.

Richard had been cunning. He made a point, as a rule, of taking charge of a homicide himself. He had dodged it, so that Castang would be caught between the judge and the local commissaire of the urban police. Dodged it, probably, because recently there had been a scandal in Soulay! In fact apart from the archaeological details supplied by Sabine, the scandal was all he knew about the place. A typically small-town scandal...

Soulay was in fact a thriving little town, with plenty of light industry. But dull. To introduce some sparkle they'd been trying to attract tourists – especially since their fortifications, which they had never noticed, had been declared a monument. It was all very well to be dynamic about tourism, but there was a shortage of hotels. It happened that the mayor owned the biggest hotel. In the name of tourist infrastructure he had cornered municipal funds to get a car park built opposite his own establishment, and some local people thought this went a bit far. A complaint had been registered, and not with the sub-prefect, where the mayor was assiduous at bridge and mellifluous with the ladies, but with the Prefect – Up There in the City.

So that local justice – dragging its feet ever so slightly – had been obliged to intervene. Charges, it appeared, would have to be preferred, and though it took time, for the mayor was strongly entrenched, charges were preferred. Traffic in influence: corruption of public functionaries: falsification of written records.

The judge of instruction, and the prosecutor, had been luke-warm about all this. The latter was unworried, being a local notable from an old family, very happy where he was in posses-sion of inherited wealth and a fine house. But the tergiversations of the judge vexed an authority in the city, who took a dim view anyway of 'these little country combines'. The judge was asked tartly what was taking him so long.

The ambitious hotel-keeper had finally been disbarred from further public office by a year in the jug, suspended. The judge had been anxious ever since to retrieve his position. Now that he had a homicide to give scope to his talents one could be sure that he would make himself insufferable to the police, his creatures.

Castang knew all about this in the simplest way. The fraud specialists of the Police Judiciaire would have been called upon, normally, to investigate the mayor's zeal for tourism, but had been called off by the judge, who had talked about excess of zeal, bulls in china-shops, sledgehammers and nuts, and suchlike metaphors. Richard hadn't been pleased a bit.

Castang sighed, being a sufficiently experienced policeman to know all about excess of zeal in country districts. He supposed that an obscure ex-poetess, the widow of a dusty functionary in the cultural-affairs sector, was not likely to be thought a ticklish problem.

Approached from this side, Soulay was pleasant-looking, with bastions and salients and an impressive gateway. The streets of the old fortress, narrow and cobbled, led up to the citadel, where the trees in the moat made a pretty little park. On the far side, the walls had been knocked down in nineteenth-century exuberance, to build a faubourg leading to the railway station. The 'new town' with its industrial quarter and the flats of those who worked there lay across the river and Castang had no desire to push tourism that far. The 'Palace of Justice' was a heavy building in a dreary square dating from Louis Philippe, that bourgeois monarch who had such bad taste in art. He left Lucciani and the car outside, and prepared to scrape his shoe back and make a very low bow. Lucciani, not being an officer, would only have to tug his forelock.

The judge was politer than expected; even quite conciliatory, despite a bilious, irritable appearance: he was a middle-aged, concave personage with an unhealthy colour and little bunches of dust-coloured hair dotted around a high bald forehead, like thorny scrub on some African veldt. Not much shade. No lions. A hyena or two, idly playing with a rather old bone.

He had been told by Richard on the phone that an experienced officer was being sent. If the fellow was properly housebroken there should be no problem. Time enough to grind at the peppermill.

'In a certain light, yes, it's a trivial matter. Of course no homicide can ever be trivial.' Castang quite agreed. 'It is evident enough what took place. A sordid case of breaking and entering. Nothing to do with the neighbourhood: that stands to reason.

47

The village is a short distance away, but part of the – what's their word?' twirling his forefinger in a circle.

'Agglomeration.'

'Quite. Comes under the town. The local police force is competent. Limited perhaps in manpower. But to handle an enquiry of this nature is perfectly within their scope.'

Castang seemed to be wondering, with respect, what they wanted him for.

'Young thugs,' said the judge rather loudly, 'roaming the countryside. Hippies. All the technical findings point that way. We've had too much of it. This band will be well away by now. I want it found. The mobile brigade and the gendarmerie have been alerted. I want some energy shown. A suggestion has been made too which seems worth pursuing – those bands which pillage country houses for antiques. I want you to co-ordinate all this. And no little dodges. I exact a scrupulous rectitude of procedure. Discretion, you understand me, and no chatter-boxing with the press. And you're accountable to me. I expect your verbal report tomorrow morning and on subsequent days.' He paused, to look Castang up and down, seeming surprised at what he saw.

Nothing odd, surely, thought Castang. Conventional appearance, ordinary clothes. Smallish for a cop, but well muscled. Dark hair, cut short. Well-polished shoes and clean fingernails – two items he was fussy about. Leathery kind of face, neatly shaved; boxer's nose – he had been a fairish welterweight, too short to be more – and one crooked eyebrow where someone had split it. Tie, plain dark red – that couldn't arouse disapproval. The judge was feeling a bit liverish; that was all. Would have liked a bigger audience for the lecture on discipline and discretion: a whole amphitheatre full of humble policemen with downcast eyes.

'Very well, as long as that's understood. Local newspapers are always excitable.'

'Good, sir.' This sobriety of language seemed to please the judge, who gave him leave to go, in quite a polite way.

Lucciani was walking about, much bored and one couldn't blame him.

These small provincial towns... Upon a couple of benches sat a couple of old men joylessly contemplating municipal flowerbeds. Everything prim, anchylosed, arthritic. If the square had trees even, thought Castang. Or a fountain. Movement, glitter, silver music. Just brass music, say, as provided by municipal fire-brigades. Nothing here but dust; dried-out, sealed in and lamentable.

The commissariat of police was another dreary barrack, shutters covered in the same peeling grey paint as all the houses. Even in rich, cool September sunshine there seemed nothing that grew and was glad anywhere, and the pettiness of a small town struck more huddled and joyless than ever. Dump, he thought disgustedly.

He said as much to young Lucciani, who mysteriously seemed to know his way about.

'The ramparts are nice. Grass, you know, and old trees.' Yes, to be sure, where sheep might safely graze.

He had to make a start somewhere, and felt no enthusiasm.

'Yes,' said the local commissaire of police. One Peyrefitte by name. Perfid, very likely, by nature, but at present assuming a large air of tolerant indifference: no skin off his nose, all this. 'Don't know what he should want to call you for.' But without hostility. 'Pleased to help. Turn the whole thing over to you. Don't see that there's much to be done, but that's your affair. Whoever it was is miles away by this time. Commonplace sneak-thief is likeliest. Only a bit of money pinched, but got scared off. Thought the place was empty; surprised by the old lady; lost his head and lashed out, like. Somebody gave his nibs the idea of a country-house removals crowd, but I don't see much in that: they come with a truck.

'Anyway, his nibs phoned me, and I have it all for you here; photos, sketch-plan, measurements – and the papers of course – doctor, witnesses, for what use they are in a thing like that.'

He was a rough-cut, heavily-built man, who came on a bit strong with the local accent and the rustic behaviour: a suggestion of 'I'm only a country hick'. Making a thing of how straightforward he was. Have confidence; rely on Joe. The local expert. 'Born here: know everyone. Not like a foreigner – I know what's said, and what's left unsaid.' This sometimes concealed plenty of dishonesty – the bluff greasiness of a grower swearing his Beaujolais is real, with a tanker-ful from Argentina standing at the back door. Peasant slyness. With the bourgeoisie, just servile and insinuating enough.

Castang thought he could probably get along all right with the man, as long as he didn't step on any toes.

The technical dossier had been shoved across confidently, as though 'what can't speak, can't lie'. He shuffled through it: it had been neatly done.

'She was found in the kitchen, I see.' Odd, surely?

'Like what would a man be looking for in the kitchen? Right, a bit weird. But her bag with the purse in it was lying on the table. Emptied, sure. How much nobody knows: the son estimated she might have had a few hundred francs.'

'She wasn't moved?'

'No, no; would have showed up. What clinches it anyhow is she was hit for sure with the iron. Stood there on the board in the kitchen. Hit on the back of the head, could have stolen up behind her like, wanting to keep her quiet. Or maybe some threat to make her turn round. Anyway he clonked her. Too hard, got a fright, and whizzed. Those shots show how the entry was forced. Common crowbar, so he came meaning to break in. Quite neat, it wouldn't have made much noise. Bedroom at the back. But these old ladies sleep light.'

'Took courage, to go into the kitchen after him.' Sabine, he thought, did have that sort of courage.

'She'd have to go a distance, to raise an alarm. You haven't seen the place.' Castang kept mum. 'If it wasn't for the crowbar I'd have thought it no more than some vagrant, a hippy looking for a place to sleep, and to lift anything handy. The gate wasn't forced – not that it proves much. But the antiques gang would have brought a van in, and grandfather clocks and stuff, take at least two men. No footmarks, but ground was dry. The only thing that gives any weight to the idea is the son claims there was a man hanging about not long ago he didn't like the look of; claimed to be a furniture dealer, and that is the way they work, sure enough. Somebody goes first, talks his way in, to have a look around to mark the good stuff down, like. Haven't had much of that around here, but always time to start.'

Castang didn't have to hide a grin at the description of himself, because he didn't have a grin. The man would find out sooner or later, but it had no importance.

'You were satisfied with the son's story, were you?'

'Hard to see why not. He wasn't on the best of terms with his ma – adopted, by the way. There was talk in the village about frequent quarrels, but raised voices to hitting Ma with the iron – no, that's over-long a step to take without strong indications. Whereas what signs there are point another way. Like the time factor. No member of the family would be running around in the middle of the night. It had always been the boy's home: he could stroll in any time. She was killed around two: she was in pyjamas and the bed had been slept in. Found next morning by the daughter-in-law, who was passing by, saw the shutter forced, thought it funny, went in being a cool young lady, found the old dame on the floor, and ran to call us together with the ambulance. I was there by nine. Now even if there was premeditation – why the middle of the night?'

'Break-ins are easy to fake,' said Castang loosely. Peyrefitte shrugged.

'Maybe, but common sense is against it.' His face said clearly that if one wanted a fancy story, the facts could always be stretched.

'Sure. Just looking from that angle for a moment. I agree; it doesn't fit the facts.'

'Homicides aren't exactly our bread-and-butter,' there was no use in being touchy with the PJ, 'but I hope we know how to be thorough.' Since the PJ had been wished on him, that was.

'A stranger might have expected a dog.'

'Took a chance. The house could as easily have been empty. It has that neglected look. Rubbish everywhere – you'll see. The odd thing there is I advised her to get a dog.'

'You did?' said Castang, who'd been wondering whether this episode would be suppressed.

'I thought it meaningless then,' said the commissaire, 'and do now. She came to me a month or so back with a tale of neurotic fears. Had a row with the son, got worked up. Felt abandoned I dare say – sense of loneliness. You know how old women can be. And typically obstinate; living alone in a house too big for her, just because she always had.'

Yes, it was the voice of common sense.

'I suggested a dog: company, like; no need of a guard dog. Something to get attached to, you take my meaning, fill the gap. She'd have none of it. What could I do? Told the patrol to keep an eye open. But it's a quiet corner, bar the local drunks.'

Sensible if unimaginative; Sabine was not the person to get attached to dogs or canaries. She had rejected the well-meant piece of advice a bit too brusquely, and lost his sympathy. 'The woman didn't want to be helped.' Sabine's tactlessness put people off. She had no idea how irritating she could be.

'What about this bickering in the family?' asked Castang lazily. 'D'you know them at all?'

'Nothing to know. I checked up, in view of this talk of being bullied and terrorised. No family bar this son, who's adopted like I say, but that's ancient, twenty years ago. Boy's nervous, maybe, shouts at people, easily irritated. Nothing criminal about that. More to the point – regular job, doesn't drink, doesn't gamble.'

You know your job, thought Castang.

'Likes fishing. Got a young wife, two kids. Loan from finance company on the car – payments regular. No housing trouble – had a free cottage from the old lady. You know how it is – one looks for something odd in the pattern. Nothing. Had words with his ma – and who doesn't? She was over-prone, maybe, to well-meant advice about bringing up the children and such: lived too close by.'

He agreed with every word, and if he himself had not met Sabine... But that was a straw, a dead leaf down his shirt. Castang had the feeling that Peyrefitte had everything right, and that the best thing he could do was make a show to keep the judge happy.

'Great,' he said. 'These are copies? – can I hang on to them for our file? So I'll look at the ground; maybe do a few interviews. Show zeal for the judge.'

'Interfering old bastard,' said Peyrefitte comfortably: He had no worries, or he'd never have said that openly.

'He blocked us off from looking up the mayor, as you no doubt know, and now he wants to show Paris how thorough his investigations are.'

'Your bad luck,' said the commissaire, much like Richard before him.

'My boy can talk to the villagers – something for him to do. And we might turn something up on the antiques-gang angle: we've a file on it at home, but I'm placing no reliance on it. The house under seal or anything?'

'No – the judge saw no need. Just locked – here, keys. I told the boy not to roam about without permission, but it's scarcely a felony if he does. It's all his now. Judge phoned the notary to see if there was a will. Another old bugger. Gives you a long answer and you've still got no idea at the end was it yes or no he said.'

'I'll keep everybody happy,' said Castang.

Starting with you. Fair words, to keep local police commissaires from thinking we might go interfering, or making a report, which would lead a judge or a Proc to make sarcastic comments about police administration. He left Monsieur Peyrefitte sitting comfortable and greased, with no hot little frictions under the collar.

And the commissaire thought much the same. The PJ, in his experience and he'd had some, was rarely tiresome unless it thought it was being got at. Or suspected that things had been concealed.

A muddle there might be. Anything tricky or troublesome – no. Those tales of family grievances originated if you asked him in old mother Lipschitz's tiresome little ways. Vague. And she liked rows. She'd made a row with him, not that he'd been provoked. Artists! They were a pest: they didn't know what they wanted. As long as they stuck to art they were all right, he supposed. Beyond that... Like grit, for a hen's digestion.

CHAPTER NINE

Fickle weather. It had clouded over again, making Castang hope it wouldn't be one of those enquiries spent with permanently damp trouserlegs.

By the map the village wouldn't be over seven or eight minutes, but it took their car double. The familiar phenomenon; roads carrying double the weight they were designed for. These quiet suburban gardens aroar with the stream of heavy trucks. Innocuous country crossroads which had accumulated so many accidents that traffic lights had had to be put in. This wasn't country; this was suburb. Even the last bit of side road – oldish villas masked by high walls - was unsafe: far too many blind bends. Another argument against high stone walls, now considered as grossly antisocial.

They certainly hadn't helped Sabine. Artists had this mania for privacy.

The village, looking just as when he had last seen it. Young Lucciani could make himself useful here.

'I want to go over this ground. Those technicians - it isn't that they miss things. But they think the wrong things important. Thorough about stuff that's not even relevant, and miss something out just because it's hard to measure.' Lucciani was putting on the unjustly-beaten-dog look.

'So do all the houses overlooking the square. Movements, visitors, anything outside the ordinary routine, and not just the night concerned but for a couple of weeks back. And write it all down. And if people are out, go back till you find them at home. See you about one, here in the pub. We'll eat there if we can; it looks clean enough. Right?' They had parked the sober, dirty car under Sabine's wall.

'I'll be in here.'

The gate was overlooked by half a dozen houses. It would be surprising if any comings and goings were not noticed by the good folk across the way, and that alone was enough in his eyes to rule out the antiques gang. Otherwise it would be feasible enough, but country-house burglars disliked places with neighbours, who might have nocturnal habits and restless dogs.

No – one couldn't rule it out. Sabine kept her grille locked, but the lock was simple, and once inside a station-wagon or even a van would remain unseen behind the wall. The local police said blandly they'd had no cases of this sort, but that statement might bear checking. What had given the boy the idea in the first place? Surely not just Sabine saying he was a furniture dealer?

The hippy idea on the other hand was plausible all round. The wall was not hard to climb. And the type was commonplace now. Anaesthetised to bourgeois notions like property, financing themselves with small portable objects easy to sell. Hitch-hiking loosely about, thinking nothing of busting a shutter that looked a bit old or shaky.

This sort, if surprised in a house they had thought empty, might easily overreact out of fright, and clonk an old lady to keep her from yelling.

Even if not true, it was hard to disprove. Nobody knew better than Castang that one never laid hands on people like that unless they were silly enough to pinch something easily identified. A few hundred francs from a handbag left no trace. What would you do – arrest all the casual labour on vineyards within three hundred kilometres? That would certainly make the judge happy!

Castang felt for keys, opened doors, turned on lights, made himself comfortable. Not a very promising terrain for technicians: Sabine had been an erratic duster, polishing some things absent-mindedly and never touching others at all. As he recalled from his visit the floor had been clean. Far from clean now. There wouldn't have been footprints anyhow. Even the stupidest, most inexpert burglar doesn't wear shoes with nicely patterned ridges. Worn tennis shoes from the Prisunic, which they wipe politely on the mat.

He had to come to terms with having been here before. It happened often enough that policemen walked about people's houses making pretty free and being nosy. It was unexpected, something of a shock, to be strolling in here where he felt Sabine's presence so strongly, pervading everything; like the strong scent, rich as plum cake, of the old house.

The geography was as it should be. This lobby shutter had been the one broken. Nothing in that; coincidence. Might have looked weaker than the others. Wood warped, say. Of course it must have been a burglar, and a stupid one at that. Who else would go breaking a shutter? So he busts the shutter, and presumably then the door is unlocked, or he'd have bust the glass pane to turn the key, which was in the door but told Castang nothing, having been turned and re-turned by innumerable policemen. But either way it wakes the old lady up.

So now reconstruct. She comes downstairs and sees at once – how could she fail to see? – the broken door. Now why does she not run out, to raise the alarm? However, being Sabine, she goes instead to pursue the malefactor. Who has hidden; that was quite reasonable. Might not be an old woman, might be a man with a shotgun. He retreated, and looked for a weapon. As Sabine came into the kitchen he clonked her.

It sounded strained, and artificial. Castang sat there sullen and hunched. The fellow went into the kitchen – all right, he was looking for a knife or a poker or something. But...

He turned his head: he had the sensation of being watched. A woman was standing in the doorway. A young woman, good-looking in an unkempt way, dressed in gipsyish fashion in sandals and a long cotton skirt, with a cardigan on top. A full roundish face with a suspicious pouting mouth and two steady unfriendly eyes which looked at him with no sign of fear.

'Who are you? What do you think you're doing here?'

He got up stolidly.

'Police officer,' showing his 'medal'. 'Come to that, what are you doing here?'

She was not in the least taken aback.

'I'm Madame Gérard and I've every right to be here: I'm the owner. And,' aggressively, 'I've not seen you before. The enquiry's finished anyhow: you've no possible business here.'

'Sorry, Madame, to have to tell you you're mistaken, both ways. The judge has called for an enquiry by the Police Judiciaire, which is me, and it's you who have no right to be here: nobody has, without the judge's authorisation.'

She stood her ground, heavy jaw thrust out.

'I'd like to see the judge or anyone forbid me access to my own house. Anyway, the door was open. You don't expect me to walk past without looking.'

'You're Madame Lipschitz's daughter, are you?' being deliberately obtuse.

'In-law,' she said curtly.

'My name is Castang.'

She decided to be polite.

'Well, I suppose that's all right then. Though the judge might have had the politeness to let us know, it seems to me. What does he want with another enquiry, anyhow?' She stood in the doorway in a peculiar sidling way, as though unwilling to come any further, something after the manner of a cat rubbing itself against a wainscot or a door jamb. Castang had no cats, and no feelings about them. But there was something dislikable about the movement. He had nothing to say to her last remark. But her curiosity, or suspicion, was tenacious.

'Well, now that I'm here, or you're here, whichever it is, is there anything I can do for you? I may say that all this furniture, and papers and stuff, has been rummaged through already. There wasn't anything missing. Only a little money. Surely you don't intend to begin all that photographing over again.'

'No,' he agreed politely. 'I was just looking around. My colleague is interviewing a few people in the village.'

A small child appeared, saw him, stood clutching its mother's skirt and sucking its thumb: she paid no attention.

'Why didn't he come to see me? I live next door. My husband isn't back yet. The children play here in the garden. I came to see what they were up to. The door was open.'

'I was hoping for the pleasure of meeting you in due course. Now it's done. So you came by. As I understood it, wasn't it much the same way in which you found Madame Lipschitz had been attacked?'

'Much the same,' fairly curt. 'It was earlier in the day. I was getting some kindling wood. The shutter was open. I thought nothing of it, since she was always flitting aimlessly about, till I saw it had been forced... I've told this story at least three times.'

'Just getting the background,' said Castang politely.

The child plucked at her skirt: she decided to take the excuse.

'I've no time at present, I'm afraid. My dinner's on the stove. If you've still anything you want to ask...' and in a rush, 'my husband will be back in a while.'

'I don't want to keep you.' It was not received too graciously:

she did want him to keep her. Castang thought her a stupid young woman, and he hadn't liked the faintly contemptuous way in which she spoke of the dead woman: insensitive, he thought.

'You didn't care very much for your mother-in-law. Am I mistaken? It's just an impression.'

'I make no pretence at hypocrisy – no I didn't. I had good reason not to. Of course I'm shocked about this – this crime, I mean. And I'm sorry about her death, because in point of fact I had considerable affection for her, though I may say I didn't get much encouragement. The truth is she detested me. She lost no opportunity of abusing me, and she spread all sorts of tales around. I daresay you'll hear some in the village, and all I can say is I hope you keep some sense of proportion. In the village they thought her a sort of ill-used martyr. I've no intention of bothering to contradict malicious slanders, especially now she's dead: I hope she may rest in peace. At least now we may get some peace too, from petty backbiting and insane jealousies.'

'You needn't be afraid I'll listen to gossip.'

'Who said I was afraid?' tartly. 'There's nothing to be afraid of. It was and is obvious to anyone of intelligence that she thought I had supplanted her in her son's – who wasn't even her son – affections, and that she couldn't endure that. One doesn't have to be especially clever to grasp what went on – just unprejudiced.'

'She adopted him, as I understand – quite late, wasn't it?'

'And didn't she just rub it in! I took you out of the gutter and this is my reward; morning noon and night it went on.' The young woman had forgotten the dinner-on-the-stove and aired her own grievance with some heat.

Yes, he thought, Sabine was a tiresome old bitch. One could see the two women, each clutching her grievance, cherishing it. But of the two, which would have had the generosity to say 'I'm in the wrong. Forgive me. Let's both understand that it isn't easy for the other'? He had known Sabine scarcely at all, and this young woman he had barely met, but there was one conclusion he could reach: the one had been a giver, and the other a taker.

He had to listen politely: the girl was in full flood. He was there to see about justice: she was by God going to see that justice was done her. It came largely from a feeling of guilt. She had been consistently horrible to Sabine, who was now dead. She had to justify herself. 'She led him a dog's life, and he's had the patience of Job. He was always treated as a sort of slave: the smallest sign of needing a bit of normal independence, of wanting just one day without the continual interfering, was the pretext for a big emotional drama. After we married her behaviour became even more insufferable: creeping about in slippers and keyholing, to know whether a remark would ever be made in sheer exasperation which she could seize on, to proclaim from the housetops that she was being abused again. And he just went on putting up with it.'

The sad thing was that it all might well be true.

'Seems to me that you had a remedy,' said Castang mildly. 'To go away, quite simply. Withdraw from the source of conflict.' If you could bring yourself to kick the free house in the teeth – but he left that unsaid.

'As though I hadn't urged that continually,' with contempt for the stupidity of his remark. Had there been a trace of sarcasm in his voice or his face? Why did she have to explain it all to him? Why so tumble over herself to justify, when there had been no criticism?

'My husband is a very sensitive and impressionable person. And ridiculously easily led. She brought him up to be very clinging and dependent, with orgies of maternal self-indulgence. He just couldn't resign himself to stop believing in all the simulated weeping about poor old her left all alone. I suppose you find me hardhearted and unjust, but I simply don't care. You hear the truth nowhere else; you'll hear it from me. I've had to fight for bare existence. I married a boy with no confidence in himself. He was talented and they kept telling him he was a lazy bum. Well, I determined I'd do something to build him up instead of sucking his blood, and that's what I've done and I'm not ashamed of it, even if people do go telling you how I set him against his ma.'

Castang held his tongue.

'And as for going away... I don't know what you think a junior functionary in the municipal administration gets paid.' Squelch: he did, too well. He lived himself in a flat too expensive for him, but didn't feel particularly won over. Too much self-pity, and too noisy with it. And all the time he saw Sabine, fidgeting with her glasses and apologising for being a pest.

'I'd go out to work, despite the children, but if you're capable of grasping a simple fact you'd know a man who's had a rough childhood doesn't want his wife to work. He feels too insecure, and he wants a proper home to come to, and at least he got that from me. Oh, I suppose you go wondering why I tell you all this.'

No, he didn't. People in homicide cases did go blurting out the most personal things to policemen. It is a kind of catharsis. He didn't need to say he was interested: she just swept on.

'He had a wife that was there, and ready to fight for him, even when he didn't want her to, even if he wouldn't let her because of his previously formed – misformed I ought to say – attachments. She would not let him go, but went on clinging like an octopus while telling all and sundry – even the baker – that he was heartless and faithless and cruel to his poor old mum. The innocent artist with no worldly wisdom... in reality she was as crafty as bedamned.'

'All right,' he said mildly, 'I take the point. Maybe now she's dead there isn't quite the need to be so vehement about it.'

'There's that,' recovering herself. 'I don't know why I'm telling you my personal affairs, either.'

'You'd finish by telling me anyway.'

'Huh?'

'Look, suppose we leave this.' The child had come back, and was hanging again on her skirt.

'Thierry, go and get your horse and cart.'

'Don't want to.'

'Do as I say and at once.'

'What did you tell them?' asked Castang as the child trailed off, thumb in mouth. She stood there tight and restless, arms crossed over her breast, hands pressed against her ribcage as though she felt the cold despite the midday sunshine coming in now warm and bright behind her.

'That she was in hospital.'

He nodded. It did not make much sense – didn't the woman realise that she'd been shouting her head off, and that a child, even when playing, has sharp ears?

She was frowning at him.

'What did you mean, saying I'd tell you anyway?'

'I'd have come to you. I'd have asked questions, some personal. It's my job. I'm conducting an enquiry, into a homicide. It's a crime against the person, and that's by its nature a personal affair for the family. It's not like a robbery, say, which is only an offence against property.'

'I don't get you,' she said, puzzled. 'It was accidental, surely, in reality.'

'Was it?' bleakly.

'You don't have to sentimentalise: I'm not a perfect fool. Somebody broke in, which is violent, I suppose, but you aren't telling me they intended killing anyone. She just happened to be in the way. Rather like a road accident.'

'Irrelevant,' he said indifferently.

'What kind of knuckle-headed remark is that?' Didn't like to be contradicted, this young woman.

'A person is killed. It's accident or design, his fault or hers, you're glad or you're sorry; that's all irrelevant. My concern is with what took place. With a road accident one knows and here one doesn't. My function is to establish and to verify. The rest concerns the judge.'

'Well, you're wasting your time here. I told the commissaire all I know about this, and I've nothing to add.'

'I have, though.'

'That's a pity because I've no time.'

'Nobody's hurrying you, Madame. This afternoon will do.'

'Will do for what?' exasperated.

'To know for example how Madame Lipschitz's death will affect you.'

'Whether I'm glad or sorry – that's relevant now, is it, all of a sudden?'

'Whether for example you're planning a move.'

It stopped her dead.

'Would you care to explain the relevance of that?'

'This house, apart from whatever value it has, is larger and more comfortable. You'll be moving in, I dare say.'

'That is no business of yours.'

'I'd only say don't make any plans yet awhile,' politely. 'Until the enquiry is over.'

'We will do as we see fit with our own property.'

'Incorrect. Not yet your property. Ask the notary – or the judge.'

She stood looking at him, head held down, pressing the heavy jaw into a double-chinned look; angry, obstinate, prudent. Alert little mind there racing along, thought Castang. Small maybe, but quick. Sees further than her nose is long.

'If you've anything further to say or ask, Mister Whatsit, I'd advise you to go about it in a different way. I don't know what the so-called powers of the police may be, but they don't include slander, nor intimidation. I know how to protect myself.'

'Oh yes,' drawled Castang. 'You mean consulting lawyers and

so on? By all means. You could even ask the judge to inculpate you formally. I'd have no further right to ask you any questions at all then. I hope your dinner isn't burning.'

She was staring at him flabbergasted.

'Inculpate for what?'

'How should I know? I've only just come into possession of one basic fact. That a person was killed.'

'Well, I'm sorry,' slightly quelled. 'I dare say I was over-hasty. I realise you've your job to do. The fact is that this has upset me more than I care to admit. My husband too. He was devoted to her, whatever you may think. Blazes, it's gone the hour; I must rush.'

'Janet?' came a voice. 'Janet!'

'Yes, I'm here,' shrilly.

A man came round the corner and stopped short. Castang had seen him before.

'What the hell goes on here? Those children are running wild and eating biscuits. What about the dinner, for God's sake?'

'This is a policeman.'

'Another one,' said Castang helpfully.

The large pale eyes did not flicker at all. The man walked up as though to take a good look, to feel quite sure, not in the least fazed. He stopped, put his fists on his hips.

'Well, blow me down! Wouldn't you just know it – isn't that just absolutely typical!'

'What is?' asked the girl, puzzled.

'I'll tell you later. But buzz now, and get that mob sorted out. Leave me to handle this.'

Castang patted his pockets for a cigarette, enjoying the midday sun coming dappled through the trees. The man stood tense and bristling. The girl looked from one to the other, not understanding the sudden tension. She made up her mind and ran with a supple youthful movement towards the corner.

'Nice out now,' said Castang.

'You'd care to explain?' tightly.

'How about a jar at the "Bons Amis" before dinner?'

'I don't drink. You trying to evade the question?'

'What question? As you heard your wife say, I'm a cop. Castang, Criminal Brigade – here's my card. No concealment.'

The man stopped looking as though about to hit him, took the card, read it with his eyes flickering continually back to the face. He put the card in his pocket carefully as though it were evidence of something, put on a sarcastic smile, and said, 'Well now, isn't that interesting!' in a meaningful voice.

'Lot of adjectives,' said Castang. 'Interesting and typical, but why not fill me in?'

'As though you needed telling – but I'll spell it out so that you can't pretend to misunderstand. I thought then that some conspiracy was being cooked up; she looked so guilty with her tales about the furniture dealer – one of those sly little back-passage tricks she was so expert in. I oughtn't to be surprised, I suppose. It's a bit audacious though, even for her, trying to get the police to believe in the horror stories.'

'She'll be pretending to get herself attacked next.'

'Meaning? –' stung.

'For such an expert weaver of fantasies something went wrong with her scenario.'

'That! Don't be silly, man, anybody can see at a glance that it's a pure coincidence. A tragedy of course, and deplorable. But a coincidence. Inevitable, if you like. She was perpetually dramatising and then this happens. Like the people who are always talking about road accidents, and then are hit by a car.'

Odd that they should choose the same illustration. Or more likely no, not odd. There was something shrewd though, about the remark. And a certain truth.

'You don't feel like a tonic-water or something?'

'No, and don't try to dodge. I don't know what my mother told you or what you think as a result, but I'll take this early opportunity of getting any cobwebs out of your skull you might have stuck there.'

'I'm an officer of police,' said Castang woodenly, 'appointed by the judge to conduct an enquiry.'

'Now look, you were here several weeks ago, and I've the right to know exactly what you were doing here and by what authority.'

'Yes, you have the right. Don't shout and I'll tell you. I just don't want to dramatise the occasion or give it undue weight. You might be well advised not to do so either.'

'More accusations,' contemptuously.

'And there you go, straight off. You're like a girl at the street corner, convinced all the boys who pass are talking about her.'

The boy took a step ready to throw a punch, looking wild and sweaty, took hold of himself and his voice.

'Cut it out.'

Castang looked at him with some curiosity.

'Madame Lipschitz came to see me some time back. In a state of fatigue and tension.'

'With a dotty tale!'

'No. Discouraged. Over-anxious, maybe over-excited, to go to all that trouble. Why be so quick to say dotty?'

'I know what's coming, that's why. She went to the police here. I know because the commissaire told me. He knew it was all moonshine. A set of hysterical claims that I was pestering her, complaints about my ingratitude, all the usual. All unprovable and all malicious. That's dotty! It's persecution mania.'

'No.'

'Swallow that guff and you'll believe anything. If you're really that credulous you'll be suspecting me next of knocking her on the head. She'd have been capable of claiming I tried. I wouldn't have put it past her.'

Castang had been wanting a drink for some time. Now he was beginning to need one.

'You throw yourself about as recklessly as these bits of terminology you make free with,' he said. 'Talk about what you know. A person who is showing a capacity for restraint and balance, who is making efforts to be objective, is not suffering from persecution mania. An open and generous person is not systematically malicious. Anybody can be embittered, and can have good reason for it. You for instance. But you're quick to throw abuse at a dead person. By your standard I'd be accusing you of persecution mania.'

'When you come here trying to browbeat me and questioning my wife behind my back it strikes me I've grounds.'

It is a truism to any cop. The public, even when treated with quite exaggerated politeness, always feels guilty of something or other, and takes refuge in feeling browbeaten. Since there are plenty of cops, as well as all the other sorts of petty functionaries, who do have a bullying manner this is just too bad for the good ones.

'Listen carefully,' he said. 'When people come to us with tales of fears and anxieties we don't jump to a conclusion. We try to look for a base in fact. And that was the purpose of my last visit.'

'And did you find any?'

'I found no ground for interfering with anyone's private life, including yours. This time though, I'm on a different footing. This is an enquiry ordered by a magistrate. Enquiry into a death. That's a fact, if you like, and a grave one. I ask any question I see fit, of anybody I like, and they're bound to answer. This is a judicial enquiry, not a cop asking to see your fishing licence. And now you want your dinner, and I want mine. I've nothing to ask you at present, and no idea what I might ask you in the future. So don't get worked up: nobody's persecuting you.'

That's a tiresome boy, thought Castang. Easy to see why Sabine found him a strain. Anybody would imagine she'd died just to spite him. And to be fair, he had found her a handful too.

CHAPTER TEN

The 'Bons Amis' could have been worse: an ordinary village pub, a bit offensively modernised in slaughter-house red plastic. A few belated villagers in no hurry to get home to their wives were having a third quick one. A noisy group of builders' workmen, whitened with plaster, were slurping soup among bread crusts and beer bottles. An old man with no wife to go to was standing at the bar drinking red wine and gazing at a far horizon. Young Lucciani was sitting at a table in the back writing up rough notes in a professionally important way to impress Castang, the eye a bit glittery already from gazing into the aperitif bottle. He'd got organised; the table was laid.

Along with Castang appeared a basket of bread and a jug of white wine: he poured out a glass standing up, for a swig he felt he'd deserved.

'Pastis?' asked the fat woman, changing the ashtray.

'This'll do.'

'Soup or rabbit paté?'

'What comes after?'

'Grilled andouillette, stew. Steak's extra. The andouillettes are good.'

'Bit piggy after paté.'

'Stew, then.'

'Me, soup and andouillette,' said Lucciani.

'And a jug of red. Need fortifying. Those two were a pest. What did you get?'

'A lot of chat,' filling his glass.

'Go easy – you're at least two ahead of me and the day is long. Sum it up briefly.'

'Madame Lipschitz was much liked in the neighbourhood. General opinion was "a sort of saint".'

'What sort of saint?'

The rabbit paté was good. Not over-seasoned, not too greasy. Nor dry. Fresh thyme in it. A pleasant surprise: the 'Bons Amis' was a find. It's police aphorism number one: criminal investigations depend a lot on the local pub being good.

'What sort of saint?' again, tearing off bread. Lucciani's mouth had been too full to answer.

'Oh, you know, always kind, thoughtful to other people, nice to the children. A real Christian. You know, the others go to church, but she behaved as though she meant it. It spread over into daily life.'

'Rare, that sort of saint.'

'Too true. Some oddities, with all that. Pilgrimages and apparitions of the Virgin. I mean, sort of superstitious. Went in for stars and horoscopes.'

'Nothing very eccentric about that. Whole damn country's given over to fortune-tellers.'

'Absent-minded,' eating soup noisily. 'Always forgotten her purse or her glasses or both.' It was vegetable soup. Smelt good. As usual, Castang thought he'd given the wrong order. But the equation was difficult. Vera made soup every day, whereas young Lucciani lived alone and soup was a treat. Vera's stew was good too, but it was Czech stew, and this would be different. The equation was too difficult and he gave it up.

'Go on.'

'All right, well, picking witnesses at random: generous, tenderhearted. Naïve. One I thought you'd like; "childishly direct and innocent" – the butcher, that. Hey...'

Castang was tasting the soup from the ladle, with a nod of approval.

'"Nobody would have wished her harm". Now the children – the son and the daughter-in-law – they aren't so well liked.'

'No, and I can readily understand why.'

'A few more adjectives,' helping himself to more soup and gazing accusingly at Castang because the plate wasn't full, 'arrogant. Stuck-up, suspicious, quarrelsome. She's from Paris, by the way. "Behave like tourists", "think themselves too good for us", "knows it all" – that's the butcher again. And the woman right opposite – "Madame Lipschitz spoiled that boy out of the goodness of her heart."'

'Nobody suggests, of course, that they knocked her on the head.'

'No, and that's reliable, isn't it, since they aren't too popular.'

'Good; that's what I wanted you to get at. Confirms what the local fuzz say too.'

'There were a lot of noisy rows, but nobody thought much of them.'

Castang, the fatigue and tedium of the morning thrown off by two glasses of mediocre white wine, was mentally composing his report for Monsieur Richard:

'Possibilities: one, the organised gang of professional burglars. To my mind can be ruled out.

Two: the amateur burglar, vagabond or layabout. Unsupported but remains a likelihood. Sole proof obtainable, a similar pattern in the countryside showing similar features.

Three: a family affair: be it conspiracy, meaningless squabble, or sudden nervous breakdown. Remains a remote possibility, but on evidence and interrogations so far collected, both evidentially and psychologically highly improbable.

Four: a solution not hitherto thought of. Nothing thus far come to light gives this any weight whatever.'

Bugger number four, thought Castang. Bugger all the others too, while you're at it.

'Good,' he said. 'That's enough literature. A few facts now.'

Facts were impeded by the arrival of andouillette, at which Castang gazed greedily, all juicy in its mask of crisp breadcrumbs, nestling on a sweet gentle bed of mashed potatoes. He was only cheered by Lucciani's glaring hungrily at his stew: each sighed loudly and went with resignation back to his own plate.

The stew was good. Generously, Castang suggested a swap, halfway through. The red wine was not as good as the white: a fact, that, for future reference.

'Nothing to offer, about the time in question. The muffled shrieks and stealthy footsteps are right out. Everybody asleep, and there isn't a fact anywhere mentioned by two witnesses independently. Tales in plenty – the vandals at the Saturday-night dance, the monument to the General, covered in red paint by persons unknown, and the Free Brittany people, who covered the Prefect in cowdung. Break-ins, burglaries, tickles in general, here in the district – zero. Lucky them. I can't get outlying districts without a print-out from the computer.'

'This evening. All right, no corroborated witnesses. Be too much to hope for anyhow. Let's have the old biddies. Must be a legless ex-soldier somewhere in a wheelchair with nothing better to do than look out of the window – there always is. And sleepless, with any luck.'

'Yes, there is. I quite like him – don't know if you will. He said "Your boss has been here before, hasn't he?" Well, I didn't know. I just said "I don't know; has he?"'

'He has,' said Castang, 'but why shouldn't I like him?'

Pleasure at Castang thus falling into the pit digged.

'Well, he said "Who's that little bugger like a groom? I've seen him before." So I thought quite a good mark for observation.'

'What other little buggers has this admirable observer reliably observed?'

'A car parked, that night. Seen it before, he says, and a man going in to the old lady. I thought that worth pursuing. Dark blue Peugeot, the "Big model". Injection engine, because that's written on the back, and sheepskins on the front seats. Number not noticed, but registered in this department. Man described as prosperous businessman type. Sort of Homburg hat, dark colour. Silk scarf, dark suit, no overcoat. Same on both occasions. Evening of the crime, between ten and eleven p.m., that's the nearest he'd go. Could be out half an hour either way. Car parked here in front of the church where it's forbidden: nothing concealed or furtive.'

'Good. Get anything else?'

'Not much. A few weeks ago there was a junk dealer, said he was from the city, asked everyone for stuff out of the attic: furniture, the usual. Grey Citroën Safari station-wagon. Man described as fat-faced, dark or greyish hair, ingratiating manner, persuasive and obstinate. No evidence whether he got in to the old lady's house, but he wormed into most houses.'

'Sounds genuine. He leave cards?'

'I thought of that. They'd all been thrown away, but the name began with "do". Domicile. Domodossola.'

'Do re mi. He actually buy stuff?'

'Yes. Paid cash – no cheques.'

'Country people don't like cheques. What exactly is a few weeks?'

'About two, in mid-week.'

'Fresh stewed pears,' said the fat woman, 'and a nice Camembert.'

'And coffee,' said Castang. 'Got to be checked; phone it through.'

'Didn't young Lipschitz have a story about a phoney dealer calling?'

'Yes, and like the groom it turned out to be me. Go on with it this afternoon; I want it really thorough.'

'You going to stay here? They've a couple of rooms.'

'They'd be delighted, no doubt. Every sip of coffee scrutinised by every eye in the village; thanks. No, drive me into the town; I've got to be there anyhow. We'll find some commercial place.'

The Hotel Central was correctly commercial, dreary and even quite central, meaning a hundred metres from the railway station at the outskirts of the 'new town'. Castang went into the tobacconist's next door and found a guidebook, which he would not have bothered with had the author not been called Vincent Lipschitz. It was the usual flowery rhetoric about persons and objects of historic and cultural interest, and he'd given a good write-up to his friends!

The Hotel Central supplied the local phone book, and the regional directory: both much annotated in every kind of ballpoint known to the human race. Castang added his quota and walked over to see the notary.

This gentleman lived in the 'old town', in a fine dignified town house of the seventeenth century, with panelled rooms. In the waiting-room the usual buyers and sellers of house property were crowded dispiritedly, until Maître should find time to read them their conveyancing deeds and witness the signatures: as Castang expected, curiosity helped him to jump the queue.

Maître was silver-haired, elderly but not yet gaga, with an air of belonging to the local gentry and not intending that it should escape notice. An art connoisseur too: lithographs by Daumier and Forain enlivened his panels.

Maître, being curious, was very polite. Said of course Monsieur Uh was not a disturbance, and that his ear was attentive. No, he had not had the honour of knowing Madame Lipschitz personally, but there had been professional dealings. He could call his clerk for the dossier if Monsieur wished, but there was no real need. His memory was excellent, praise God. And subsequent to this tragic and deplorable accident he had refreshed it. At the request of Monsieur le Juge; quite so. He would be happy now to recapitulate.

No no, no, not a shadow of query upon the title to the property. His own father, predecessor in this study, had drawn up the deeds. For Madame Lipschitz's father, exactly. Unencumbered – mortgages, loans: perish the thought, dear man. And he had made a will. No real need, no, but the late Monsieur Lipschitz, with whom he had had the pleasure of being on terms of acquaintance, had been a man of business habit. During her lifetime, all property mobile and immobile to Madame Lipschitz, and in event of her death before such a date in trust – skip that bit. All firm as the rock. Which rock would that be, haha? The rock of Good Hope, perhaps; inheritances you know, haha.

And the adoption of the child: oh, absolutely legal. Maître had seen to it himself. As a consequence all property, including that from Madame's father and brought into settlement at her marriage, descended to the young man Gérard. Enjoyment and usufruct during Madame's lifetime, quite so.

Oh that was all splendid, said Castang (approximately). And by the way, since Maître was a local dignitary, a Pillar, and generally the repository of every secret – aha, haha, nothing there for the police of course, nono, hoho – and since also (spiderlike, Louis XI listening behind the arras) Maître was such a patron of the arts, perhaps he could suggest some people in the neighbourhood, who had known the family Lipschitz fairly well, say.

The old boy fell into guide-book language straight off. Now let's see: there had of course been dear old François-Xavier, Poet of Our Region. A great family friend, and the child's godfather. Now alas deceased. And dear old Canon Rampon, archpriest of Our Cathedral – most delightfully Proustian figure, great expert on etymologies, but alas also deceased, dearohdear. Now really the only person actually, who could still be thought of – still alive, nominally anyhow – might be Monsieur Barde, the well-known local gentleman farmer. Who was still in robust health, he was glad to say. A most delightful person whose every pore, so to speak, breathed perfumes of true civilised living. A littérateur, too, my dear man, of note. Formerly a contributor to literary reviews. Ah, days gone by! Golden youth and sweet virility never more to be recaptured. Ah, and now that he thought, Mademoiselle Aubrienne the noted sculptress: he couldn't quite say but he rather thought she might still be alive.

Profuse thanks. Maître was too good.

My dear man, think nothing of it, I beg you: had you no hat?

No hat. But Maître did not by chance know someone owner of a Homburg hat and a dark blue Peugeot with sheepskins?

Dear man, don't ask me about cars; I know nothing about them. I have one, naturally: an English one, of course; a Rover, I believe it must be called. French cars are for the base populace, and German cars for successful butchers. And Italian cars, somehow associated with living upon immoral earnings.

There remains to be sure the Ross-Royess, but apart from one or two elderly ladies of his acquaintance nobody bought them but pop singers. Homburg hats?... wear one myself. Delighted, dear Monsieur Uh, and my compliments to the Judge.

Whom we'll all be seeing, Castang told himself, at the

Wednesday evening bridge table at Monsieur the Procureur's. They live here as though it were still nineteen thirty-five, tut-tutting away about housemaids and the Stavisky scandals.

Monsieur Barde farmed, in his gentlemanly way, about three kilometres off, in his country house upon his estate. Castang was tired of gentlemen already. He had kept the car though: do young Lucciani good to walk a bit.

Mixed feelings. This affair was full of provincial celebrities, and Castang had learned early in existence that they are the biggest bores on earth. But it was his very first independent – truly independent – homicide, without Richard breathing down his neck while pretending not to be interested. That counted. Make something of this, and it will be some needed good marks.

And however provincial this ancient but tiresome town may be, this is still a homicide. Sabine was killed. Sabine was murdered.

CHAPTER ELEVEN

Monsieur Barde's house was a small country manor. Something like Sabine's, in fact, but much grander, more bijou, gayer, and lots more paint on the window-frames. Money inside, too, no doubt. The wrought-iron grille was rococo openwork, and a formal French garden could be seen, with a geometric maze of box hedges going from square to circle through octagon. On either side, trees. None of those huge, wet dripping trees, whose roots tripped you up, thrusting awkward humid fingers through the bedroom window. Lush, but trimmed, bowers, with showers of flowers.

The manor had a dinky pepperbox turret amongst other nineteenth-century follies. A stable, too, and part of this was a garage. And in the garage, a shiny dark blue car, with sheepskins on the seats. Not, though, a vulgar modern Peugeot. One might have guessed, at that. Gentleman's car, 1937 or thereabouts, Delahaye. Regretfully, nobody would mistake it for a modern one: its lovely radiator was well back of the elegant front wheels.

The front door was opened by a phenomenon, a young pretty girl in a black frock and white swiss-embroidery apron; a maid, no less, and whose nubile charms were set off by the harness. A soubrette. Castang gave her his card.

'Like to see Monsieur Barde. You could say I've an introduction from Maître le Tarentais.' The soubrette smiled winningly and tripped off: he couldn't remember ever having seen anybody tripping off before. He stood in the hallway, where swords and things decorated the walls. She came back and hooked on, and towed him along.

A large, light room, the depth of the house, window in front and French window onto terrace behind. Pretty and pleasant; stucco ceiling, painted panels of Pompadour pink and apple-green, like Sèvres china. Furnished in English style with low sofas covered in chintz, and a marble chimneypiece with bright brass fire-irons, and a fire too of logs smelling of fruit-wood, even on this warm afternoon. He was taken aback by the warmth, both of the room and the welcome.

'My dear Monsieur Castang. Come along in. Sit down, do; make yourself comfortable. And let's be talking, as Mrs Kenwigs said. You don't know Dickens? Pity, you'd like him. Now, what can I offer you this chilly weather? A whisky would be just the job? Or would you rather a glass of sherry?'

Overwhelming. The wave, arriving while one wades gingerly out from the beach, water striking a bit chill round the gut, so one takes one's time. The wave sends you spluttering and feeling for a footing. No harm done. Just you'd have liked to choose your own moment to get soused, less boisterously.

'It all sounds very English,' he said feebly: there was a big boom of laughter.

'Terrible country, England. I like it, even the warm sherry, and a fuss about decanters. Now here you are.' A cut-crystal glass shaped like a thistle-flower. Castang, who had seen this object embroidered upon the shirts of Scottish rugby players, drew the right conclusions and got another boom.

'Splendid, and shows you're a detective. Right, right, we

should have water too from some beck, but since there isn't any, we drink this as she comes. Not going to abuse this with frightful ice cubes. So fall on, as the English said to the French when they fixed bagginets. That's Sam Weller. Tell me what you think about that.'

'Sensational,' rightly guessing this meant the whisky and not the mysterious phrases in English. 'Doesn't taste like whisky though.' Third boom.

'Not like that blended muck they give you in bars, no. Single malt, my dear boy.'

'You aren't English, are you?' still feebly.

'Certainly not. Or parish pump French either. A Norman, my boy, Norman as Maupassant.'

Castang took a swig to give himself countenance. He had got a frame of reference by now. He knew a wine-shipper down in Aquitaine, where they talked about Queen Eleanor, gave their dogs English names, sent the children to Cambridge to polish their accents, and were snobbish about the Rothschild family.

Monsieur Barde was tall and massive, with pale straight features and pale brown hair. He was surely sixty, and the hair dyed, but he didn't look a day over fifty, and with excellent digestion. He wore a shirt with an open collar, a cashmere pullover the colour of a Victoria plum, riding breeches – beautifully cut. And boots which would cost two months of Castang's pay. There was money in the family, one might say. Broad acres, pedigree cows, thoroughbred horses, all very Norman. And literature too. Who was Sam Weller, anyway?

Humbled by the boots and the whisky he felt like a stable-boy, being congratulated after the owner has had a good win at Cheltenham. This sofa was too low and the cushions too thick. And Monsieur Barde... standing in front of that fire, warming his behind and sipping at the single malt, whatever that was. All affable and patrician. Castang didn't want to be towered over. He got up.

'We've had a death in the neighbourhood.' Parochial. He put his glass on a silver tray, presented no doubt by grateful foxhounds, and lit a vulgar, parish-pump Gitane with a filter tip.

'You mean poor Sabine Arthur. Very sad indeed. And I'm in burglar alarms up to here, and I just hope they do me some good.' He saw from the policeman's civil-service facial expression that it sounded a bit too tittuppy. 'Poor Sabine. She was an old friend. I was deeply distressed.' He wasn't pleased with 'deeply distressed', thought about it in a search for something better, gave it up. All those funereal phrases sound insincere.

'But you haven't had any trouble round here with housebreakers? Wealthy neighbourhood – looks tempting from the road.'

'No. No. Not to my knowledge. I didn't go to the funeral, I'm afraid. Should have. Smell of chrysanthemums affects me like ether. Felt guilty about it.' So one saw. Why else all the excuses, and the emphasis on how deeply he'd been distressed.

'Had any calls, from furniture dealers, or purporting to be such? In the last couple of months, say?'

'Not that I know of. My housekeeper wouldn't bother me with such. And if I want a dealer I go to the Quai Voltaire. Local people's prices are too high.'

'And you've never had a break-in? Can I ask the servants, whether they've seen people wanting to buy or sell things?'

'Of course. Ring for tea by and by; ask what you like. But is this visit just a warning to look out for phoney dealers?'

'The notary mentioned your name, as an old friend of the Lipschitz family.'

'I see. The burglar after objects of art – that's the accepted theory, is it?'

'More or less. I've only just begun.'

'Of course. Yes, well, Le Tarentais is a bit of an old ass, you know. Country notary's business – nothing much to stretch the brains. Dear old gentleman but the grey matter gone a bit to seed, like a dandelion. True enough, Sabine was an old friend. I haven't laid eyes on her in donkey's years, that's all. In the far-off glorious days of youth we used to sit up talking till all hours of the night,' sentimentally. By the fireplace was a broad ribbon ending in a tassel: he pulled it and an electric bell sounded faintly.

'She decayed, you know,' said Barde. 'Dusty little province this. I would myself, without effort.'

The door opened and the pretty maid stood waiting, well trained.

'Tea, for two, would you tell Céleste, and would she help bring it because I want her... delicious crumpet,' fruitily, as the door closed. 'That catch-hold-of-me-bottom walk... Sorry, rather a sudden pull up, Sammy, ain't it? Tony Weller.'

Janey, he's being Dickensian again.

'Still – you can ask Céleste if there've been any hawkers. She's a cranky old devil: if I wasn't here she might refuse to say, or invent heaven knows what. Called Melanie really: Céleste is after Proust of course. But to go back to what we were saying – Sabine when young, dear me yes. Swiftness, supple phrase, the swallow's wingtip, absolutely. A felicity of wit in that gentle voice. But she got old, poor dear.'

'You knew Lipschitz too?'

'Indeed I did. Can't exactly say we were all students together **t** but we were contemporaries.' Would put him at about sixty-five, thought Castang. Must be all the bottom-pinching keeps him young.

He must have had a mental arithmetic look, because 'I was a lot younger really,' added Barde, 'but seems contemporary at this distance. Poor old Vincent.'

Why was he so overwhelmingly loquacious? They were always like that in these small towns – nobody to talk to.

'Had talent; undoubtedly he had talent. All renounced for love of Sabine. Her roots were here in the countryside: she detested Paris, poor thing. And Vincent as poor as a church mouse. Had this thread of erudition, a taste for archaeology. Stuck to this small affair and worked it up, quite brilliantly I'm bound to say. Can't think of a provincial museum more excitingly displayed. Oh, here's tea; do praise it: the old dear will be ever so pleased.' The corners of Castang's mouth were turning down a bit. There was something about Monsieur Barde's praise of others that was approval of himself... Provincial celebrities! Sabine had not been like that. Somehow it put him on her side. Simplicity, the navy blue pullover, the shabby trousers, and the alert eye that took things in.

The pretty girl brought in the tea with a hobbly but spry old witch to supervise while goodies got circulated: scones and things all very English. He took something to be polite. Barde, who as he explained – everyone would be interested – got up early, and lunched at twelve, and always did, and was busy with unspecified but energetic things concerned with horse and hound, sabred away at the honey and stuff. His mouth might be full, but it didn't stop him talking, and supplying the answers too.

'You've never had any phoney antique dealers here come to the door, have you, Céleste? I felt sure you hadn't, or you'd have told me about that, wouldn't you?'

Castang had a feeling of being carted. Bit of a dealer in fake antiques himself, this Barde.

'Lipschitz was a bit of a disappointed man?'

'What makes you think that?'

'I don't know – an impression. Childless couple too. This boy's adopted from what they tell me. Sole heir, if I understood Le Tarentais aright.'

'Yes?' vaguely. 'I saw little enough of them in these last years. Know what you mean, of course, that the boy was a disappointment – true, I think. Vincent didn't talk of it, and Sabine was always an intensely secret person. I say though: you're digging away at ancient history, aren't you?'

'Tidying,' said Castang. 'A good thing to check up on, when there's an unexplained homicide, is to see whether anyone had a financial interest.'

'Oh quite. Have another cup. Oh, nonsense, man.'

'But this boy's sole inheritor. No conflict of interest there.'

'No, I suppose not.' Castang had thought Barde would gossip, but he seemed disinclined.

'I don't know much about it. You should have asked old François dear old man, if rather a bore.'

'Who?'

'François-Xavier Martigues, Poet of Our Region. He was close to them. Took an interest in the boy and all that: I'm vague, myself. Sabine was very headstrong about it all, as I remember: dare say she came to regret her impetuosity.'

Not much use, this Barde, as a source of information or even of gossip. He was nicely embedded in honey, and it gave him eternal youth, and he wasn't going in for children, thanks. Noisy objects, tiring, tending to break china or come bursting in just as he had his hand up the parlour-maid's skirt. Not that that was police business.

Very polite though; insisted that he take a cigar.

'One last thing, by the way,' said Castang. 'You asked whether the burglar notion was the accepted theory. You might have had a faintly sceptical tone, saying that? I dare say I'm mistaken.'

Barde was looking surprised.

'Don't well see what else it could be. I'm not a policeman, naturally.'

'You find it plausible, though? Good stuff in the house for example? Looked nice to me, but I'm no judge.'

'Yes indeed. I've not been there in ages but Vincent had taste. Nothing outstanding perhaps, but good early china, some fine old country furniture, not to be sneezed at nowadays. Worth a pillager's trouble, no doubt of it. They wouldn't touch the Gallo-Roman stuff.'

'Many thanks. Lot of help.'

'Pleasure, dear man. Chap gets bored. Police make a nice change.'

Not everyone's sentiment, maybe, but in this small-town world one could see what he meant.

CHAPTER TWELVE

Castang had taken one sandwich – cress and parmesan, nice – and no cake, and stood in no need of exercise. This country road was pleasant, though, on a late afternoon of still autumn sunshine, now westering. There would be a fine red fireball over there above the low hills crowned with woods. He wanted to shake off the stuffy feeling, a flavour of cigar and Barde's faintly ignoble personality. He understood Sabine saying she had no real friends left. He strolled a way up the road with his hands in his pockets: not even a policeman would be insensitive to the smell of burning leaves and moist earth.

Hm. A quarter out here for the folk who'd got it made. Villas, mostly newish along this side. Double garages and immature trees. Hedges still thin, and a glimpse here and there of a swimming-pool. The other side older and bigger houses of a former era, not without attractions either. Paddocks, tennis courts. English gardens. Burglars or an antiques gang would have been busy along here, surely. Barde had said not, and he would know.

Countrified road with no pavements; a lane. Called rather grandly the Route des Crêtes – what summits? Those little hills? Or these villas, prosperous with their tall hedges and high gates and names like 'Green Gables'. Successful undertakers as the notary said, big Mercedes cars. Grand piano belt, this. Somebody had made a lot of money carving up that terrain opposite: living out here had 'standing'.

There was a soft noise of hoofs. He turned his head idly: a horse was being walked, a girl in the saddle wearing jeans and a sweater. Prettyish girl with fair hair down to the shoulders. He felt a fool, because she had to turn in at Green Gables, which he was staring in at open-mouthed, and he caught a haughty glance, cavalry to infantry, as she reached over to release the gate-latch. Daughter of the rich. She did not glance back, but he shuffled off shamefaced as though he had been caught peeping.

He had work to do anyway. His work on directories had given him the local house agents: he sat in the car and studied his notebook.

That was why it had seemed familiar! Pierre-Paul Thonon. Number Four, Place d'Armes. Private address, 'Green Gables, Chemin des Cretes'... Trust a house agent to have made good money. He would twist Monsieur Thonon's tail a bit, just to be spiteful!

He left the car on the faubourg outside the Hotel Central, where Lucciani would see it. He walked the few hundred metres to the old city gate. The Place d'Armes was the centre of the 'old town', a formal square in the severe manner of Vauban's time, with an arched arcade spoilt by the self-advertising vulgarity of a row of shops. The Agence Thonon was one of them, inoffensive with the usual window full of typed cards and photographs of desirable residences, with agency shorthand about their insides. Within was a small office, with a secretary at a desk, architects' plans and elevations on the walls, and two dinky dollshouse maquettes of what the new block of luxury flats, In This Exclusive Neighbourhood, would be like once it stopped being a hole in the ground.

None of this was very interesting: what he was staring at had caught his eye through the window: a heap of cars parked on the square. Vauban wouldn't have cared for that, no, but more to the point was that one was a dark blue Peugeot with sheepskins on the seats. This cheered him up. It existed, and its owner would be back to pick it up if he hung about till six. Come to that...

The girl put down her phone and asked could she help him? He'd like to talk to Monsieur Thonon? Well, he was with a customer but wouldn't be long. He didn't mind waiting five minutes?

Castang, feeling lucky, didn't mind five minutes.

'Thought I'd catch him – isn't that his car, the blue one?'

'That's right.'

A real little stroke of fortune, making up for all that time wasted tea-drinking with the bourgeois. He was to windward of a chap he wished to question. Ho ho, Thonon, dear old Popaul. He had too much experience to think everything was going to be this easy, but it was a breeze to sail under.

A fitful breeze. The man had parked there openly. And Sabine herself had told him about the energetic house agent. But at least the fellow had been there that evening. He'd be able to throw a little light on what Castang wanted to know. What had been Sabine's activities that evening? Maybe movements? Maybe thoughts?

The five minutes dragged but he didn't mind. He had five or six agents on his list and this might have been the last call, if he hadn't taken that little stroll down the road. And it might so easily have been somebody else come to hustle Sabine: an architect, or a builder, or someone from town planning. Or a man about a dog.

A loud busybee noise on the pavement made him look. A Japanese motor scooter with gay paint; agreeable toy. A girl in a scarlet trouser suit added to the colour scheme and the notion of agreeable toys: she came in on a high wind.

'Dad there, Marianne?'

Popaul's daughter. Hell, he'd been slow! The girl on the horse… Castang remained turned towards the window, vastly interested in Japanese motorbikes. He'd been caught once that day.

'He's got someone. Oh, only old Sallebert worrying about his sewer pipes, but there's…' Meaning cough, meant for him, so he paid no attention. Even if she did recognise him – what importance had that?

'Oh, it's nothing much. To pick up my eiderdown from the cleaners – such an awkward big parcel, and it's on his way home. You won't let him forget, Marianne, will you? He'll grumble, but I don't care – here's the ticket. I'll fly, then.' And whizzed out, still with the high wind.

Accelerating like a mad thing, apparently intent on kicking the clutch to ribbons: teenage girls! Imagining it was a Harley Davidson. Bourgeois Miss of about nineteen. Nice, though. He felt indulgent. Small coincidence number two: they generally came in threes, like aeroplane accidents. Still a bit fat, spotty and awkward, but would be really pretty one of these days, mm. The detective daydreamed of lecheries, and woke to find Popaul on deck.

'Ciao then, and I'll give you a buzz as soon as I hear… sorry to have kept you – would you like to come in?'

'Oh, Monsieur Thonon, Martine dropped in and I wasn't to forget to ask could you pick her eiderdown up from the cleaners?'

'Oh, blow her old eiderdown; why can't she do it herself?'

'Too big, she said, to go on the back of the bike.'

'Oh nonsense, she'd only to ask for a bit of string. Too big and also too lazy. Sorry,' with a quick easy smile to Castang, 'these domestic hitches… Do sit down,' picking up a pipe and beginning to fill it. 'Advice on bringing up daughters is free, or haven't you any?'

'Not officially,' pushing his card across the desk, getting a laugh round the corner of the mouth which was getting the pipe to draw. He glanced at the card, didn't look fussed.

'Well,' leaning comfortably back and wedging the pipe between firm white teeth with two gold crowns, 'what's your problem then, or is the card to get the price reduced?'

Castang embarked on a vague tale, about burglaries and bourgeois houses with exterior signs of wealth like tennis courts; along the Chemin des Crêtes, for example. Thonon listened with no sign of haste or impatience. The description was right as well as the car: 'prosperous', youngish but formal in a middle-aged way. Dark suit, gold cuff-links, subfusc tie, and the Homburg hat hung upon a hook.

'Nothing much,' he said. 'An outbreak of break-ins – sorry, not trying to be funny – a few years ago. Two or three houses suffered loss and damage. An enterprising locksmith did good business afterwards with deadlocks and pressure pads and stuff. What took you out there?'

'I was talking to a Monsieur Barde.'

'Oh, I see. Bit of an old woman. Supposed to have an erotic picture worth a lot, Boucher or Fragonard or something. Probably a fake; he's a bit of a fake himself. His house bristles with electronic alarms and whatnot. Don't know that I'd put much faith in them. Might discourage an amateur, and at least you avoid the damage and the vandalism. Not that I've anything much worth pinching. If I had, I think I'd have more faith in a couple of lights left burning, maybe a radio on low.' He smoked the pipe with small even puffs, and didn't seem to be getting tense, despite the transparent silliness of Castang's story.

'Did you by any chance know Madame Lipschitz?'

'Who got slammed by an intruder? Certainly I did. And of course I knew that this was the real subject of your interest, Inspector.'

'News gets around.'

'What d'you expect? – Place this size. Just surprised to hear that the PJ were dragged in on it. Something fishy?'

'Not as far as I know. Judge making a slight fuss. We mostly do get called, you know, when there's a homicide. It's more than just another burglary.'

'Oh, of course. And the judge got a black eye over the mayor's parking lot. But you're trying to draw me out – I'm not vexed, don't worry. Am curious, though.'

'I'm trying to find out what I can about her movements that night.'

'Ah... now I get it. Somebody saw me, is that it?'

'Oh, it was you, then?'

'Stop being crafty; you were waiting to see if I denied it. Those villagers! They notice everything.' He sounded amused, like a man with a clear conscience. He took the pipe out to stop the tobacco with his finger. 'Well all right, I admit it, I suppose I should have come forward like a good citizen. Nothing to hide. But nothing to contribute either, and frankly, around here you learn that discretion isn't just better than valour: it's better than pretty well anything.' Rattling on though rather; overacting somewhat. 'Good,' holding his arms up and making a comic face, 'you've tracked me down. I'm at your service, naturally.'

'I'd like to know your business, and why you were doing it that late. You might have been the last person to see her.'

'But I left her in rude health.'

'Nobody's denying it.' The two pairs of gentle brown eyes looked at one another with the utmost sincerity. 'Of course you should have come forward,' said Castang mildly. 'I'll make no reproaches about that if you'll now be perfectly open about your concerns.'

'Fair enough. Nothing difficult about that. I've been dickering with her one way or the other for a year. Tiresome old lady, as they tend to be. You know; blowing hot and cold – now she would, now she wouldn't. But it's a good bit of property there. Worth my time and trouble – worth anybody's, and I mean anybody, and I hope you understand why I prefer to keep this dark. And why I didn't come forward: she got herself killed. For which naturally I'm personally very sorry, but for business my pitch is queered.'

'I'd like you to go into lots of detail,' said Castang. 'Who, what, since when?'

'All right. As I say then, I had a shot a long way back and she was very unforthcoming, but I did manage to get a first refusal out of her. Then she got the house classified: not historic monument but typical traditional dwelling-house. So it can't be knocked down, and the price goes up too: crafty move. Her husband was something in Cultural Affairs – she must have had a line to them. But I'm a tenacious bugger, and there's still plenty to be done with that huge garden where she never sets – sorry, set – foot. I murmured at her about that, but no soap. Then a week ago, you could have knocked me down, she comes sailing in here. Was I still interested? You bet, and exclusive, so no commissions to split. As for sneaking about like Dracula at dead of night, she suggested it herself.'

'Interesting.'

'Is it?' asked Popaul innocently. 'You may be right. Didn't strike me particularly, but maybe you're not as used as I am to the oddities and suspicions of old women who sell houses. Under the civilised exterior, you know, she was a very peasant sort of woman; intensely roundabout and full of chicanes. Didn't want anybody to know about my visit. And of course I was seen; just shows you.'

'Anybody in particular, or everybody in general?'

'Blowed if I know. Gave it no thought. Well yes, I did actually, but from another viewpoint. Meant to me that I might be getting somewhere. And why publicise that? A business like this, one has lots of friends who love you dearly, and the thing they love dearest is poking a stick into your bicycle wheel, strictly by accident.'

'Was she ready to sell, that night?'

'Heavens, man, we didn't get that far. A great deal of what about this and what about that. I felt optimistic though, that it was a matter of patience. And then she has to go and die,' said Popaul tragically.

There was a moment when Castang thought his enquiry was already over. The fellow's patter was so smooth, and sounded so well rehearsed.

'What about what this, and what that?'

There is a deal of talk in the Code of Criminal Procedure about interrogations, principally concerned with protecting the individual's rights. Lawyers, worrying about this, put in so many safeguards about not hearing, as witnesses, people against whom grave presumptions might be said to rest, that the cops could not do any work at all. There is, luckily, a safety valve. A witness in the office of an examining magistrate can be put on oath and threatened with a lot of penal sanctions. But a PJ cop conducting a 'prelim' knows anyway that everyone is telling lies. He expects it: would be astonished if they didn't.

He had to go easy. The fellow having simply 'been there' that evening was not a proof of anything. It was perhaps a 'material indication'. But that is not a rope you can trust your weight to.

Thonon fidgeted, and peered into the bowl of his pipe for inspiration.

'Do I have to tell you?'

'Tell me nothing if you prefer,' said Castang, bored.

'If it had any point – but it's all irrelevant.'

'Tell a lot of lies, if you think that would be cleverer.'

'I'd like to know what you're aiming at.'

'My reports go to the judge. He convenes you as a witness and questions you himself, if he sees fit. You've a lawyer to look after you.'

'Good God. You mean you suspect me of...?'

'Then stop being evasive.'

'Just that the judge, saving your presence, is an old nosy parker. Gossip with the notary, with Barde, all that gang. Look, if I'm straightforward with you, will you give me some assurance that it stays between us?'

'I'm as discreet a man as you are.'

'Not you I'm worried about, but this bloody small town.'

'See this impersonally,' said Castang patiently. 'X is dead. We enquire. So-and-so saw X at such a time. The subject of the conversation may as you claim be irrelevant. It is though germane to the enquiry. Obstruct me; I tell the judge you're a recalcitrant witness and ask him to treat you as such.'

'All right, all right,' irritably. 'I was hoping to make a deal, and still to make it with the old lady's heirs, but if this all gets into the press what chance have I?'

'I haven't spoken to the press: haven't even seen any yet. When I do I'll tell them what I see fit, which can be precious little. The judge is bound by professional secrecy, like a doctor. And I'm stretching this for you a long way, you know.'

'I was hoping for two separate deals,' sulky, 'one for the garden to develop as building land, and one for the house.'

'She sign any agreement?'

'You'll be claiming I had an interest in her death, next. Look, we were talking about getting an architect to design a wall – protect the amenities.'

'You've had contact with the heirs, on this subject?'

'I scarcely know who they are. The son next door, if that's all there is. Got to be tactful; can't just storm in while they're still arranging the funeral.'

'So you've nothing signed, no bit of paper?'

'It may sound strange, but she was an old-fashioned person, the sort who gives her word and keeps it. I relied on a verbal agreement. A written order to sell is of course legally necessary to the agent. I don't know whether that would be legally binding on the heirs. I've nothing, now.'

'Better. This has a more convincing ring about it.'

'I hope you now understand that I had certainly no interest whatever in her death.'

'Tell people they sound truthful,' said Castang, 'and they rarely lose an opportunity to embroider, to sound more truthful still.'

'Oh, for God's sake,' said Thonon crossly. 'Cops!'

'Cops are used to lies. Even when it's the truth, it's rare when there's nothing added, or nothing left out.'

'You're not seriously thinking I killed her, are you?' shaking his head disbelievingly. 'Or had something to do with it?'

'I don't have any preconceived ideas, Monsieur Thonon.'

'Was the press report all nonsense? I understood that this was a straightforward thing. Somebody broke in, and was caught by the old lady, and bumped her with a bottle or something, probably sheer stupid gratuitous violence.'

'That's correct, and that's the probability.'

'The sort of thing,' said Thonon seriously, 'which might have looked improbable a few years back, but now is only too believable because only too frequent.'

'As you say. Frequent. Believable. Likely.'

'You're doing your job. Exhausting all the possibilities. All right. I've given you all the explanations I have. Satisfied?'

'Sure,' placidly. 'I understand your wish for discretion, I understand your getting irritable. I'll hope to worry you no further.'

'I can take it that the police, or the law, or whoever, have no objection to my pursuing my business activities?' People are always sarcastic with cops, when they have felt frightened. 'You'll see nothing suspect in my trying to salvage this deal?'

'As long as you realise that while a homicide enquiry continues the material assets are frozen. A formal rule: it's not aimed at anyone. Means you can't yet put the deal through, but there's nothing to stop you setting it up. I won't gossip about your affairs.'

'Thanks.'

'Just out of interest, can you do business with the son?'

'I can try.'

'Know him at all?'

'Very slightly. Works for the municipality – I've seen him there.'

'What's his job, do you know?'

'Equipment – planning permissions and building permits,' with a faint grin. 'But in a junior capacity – don't get any wrong ideas.'

'No business of mine,' said Castang.

'I'd like to close up now,' a bit wearily. 'You'll not take it amiss if I say I've had enough.'

'Not to forget the eiderdown.'

'Damn the eiderdown... All right, Marianne, closing time. You'll not forget? – I count on your discretion.'

'Don't worry.' It was the truth. There would be a bustling local press man nattering at him, but that could be fixed with patter. As for the judge... well, one would see.

CHAPTER THIRTEEN

Young Lucciani'd had a nice quiet day, breaking off in plenty of time, under the pretext that the bus was only every half-hour, and he'd had no car. Primed now with a lot of stuff to show how hard he'd been working.

'Feel like a beer?' he suggested generously. 'And Peyrefitte's been asking for you.' Castang gave a grunt, to both, and went to ring. The Commissaire had been showing zeal.

'I've been looking up everyone with a record for violence as well as for larceny. The judge wanted a real purge, so we've looked at everyone round here. All verified and no soap.'

'Mm,' said Castang. What's he telling me for?

'That's that then,' he said aloud with a lack of warmth.

'Yes, but the computer turned up something interesting. Somebody'd asked for a print-out of the file at headquarters.'

'Lucciani was looking after it.' It had been a long day and there was something dulling about that computer. Or perhaps numbing.

'I had a telex half an hour back and I thought it worth seeing the judge about it. Some people, sort of gipsy characters, a bit out in the country. We've a file for a dozen misdemeanours, affrays and stuff, but no felonies. But the computer turned up a larceny with violence at Douai.' Interest quickened but very slightly. That was typical of the computer. It was always turning up peculiar things that had happened at Douai.

'The judge is pretty excited and is thinking of pulling them in on a mandate.'

'Too late now, surely.' The police can only use search and seizure warrants in daylight hours.

'Arrest them and be done with it, he thinks. He hasn't decided yet, but I'll keep you in touch.'

'Fair enough.' Castang was beginning to see light. Monsieur Peyrefitte would be pleased, and feel refreshed, if he managed to arrest all these frightful criminals while the PJ was stumbling about holding up its trousers with both hands.

'Peyrefitte's arresting a crowd of names he got off the computer,' drinking beer. 'He must have something else he isn't telling yet. He's preparing a triumph. What about you?'

'I phoned through. Richard says the dodo man is identified. Bona fide junk dealer. You know, selling stuff to Parisians who'll buy anything as long as it's wired for electricity. So that's out. Then this computer thing – some people to be verified by the gendarmerie. And they'll look up any other complaints made concerning vagabonds and hitch-hikers, all that stuff. And I said we'd be here, so he just said continue that way he has.'

'The village buttoned up?'

'I think so. But whatever they saw, thought, or imagined...'

'Or invent in order to sound interesting.'

'Anyway nothing fresh. By the way,' elaborately casual, 'the dark blue Peugeot – it's a local estate agent. I did some work on it.'

'I've just been talking to him,' without admitting he'd done no work on it.

'Oh,' said poor Lucciani, who'd done more than he admitted. 'Well, in case you hadn't known.'

'On the contrary, good. Anything known about him?'

'They say he's honest and you can rely on him. Clean reputation.'

'You have anything to conclude, about all this?'

'I think,' not sure whether he'd be jumped on, 'that the vague talk about vagabonds and hippies is just wishful thinking. What would they be doing in this neck of the woods anyway? They stick to main roads. Pass unnoticed there, but here surely – in the village – they'd draw attention. Nobody'd seen any: it was always someone else who had.'

Castang nodded.

'I'd agree. Write it all up anyway in précis form, so that I've something to show the judge for his trouble. Can't write it off. You'll have to go through all the gendarmerie reports tomorrow.'

'If I'd killed anyone, I'd get out of the district quick.'

'They don't always reason. Think they're invisible. Disdain for stupid cops. An incredible vanity even when they aren't on drugs.'

'If nothing got pinched but money there's no way of tying it up.'

'Can never be sure. This year one walked into a shop and bought a transistor radio: he hadn't had a penny the day before. Anything that turns up – breaking into an empty house is likeliest.'

'Except that it isn't noticed, often, till the owner comes next weekend.'

'I agree it's a bore. There's nothing for you to do here, though, and little enough for me.' The boy was in his first year of PJ work, and still made faces at the idea of an 'enquiry' petering out into days at the office, searching through piles of typed flimsies, straining the eyes and crooking the back. A computer could turn up a 'coordinate' in statistics of, say, condemnations, but could not handle the innumerable petty-larceny complaints. Young Lucciani still had visions of himself on the Violence Brigade, flat on the pavement outside a bank while bullets whistled, and wore his gun while behind a type-writer to show he was a cop.

CHAPTER FOURTEEN

Castang went to have a shower. Getting downstairs again he drank a mouthful of Lucciani's beer and went out to buy a paperback thriller before the tobacconist closed. Evenings in a town this size…

There was thinking to be done, but so little. One stayed still, let the day's work sink in. Maybe a breeze would blow and give a direction to next day's footsteps. What did the local people do in the evenings? Watched the television, heaven help them. The cinema. A beer at a café. Playing cards or studying racing form. The odd one might read a book. And many went away into little private worlds, rubbing an already well-cleaned shotgun, mending fishing tackle, watching a pigeon-loft or just 'with the collection'. Or with simple fantasy, which cost least. A few would go out and defeat boredom with petty crime. Not much of that hereabouts, bar breaking the speed limit. And Castang would go to bed with a gangster thriller.

Seven in the evening, when this already means nightfall, is the best time for looking at provincial towns in Europe. The animation is highest: the women who have worked all day are shopping: the street lamps hide the ugliness and the dreariness.

Best of all when it rained, and each shop offered a glowing haven from the raw air, and faces were seen through the glass of these brightly lit aquariums, laughing. Tonight it was chill, as it is in October after sunset; a dusty draught blew along the ugly little faubourg. But one did not see the mean ramshackle façades, and the leaves on the chestnut trees were turning, not yet fallen, and he felt content.

The Hotel Central was full by now of folk in for a quick one, as well as serious, heavy-footed billiards players, a smell of pork chops, and Lucciani reading that morning's Paris paper, the local one an exhausted wreck beside him. There had been a little paragraph about 'Judge calls in PJ', but no hawk had been around yet for any hot news. The local hawk would be too experienced, and too lazy, and knew there wasn't any hot news. Perhaps Peyrefitte was preparing some, but meanwhile the big story was the cracks that had appeared in the new swimming bath. 'Enquiry ordered.'

Castang pulled a chair out, asked for an Alsace beer and looked at it languidly.

'We'd better eat here. Peyrefitte won't arrest anybody this time of night. What you going to do?'

'Oh, go to a movie. Sex films again – never anything else in a place this size. What you got there? Pass it me when you've read it.'

'Phone for you, Monsieur Castang,' called the patronne from the bar, poking at her over-elaborate provincial hairdo, being slightly coquettish with the cops. 'Well,' passing him the phone, 'I'll have to get you to enquire into what the laundry does with my towels.'

'Man or woman?' half-hearted. Peyrefitte fussing again, or Vera, having a housewifely check-up?

'Woman. Dinner when you like.'

'Yes, Castang.'

'Are you the police inspector?' Not Vera!

'Himself and who are you?'

'Martine,' rapid and tense. 'You know – horse, motorbike.'

'Sure, but why the coy approach?'

'Don't fool; one never knows who's listening.'

'Somebody your end?'

'No but – I don't want to do a lot of explaining. Can I see you? Would you buy me a drink?'

'With pleasure. Not here though.'

'No, no, listen. D'you know the Rue des Remparts? In the old town. Behind the wall.' All very important: young girls thought themselves so extremely important. He had to collect his scattered wits: she was getting impatient at his stupidity.

'Ramparts, yes.'

'There's a little place called the Green Bay Tree. Two sort of tubs on the pavement. Meet me there. In half an hour.'

'I've had nothing to eat yet.' The sizzle of pork chops was making his stomach rumble.

'Neither have I,' irritably; when would these cops stop thinking about their stomachs? 'One eats well there.'

'All right, long as it's not too dear.'

'Oh, I'll pay if that's what worries you.'

'We'll manage.'

Lucciani was staring at the dregs in his beer glass, hoping to get another bought him. Castang didn't take the offer up. Not mean; just prudent.

'Go eat your dinner. I'm going out.'

'Office in a flap about something?'

'A bit of possible business. Go see your sex movie; I won't need you. Tomorrow morning around seven-thirty: be all bright and fresh then.'

Foggy, a little chilly. The weather was changing. Minute beads of moisture formed on his eyebrows, not enough to wear a raincoat for.

The Place d'Armes, with some economical floodlighting on

the classical façade of the town hall, once the Hotel of the Military Governor. Not a cat to be seen. Small provincial town. But he was a small provincial cop.

The Rue des Remparts was narrow and picturesque, with cobbles and antiquated street lamps, and seventeenth-century military architecture: low heavy arches with deep embrasures. Castang had a vision of vast ammunition-dumps left over from the Prussian War of 1870. All armies did this, squirrelling away immense quantities of expensive material, forgetting where they'd put it, and finding it again, much surprised, thirty years after it had become obsolete.

In the embrasures were now little low shops selling goldfish or wicker baskets, and one of these was the Green Bay Tree, with a curtained window duskily orange.

Somebody touched him on the shoulder and said 'Hallo' with a sort of friendly awkwardness. Martine was quite a big girl, or maybe he was too small. He wished he were one of those tall distinguished-looking cops like Richard. She still wore her scarlet suit, with a fine bottom inside it.

'Rather nice, isn't it? I like those heavy arches, and the case-mates or whatever they're called.' Nervous, therefore talkative.

'Must have been nice when it was a garrison in the colonial days. You know, Zouaves, and Spahis, and Senegalese. All with their own special brothel.' Bourgeois girls were always fascinated by brothels.

The Bay Tree was pleasant inside; a little bar and a few tables laid for eating. Smelling of old woodwork, but clean and friendly. A thin young woman in huge horn-rimmed glasses was sitting on a high chair behind her counter. Two men in overalls were having a glass of wine, and through the open kitchen door a fat comfortable woman was chopping parsley: there was nobody else.

'Hallo Sophie,' said Martine. 'This is a friend of mine.' Castang was glad to hear it. 'We'll sit down, shall we, at a table?

There'll be people to eat, later, but it's quiet here. And discreet.' Fine. He felt better, less like a black soldier who has walked into the wrong brothel.

'Do you drink?' he asked, 'or are you a Coca-Cola girl?'

'Whatever you like.'

'The whisky's nice today,' said Sophie comically, as though it were the fish. 'You know,' apologetically, 'it's hard to get good ones.'

So it was; not perhaps Monsieur Barde's super single malt. But not bar Scotch either.

'Sit down a sec and have a gossip,' said Martine, manoeuvring to be at ease.

'Have one with us,' said Castang hospitably, already at his ease and wishing to dispel the accusation of being mean.

'All right,' said Sophie. A plain young woman, but behind the big glasses were huge luminous eyes, beautifully shaped. Close up, she was pretty.

'There are no scandals. The coffee-machine is on the fritz again. I'm scrabbling in the till to pay the phone bill, as usual. I haven't a penny – I will go playing those horses.'

'Hey, Sophie,' called one of the men from the bar, 'what'll you give me for fixing the machine?'

'A drink a night, for a week.'

'That's a deal.'

'What's good to eat?' asked Castang, who didn't want his stomach to rumble in company with all these girls.

'And not that revolting menu all out of the freezer,' added Martine.

'There's a baby goat, with which Léonie has created a masterpiece, and there's hare. Birds, but they're rather dear. And a leek flan. And oysters.'

'I don't like hare,' said Martine.

'Green light for the baby goat,' said Castang, finding it all a change from the pork chops of the Hotel Central. 'And flan to begin with.'

'And a nice bordeaux,' said Sophie. 'Nobody ever heard its name, but a real one. I'll tell Léonie.' Her gestures behind the bar had been languid, but her walk was rapid and elastic. A plain young woman with messy hair and negligently dressed, but suddenly highly attractive. Perhaps that's the whisky, thought Castang.

The young man had fixed the coffee-machine, apparently with chewing gum. He poured himself a glass of wine, drank it, said 'Good night, good appetite' and walked out with his silent friend, leaving them to themselves.

'She know who I am?' asked Castang.

'She may: I haven't told her. She'll behave as though she doesn't. I brought you here because this is a good place. She's honest. This is the only place in this filthy little town where you're accepted for what you are. Nobody cares what job you do, or who your father is – or whether you might be in trouble with the cops.' It was a high accolade.

He liked it, even if it were only young girls' romanticism. He took a good look at her, which she was unselfconscious about while helping herself to one of his cigarettes.

Martine was a good choice to spend an evening with. A big tumble of clean shiny hair, a large frank forehead, wide eyes between grey and green, a spot from overeating at the corner of her nose, an unpainted mouth.

Silence fell between them. Castang was thinking of the latest bent-cops scandal: a vice-squad commissaire, who having been surprised was now acting the astounded in front of a tribunal. He'd got on the wrong side of the press, which described him cattily in this morning's paper as having 'a dear little red mouth pursed up like a hen's arse.' Castang, who had small sympathy for his erring brother (a man wearing hand-made shirts) had guffawed.

This mouth was as far from a hen's arse as one could get. A big round chin too, and well-shaped ears. A young female straight as a young tree. Skin coloured by blood and autumn sun. He drank his whisky and made a sound of relief and satisfaction.

'What's the big sigh for?'

'Pleasure. No wrinkles. Both are rare.'

'Right. You're a cop. PJ cop from the big town. So a bent bastard. But we can be friends, perhaps. I'd like that: the thing is, would you?'

'Not altogether bent. Miserable bastards.'

'Human, like anybody else.'

'They start out that way. Like most people, they're best when still children.'

'I don't want you to start fencing with me.'

'All right. Let's be straightforward: I ask nothing better. Why did you ring me up?'

'I wanted to find out what all this is about. I thought you might tell me in private, if it was between us.'

'I see. It's simple. Elderly woman got assassinated. By an intruder, we're assuming. Municipal cops make the usual enquiry, which is inconclusive. The judge instructing calls in the PJ. Which is me. That's all. It's ordinary enough.'

'And you think you're going to catch this burglar round here?'

'We're working on it all over. Back in the town too. I just happen to be here. You know anything about this burglar?'

'Don't be ridiculous: you don't think I know any burglars?'

'So you rang me up. Just out of curiosity. Never seen a PJ cop before, and you're anxious to know how they behave. That it? We're playing truth, remember?'

'Partly. I'm curious, of course. And I'd like to know too why you're spying on my father.'

'Routine background. A query about title in the house the old lady owned. A detail. I reckoned he could tell me.'

'Oh, don't lie so stupidly,' said Martine. 'I saw you hanging around our house this afternoon. Spying about.'

Castang shrugged. People insist on believing the cops are being crafty again. To talk about Monsieur Barde, and a stroll for fresh air and to look at the sunset – no, no explanations; nobody would believe them.

'Your father wanted to make a property deal with this old lady. It's not a secret, but he wanted to keep it quiet, as a matter of business tactics. I happened to learn this. I happened to be out your way this afternoon. Nothing sinister about all this; it needn't worry you.'

'Worry – that's a loaded word; it irritates me. Like a fussy old auntie. I don't worry. I'm concerned. People ought to be concerned.'

'About what?'

'About you. I suppose you're accustomed to everyone being hostile, or else going all servile because they're terrified. Well, I'm neither. It's so old-fashioned, all that. I mean cops, living in a sort of ghetto, friendly with all sorts of foul people and claiming it's because they're sources of valuable information. Like that ghastly man in the paper. Going to the same shirt-maker as the local gangsters, garaging the car where one gets such exceptionally good – and so cheap – service. Are you like that?' Blunt. As the cliché says, bluntness is disarming.

'Not all of us. There are always a few like that. Always will be. Anywhere.'

'I can be friendly with anyone. I don't care what they do. As long as they aren't false, and incapable of being honest with themselves. I suppose you'll say I'm very naïve. I should like to know why the truth always has automatically to be naïve.'

Castang was saved answering by Sophie, who came pattering up with two plates, one chipped but both hot, and two big wedges of the leek tart. The pastry was tender, the underside not soggy. The leeks were not overdone, the cream sauce light and plain, there was not too much cheese. It was simple, natural, and tasted good, like this girl.

Castang was very hungry. He hoped his underside wasn't soggy, either.

'I suppose your family don't know you're here – or even where you choose your friends.'

'You expect me to be scornful about my family, I dare say. Petty commerce and that. I can understand people who are ashamed of their families, but I'm not. I may not always have a very high opinion of them, but I keep quiet about it. I'll be going back to the university in a week or so, but while I'm here I try to avoid conflicts. And they don't know where I am nor whom I'm with because they trust me, so I trust them back. Peculiar of me, but that's the way I am.'

Castang couldn't stop grinning a bit. She didn't notice, wolfing down tart. Healthy young appetite.

'I'm not slumming in search of the picturesque, either,' getting good and warmed up. 'Not going ooh, you're a cop, you've a gun, you shoot people, let's play with the phallic symbol.'

'I'm carrying a gun,' said Castang peaceably, 'and wouldn't dream of letting you play with it.' Aware that this wasn't happily phrased. 'We're on terms of perfect equality.'

'All right. Long as we don't sit stupidly being suspicious of each other and reading motives into everything. More in existence than just imbecile sex.'

'I'm not against it, though. Are you?'

'No, but one gets vastly bored with the village cock, whose one idea is to steer one towards the nearest sofa. Nothing more resistible, did the preening cretin but grasp it.'

'We'll lay down the arms,' said Castang. His gun was in a belt holster, pushed to the back when he sat to eat, so that it didn't get in the way of his belly. He didn't know what he needed yet to cope with this one, but it didn't seem to be a gun.

'Sorry,' said Martine, 'but that sniggering certainty that a girl thinks of nothing else, dreams about it at night – contemptible.'

No guns, and no sex – what else did he have?

'Oh, blow this corkscrew,' said Sophie by his elbow.

'I'll do it,' being male.

'If I can't make a tool work I throw it away and get another, not scream for help,' scooting off.

'I see why you like her,' he said.

'She stands on her two feet. She has a little boy; doesn't parade the child looking for sympathy.'

'Better,' said Sophie wiping out the neck of the bottle and whisking the plates away. 'Goat'll be here in a sec.'

He poured out the unheard-of bordeaux. She wanted something from him. Perhaps just information. He wanted something from her. He didn't know what himself, yet. It was as simple as that.

'You get on well with your father,' he said, 'as I saw this afternoon.'

It was perhaps not very skilfully done.

'We're fond of each other. If he has worries I'll try not to add to them.'

'I'm not using this on you,' picking up the despised corkscrew Sophie had left.

'Stupid thing,' said that lady, whisking it away and inserting the goat deftly between his elbows.

'You used some corkscrew on him though,' said Martine. 'Probably most unfairly, and he's bothered. He's said nothing but I saw, and I'd seen you at the office. Fair and square now. If you suspect him of something, it's ridiculous, and if you're trying to pin something on him, it's just abject. But maybe it's a misunderstanding. If you'd tell me I might be able to help.'

One couldn't attack these nubbly bits with anything as

stupid as a knife and fork. Castang put his down, deciding to eat baby goat with his fingers. It was done the 'bonne femme' way. Shallots and mushrooms and little cocotte potatoes. Pretty good.

'I don't have anything to suspect – or pin down,' working away at the nubbly bits, 'on anyone.'

'Oh, do stop lying,' crossly. 'What's an inspector doing hanging about here? Nobody believes in this vagabond tale.'

'Your father doesn't?'

'But why should he know anything about it? He was trying to sell her house, and so what?'

'He was there the night she was killed, though.'

'Oh,' much taken aback. 'But that's meaningless.'

'Not all that meaningless. I see you thinking stupid cop. But it could be something more than superficial. Might be a causal connection, as well as spatial. Like whose book did it suit – or not suit – that Madame Lipschitz should sell her house?'

'Are you really suggesting,' enormously indignant, 'that he might have killed her?'

'Go on eating,' said Castang. 'Don't let it get cold.'

'You must be insane.'

'I'm not in the least insane.'

'But it's preposterous.'

'You asked me to be open: all right, I will be. If by "it" you mean some absurd scenario where the old lady refuses to sell and he gets mad and belts her with a hammer – yes, that's pretty preposterous, though sillier things have been known than that. I'm trying to tell you that his being there may not be just a coincidence. I don't know what it means, if anything, but maybe something consequential. I just have to be prudent about it. Now the idea of his killing her never entered your head, right?'

'Of course not.'

'So tell me what it was that worried you.'

'Salad,' said Sophie, bumping it down.

Poor Martine, pink and sweaty, eating and drinking in a great hurry, deciding she just couldn't eat any more. And she'd been so confident to start with. But what was it the girl had fixed in her head there?

'Well, when I saw you hanging round the house like that...' He ate salad with a blank patient face.

'I thought...' Sophie took away her plate; he poured out the last of the bottle. 'I thought it must be some kind of tax thing.'

'I see,' surprised, amused, hoping he showed neither.

'I mean I thought, when you found out that he was setting up this deal and it looked sort of surreptitious... And now his going there late at night... I thought maybe you suspected some kind of tax fraud. That you'd think, I mean, it might look phoney,' getting more tangled every second.

'And is there?' She picked at her salad faint-heartedly. 'Very serious offence, tax evasion,' pompously. Filthy hypocrite.

It all came in a flood now.

'I'm serious,' she said. 'I don't like this lousy capitalist society a bit, but just because I'm a student I don't go for all that Marxist crap either. Anyway, I've learned the hard way that what you do isn't always what you believe in.'

I haven't got much further, thought Castang.

'So I'm appealing to you now as an honest man, which I think you are, even if you are part of a lousy corrupt government. My father is straight in business, even if most promoters are sharks. I've done things myself I'm ashamed of. So have you, and if you're honest you'll admit it.' Simple, complicated, candid young woman.

'Indeed I have.'

'Well, what's your answer?'

'Are we talking ethics? I've got a bit muddled.'

'If you are going to stir up trouble for my father with the tax people – well, I could find a lot of policemen who'd be hard put to it to account for every shirt they buy.'

'I'm not proud of it. In fact society can't get on without a police force, even a bad one, but we're not going to swap arguments about corruption, like what does an hour on your horse cost? It's irrelevant. If I'm corrupt and so are you, where do we go from there?'

'I thought I'd offer you a bribe.'

'You don't cease to surprise me,' meaning it. 'For forgetting about tax fiddles?'

'Yes, look, I can tell you with truth and certainty that there was nothing at all queer in this deal. There may have been a bit of finagling at times, and that's my fault. I cost him a lot of money.'

The way these children's minds worked!

'What's the bribe?' he asked bluntly.

'Me,' likewise.

All was now clear. But his existence was getting complicated.

Being offered bribes was a familiar situation. Sometimes one pretended to accept them. One of the little professional dishonesties of existence. Much like pretending to believe something, in order to get information about something else.

Being offered young girls was trickier, because one was tempted to take them.

'That's an honest deal,' said Martine. 'Nothing to do with your homicide thing, because I know my father isn't involved in that. Just to forget about technical finance stuff, right?'

'Very well,' said Castang calmly.

And if he didn't keep his bargain, her idea would be Sophie as a witness?

'Fruit?' said Sophie with a dish. 'The pears are rather hard. There's cheese. And a chocolate cake.'

He'd better do a bit of police work.

'You'll excuse me a minute.'

'Through there and up the stairs. Cake for you, Martine?'

There were a dozen people in the little restaurant, now. The stairs were steep and crooked. An old house, built into the back of the city wall. A bathroom next to the lavatory, a little landing with three rooms, marked one, two, and private. Mm. He had an idea that Sophie knew about this brilliant notion of Martine's.

He found her smoking a cigarette, and looked at her with affection. Pale and meditative.

Sophie was cleaning her glasses on the corner of the table-cloth; looked at him with the blank beautiful gaze of myopia.

'Coffee when you like,' said Castang.

'Can we stay, Sophie?' with a show of being colourless.

'Sure,' indifferently. 'So coffee, and a drink.' She went to sit on her stool behind the bar to write bills, sucking her pencil and concentrating, gazing at the horizon.

'Nice girl, that.'

'She's a good friend.'

'She stays the night too, sometimes?'

'It isn't my affair,' said Martine sharply. 'I don't ask.'

Coffee and a drink, a nice one for young girls, a delicious summery smell of sunshine on ripe greengages. Sophie's face as impassive as a policeman's.

Castang's face had a look of several pieces of leather, cut in a complicated fashion and painstakingly stitched together; some salients blurred and effaced; some shadows and hollows more deeply hatched. Corrosion and oxidisation had played a part. Disciplines, pains and constraints had cut profiles deeper, and being much out of doors had cleaned the face as though with acids.

This look, that of an old coin, can be seen in most policemen of experience.

In repose it looked severe. But if one watched him for any length of time there was a phenomenon of much charm; a sunny smile. Vera had much pleasure in these moments when an old, much tilled, eroded landscape was lit by errant sunlight.

Martine noticed it and was pleased, opened her mouth to say so, found no words, was overcome by shyness.

Her own face, round and open, conventional and a little boring, became delicate: Castang was touched. The expression of the obstinate little horse, that has made its bed and is going to lie on it however thistly, had become something more adult, and much more interesting.

'You are good,' he said. 'And patient.'

The sulky blush, at once, of the snubbed schoolgirl. She saw that he had wanted her, and no longer did. But not going to be tearful, whatever happened.

'You're laughing at me.'

'No.' He felt clumsy himself, looking for a word that would not sound insulting, or diminishing. Couldn't just pat her head and say good dog.

'You're too good to treat frivolously.' It crossed the cop's mind that Sophie might have a tricky relationship with the local cops, and that it might have been a help, having a PJ inspector around who took girls upstairs.

'Not that easy,' he said. 'But first rule when posted to Russia is don't get caught in bed with the girls.'

'Shove it,' said Martine, humiliated. 'Shit; I suppose you're right.'

'It has to be spontaneous. Like having a leg amputated on the battlefield. Go ahead and cut, you bastards: give me another drink.'

She laughed a little.

'Do something spontaneous then, to please me.'

'Like cutting my head off?'

'Oh – rape me or something.'

'You know what Bismarck said would happen, if the English army invaded Germany?'

'Huh?'

'That they'd be arrested by the police, if they did.'

Good, he'd turned a difficult corner: she put her head back and laughed. Splendid throat like a pillar; splendid tit. See what you're missing.

'On what grounds?'

'Disturbing the peace, what else?' But oh, what a dose of castor oil he'd have had to take, next morning.

'Then say something spontaneous.'

'Very well. Tell your father from me that a thing like tax doesn't interest me. I'm not the fraud squad. But that anything to do with a homicide does. Any information he has for me I'll keep discreet. The examining magistrate doesn't have to know where it comes from.'

'You're looking for an informer.' Lip curling, somewhat.

'That's right,' said Castang dryly. 'And contrary to belief, we pay informers very little. Generally they get paid in terms of their own immunity. A bad system, but the administration is extremely parsimonious.'

'I've understood.'

'You'd like me to take you home?'

'No thank you.' But she didn't say it nastily. He asked Sophie for the bill.

'Oh, you can pay in the morning.'

'I'm having another drink instead.'

'As you wish,' she said tranquilly.

'Ever come across Madame Lipschitz's son?' he asked Martine.

'No.'

'It's a small town.'

'Oh, I may have seen him, but I wouldn't know him if I did.'

'What about your neighbour, Monsieur Barde?' A busy little bee, taking in any flowers along the way.

'Barde? Oh yes, I know him.' No great interest.

'Character sketch.' She was pleased to be off the hook at last, on to something that was just gossip.

'But what's your interest in that old phoney?'

'Not much. He's an old friend of the Lipschitz family. And that, incidentally, was what I was doing out your way this afternoon. Drinking tea with Monsieur Barde.'

'I don't know him much. Wouldn't want to; he makes faces of odious politeness when he meets me out on the horse. Beds his maids.'

'Oh, anybody can see that.'

'Well, let's see. Calls himself a writer. Can't write, but does twee little bits about people who can.'

The unforgiving judgements of a girl of twenty. What would she say about himself?

'Plays the wealthy landowner. Big swagger, but not much behind it.'

'How do you know?'

'Oh, he sold a lot of land. Dad got some, and cheap. Did well out of it, too: we got Green Gables that way. We were putting margarine on our bread before, in a flat. Barde wouldn't like doing without butter. He likes exterior signs of wealth, as the Finance Ministry calls it. Yachts and racehorses and stuff.'

'Has he racehorses?' Castang was amused at these youthful cruelties.

'That old nag? Don't make me laugh. No, but a dinky girl-friend dressed up as parlour-maid. So he supplements the wherewithal with bits of literature and other crafty little combinations. Pawnbroker.'

'Ouf,' said Sophie, sitting down and kicking her shoes off. 'Rush is over. Here's your bill. Being a cop, I'm sure you want it for the expense account.' Not too maliciously.

Quite a little family party they made. It was only ten, but the day had been a long one. Castang felt like kicking his shoes off, too.

CHAPTER FIFTEEN

I t was not to be. Lucciani wasn't back from his sex film yet, but the good lady of the Hotel Central was still alert behind her bar, helping the government to collect its Value Added Tax.

'Monsieur Peyrefitte asked you to ring him back as soon as you got in.' How singularly ill-timed of him.

The voice came harsh through the phone receiver.

'I've been trying to reach you: where the hell you been?'

'Military brothel.' Fellow sounded too excited.

'What? Now hell, this is serious. I'm pulling these people, and that'll be your affair settled, likely.'

'At this time of night?' scandalised.

'Judge reckons there's enough evidence. Got a good tip. Pick you up with the car, in a few minutes: I'll explain then,' hastily, before there could be any complaining. Castang had time to think that he could, instead of this gallop, have been in bed with Martine...

Second thought was technical. A judge of instruction possesses vast powers. He can issue several sorts of warrants to the cops. Besides the convocations inviting Mr Thing to present himself, voluntarily and without coercion, there is a detention warrant, authorising the cops to consign Thing to jail. And there is an arrest warrant, which permits the cops to pick Thing up, if need be by force, at any time of day. This one is not all that frequently used. Well, well, thought Castang: these country judges can throw their weight about.

Third thought was that if Peyrefitte seemed unusually zealous it was Castang's fault and no other. The local cop would be pleased to give a demonstration of his own efficiency, and wipe the PJ's eye for it. These city boys, who think themselves clever.

If, of course, Peyrefitte had identified the burglar who had used violence on Sabine (involuntary homicide: blows and wounds resulting in death, grave crimes these; not to speak of assorted felonies like armed robbery, breaking and entering – either plain burglary or climbing-in in the nocturnal hours)... well then, of course, the judge was quite right. The forces-of-order would gallop in the nocturnal hours, and he, Castang, would be only too pleased to go home to his wife with his homicide tidied behind him.

The police car flicked headlights at him from twenty metres along the pavement. He got in at the back, next to Peyrefitte's second, a stolid man with a finger missing. Not his trigger finger.

'We think this is hot,' said the commissaire over his shoulder, 'and we're taking every precaution.'

Tyres whirred on the cobbles of the old town, through the medieval gateway – a scant hundred metres from the Bay Tree down the Rue des Remparts – over the river-crossing this fortress had once defended. The land beyond the bridge was low-lying: this was the 'new town', a dreary sector of industry and municipal housing, deserted at this hour. The road stretched out into a featureless farmland of potatoes and sugar-beet while Peyrefitte talked in choppy sentences and Castang fought against feeling sleepy. He turned around: they were being followed by a Citroën van.

'Turned out in force.'

'They are four brothers: tough group they make, too.'

'Four black bastards,' muttered the adjutant.

'They Arabs or what?' asked Castang to be saying something.

'Basques. Got those unpronounceable names. All right,' to the driver, 'cut the motor; coast in quietly. Pack of hooligans,' sourly. 'This may not be funny, and I'm taking no chances. They may easily possess arms, and they might not be slow to use them once they realise that I mean business.'

Like the man in the Rue d'Aboukir, though this was not very like the Rue d'Aboukir. An isolated small farmhouse, or rather a dilapidated bundle of outbuildings huddled round a cottage. The night was cloudy: vision just good enough to see that the cottage was oddly neat, even prim, with flowers growing round it.

The dispositions were rather more elaborate than in the Rue d'Aboukir. It was as though 'whatever Paris can do, we can do better.' Four cops with assorted weapons got out of the van: eight armed men made the black brothers seem unusually formidable, but not by terrorist standards. They didn't have any armour, or marksmen with sniperscopes. The cops scattered round the outbuildings. Peyrefitte advanced purposefully, Castang flanking. The adjutant and the driver stayed at the gate.

Light glowed through the bars of a shutter, at a ground-floor window: the bluish flicker of a television screen. Peyrefitte knocked at the door: the sound died instantly. There was silence for a count of ten: he knocked again.

'Police,' he said, in an unemotional way. Castang moved a little further sideways to where he could not be seen.

The light went out. A pounding of feet sounded on the stairs. A window opened above Castang's head. There was enough light to catch the oily glint on a pair of well-looked-after shotgun barrels.

'Now don't act the imbecile,' said Peyrefitte, tucking himself against the wall on the lock side of the doorway. 'I don't want to have to use any force.' Silence went on ticking and nothing happened. 'Let's have this door opened quietly, boys. Order from the judge. Refusing just gets you in worse trouble.'

Nobody stirred, but the glint upon the shotgun slid gently along the barrels. Castang watched them dip.

'Idiot,' he said. 'Live one and die one: the man'll blow your head off.' One was down here, and one was up there, but he was wondering where the other two were, and if they were deciding to be heroes.

'We start again from scratch,' said Peyrefitte patiently. 'If the door gets opened quietly, then nothing need be said about resisting arrest.' Castang, stifling yawns and wondering how much shotgun pellets would scatter from three metres high – in no hurry to find out – was getting a crick in his neck.

There was a dragging movement behind the kitchen door.

'No shooting?' said a soft hoarse voice. 'Word of honour?' It sounds serious, in Spanish.

'Word of honour,' said Peyrefitte.

All this talk about honour, thought Castang.

'You might just break the gun open,' he said conversationally. The glint wavered and wobbled, and then drooped with a snick. He took a couple of steps forward, turned round and tucked his gun into his belt, quite surprised to find it still there: such a strong feeling of his trousers coming down.

'Put it down on the floor.' The adjutant, holding a big Star pistol against his hard belly, advanced ponderously. The door-bolt creaked and a large man with lank hair glinting like the gunbarrels was smiling politely in the opening with a hunting rifle in the crook of his elbow. He and Peyrefitte bowed at each other like two penguins, all very formal. Out beyond the gate, the driver was dropping a tear-gas gun back into the boot of the car.

The other two were at the back. One had a long single-barrelled shotgun for duck. The other, a boy of eighteen, grinned impudently at all those cops with submachine-guns, and put down a .22 repeater.

'For rats,' he said, showing his teeth.

'No prohibited weapons,' said the eldest. 'All legal. You frightened us. No resisting arrest.' The judge would appreciate that, and so, thought Castang, would everyone else.

The Four Black Brothers were taken back two by two, while the adjutant and a couple of cops stayed for a search. They got back at around three in the morning, with an old army revolver, two-thirds of a kilo of plastic explosive, several objects known to have been stolen from a parked lorry, and a lot of gold coins.

'Too many,' said Peyrefitte, 'for a small potato farm, and nobody has four tape recorders.' But neither this fact, nor all the interrogation up to then, produced anything to do with Sabine.

Castang indeed made a face at the results of the search, and went home. Neither Peyrefitte nor the judge would lose face.

Certainly not. The Black Brothers had several activities interesting Justice, including the Basque Liberation Front, and contravention of Common Market Regulations concerning potatoes. The rummaging went on till nearly midday, turning up a packet of detonators, which are Prohibited Weapons, and also the microscopic scratches made by the previous owner of eighty-four gold napoleons, by which he could identify them. But Castang had gone to bed. He didn't believe that the four black brothers had anything to do with Sabine, despite the denunciation sent to the judge. Their contempt for the idea of hitting old ladies was too genuine: the notion was altogether against Honour.

CHAPTER SIXTEEN

Young Lucciani had missed all the excitement, but knew enough not to be talkative at breakfast. Fruity chuckles at the paper; further instalment of the misdeeds of the vice-squad commissaire. Castang, biting into a far-from-crisp croissant, reflecting gloomily that half-cooked bread was spreading like the cholera, was reading an economics article. Chocolate-coated double-talk: we are governed by poltroons. He hadn't had enough sleep. The croissant was like Tampax. As Vera said, 'The one thing one knows about the tap-water is that it's been five times through the human body already.'

Paris! As provincial as this place here. Little frightened eyes, peering over the battlements to make sure the drawbridge was lowered, chatters about the Hexagon, as though it were a wizard's star, able to keep out horned things with tails. In one paragraph of jargon Belgium was 'Over the Quiévrain', Germany was 'Across the Rhine', and England was 'Beyond the Channel'. The writer seemed grateful for all these muddy little ditches, as though they had been designed by the prudent foresight of Vauban. The English talking about 'continentals', or the

French complaining of 'islanders': who sounded the sillier, muttered Castang crossly.

Lucciani put his coffee cup down with a clank and a noisy puff of breath.

'Okay, skipper; what's the tactics?'

He loathed being called skipper, and tactics indeed. Use your bloody head is all the tactics you need.

But they never did have any head. It wasn't all their fault. Their great terror was that of all functionaries, exceeding instructions and getting a bad mark, so that one spelt everything out for them, in monosyllables, and then they were 'covered'.

'It's the slavish worship of the lowest common denominator,' said Vera. 'Seek to please everybody, end with a third-rate everything. Art. Police forces.'

He had to make an effort.

'I was up till three, wasting my time with these Spanish gangsters. Peyrefitte's delighted, so's the judge. I'm not. Now you ask about tactics. Oh, well, I'll go ring Richard.' He did so.

'To simplify,' coming back and drinking a half-cup of stone-cold coffee, 'the judge won't be pleased at my poking about in the local folklore. To distract him from my doing so, a cloud of smoke must be released. Your function. All the forced-entry jobs in the region over six months, minus whatever gets pinned on the Black Brothers. And a report drawn up. So you go home and play with the computer.'

Pride of the ministry's heart, recently supplied to Regional Services of Police Judiciaire, the machine produced huge meaningless quantities of statistics, of crushing banality. Eigthy-five per cent of the prison population is below average intelligence. Well, who'd have thought it? If it wasn't for that, as Richard remarked, they'd certainly never have been caught. Since eighty-five per cent of cops…

But to tell the truth for once and avoid cant, and state simply that eighty-five per cent of the entire population of anywhere is subnormal in intelligence – who decides what's normal, anyway? – would be heresy. Quite beyond the machine's capacities.

Who wants statistics anyhow? They provide employment. They get evaluated by other machines, and studied by other functionaries, and this creates a cheerful bustle, and calls for a large budget.

'Oh, all right,' said Lucciani. 'Be glad really to get out of this creepy dump. Still wondering what they do in the evenings.'

'Go to the military brothel.' The boy would never know how literally he meant it.

CHAPTER SEVENTEEN

Yes, the Black Bastards had put the judge in cheerful spirits.

'Ah, yes. Good morning, Castang; sit down. Good.' Sit down!

'Nothing much as yet, sir: to subtract that is from the enquiry made, or to add to the conclusions drawn. So we're left with the hypothesis of a break-in, and a homicide by accident, so to say.'

The judge said nothing at all.

'Pity about these Basques; that looked most promising.'

'I'm not finished with those gentry. But I agree that we haven't sufficient evidence to inculpate them for this.'

'It's something to give the press. And we may link them to some other unsolved cases. Monsieur Richard has asked me for a complete report along those lines.'

'At my suggestion.'

'Yes, sir. I propose to detach my associate and put him to the task of synthesising.'

The judge had no criticism of that.

'I think perhaps, with respect, that there are one or two points apart from this, which bear looking at.'

'Yes?' mildly. 'Suppose you tell me about them?'

'Maître le Tarentais was kind enough to give me his time.

'So he told me.'

'At his suggestion I had a chat too with Monsieur Barde.'

A nod: whether of approval or foreknowledge one couldn't tell. It was prudent to assume both. Thonon had been right there; all these small town personages were fearful gossips.

'Since he knew the family well in former times. I thought,' picking his steps, 'that we ought to know more about family relationships and the financial situation. I had a word with the heirs. They were co-operative enough – a bit restive. I had to explain for instance that even if no formal order were made they couldn't dispose of the property without your permission.'

The willingness to listen was getting a bit ominous. One preferred judges who only listened to themselves talking.

'I identified a man who was seen to call on Madame Lipschitz that evening as a local house agent, a Monsieur Thonon. He seems to have been hoping to get her to sell some property, but he tells me nothing definite was concluded. He asked my permission quite correctly to negotiate with the heirs: I told him your assent would be needed.'

'Good. I've spoken to Richard on the telephone. I want this report on forcible entries pursued diligently; I'm approving this suggestion regarding your young man.

'Now,' thoughtful, stabbing himself gently in the stomach with his paper-knife, 'Richard assures me that you are a prudent and experienced officer, to be trusted in a delicate matter. You will have understood that my remarks of yesterday about playing the bull in the china-shop were a reminder of the need for restraint. Now this report will take time. And we'd do best not to rely solely upon it. The investigation must be pursued if only to avoid an impression that this has been a superficial or incomplete enquiry.'

This was a great deal better than yesterday. Castang understood, or thought he did, that the Black Brothers might not have anything to do with Sabine, but were highly important. A spectacular and successful operation, which greatly strengthened the judge's position.

'I don't wish to hamper you, Castang, nor to stifle your scope for enquiry. But to impress upon you how important it may be that nothing should lead you into a situation where – you follow me – anyone wants to see you stifled.

'I think you do right to clear up any ambiguity on this point of the property; whether it was or wasn't on the verge of being sold. Plainly you had to interview these heirs: I have no criticism of your doing so. They're being touchy and righteous, I may tell you: I had the young woman on the telephone making a fuss. I anaesthetised her, but they're likely to be troublesome. I'm told,' searching for a note on his pad, 'that the young woman's mother is expected today, from Paris. A certain Madame Wilhems. The widow it would seem of some industrial magnate in the north. Hints were dropped that she possesses the ear of unidentified persons in political office.'

'They all say that, even if it's for a parking offence.'

'Quite so. I don't imagine we need take it too seriously. The point is – why should she think such remarks necessary?'

Castang was quite warming towards his judge. The obstructionist fusspot was showing signs of becoming an ally!

'Material interest, I should imagine,' disdainfully. 'The moment that is called in question these people make a great to-do about their powers of influence. I'm inclined to put it down to the young woman being officious. If this worthy lady proves obstreperous there's no harm in our showing that we aren't getting rapped on the knuckles by some manufacturer, even if she has a Deputy in her pocket. Tradesmen...!'

Castang was learning rapidly a lot about small towns. This, he guessed, was the Proc speaking; the local personage of 'good family'. Who might have been willing enough to have Sabine's dossier 'classified' – put on the shelf. The judge would have rung him for an opinion. He would have got hoity-toity though, at the bare idea of being bullied by some manufacturer's widow from Roubaix. Tradesmen!

He wasn't interrupting – the judge had lots of time this morning, and was by no means finished. In the mood for a dissertation, to which Castang would listen humbly, if he knew what was good for him.

'Certain sections of the magistracy hold the theory that judicial decisions are inseparable from politics. Some elements go as far as to say that the neutrality of the judge is a myth, that his decision will always be based upon a personal and individual set of interior mechanisms. I find this argument unconvincing. A theologian, perhaps, would speak of excessive scruple.

'I need hardly tell you, Castang, that the great principle of the law is the independence of the magistrate. He speaks without fear or favour, for he is not to be removed from his post, and need heed no pressure from political personages, who are in any case here today and gone tomorrow.

'However, the Police Judiciaire, however elite a body, contains infected sheep within the flock.'

Aha, muttered Castang towards the back of his head, another reader of newspapers.

'It has, moreover, no security of tenure. Yet this is the executive instrument upon which a magistrate relies.'

This is perhaps not the Proc speaking, nor, possibly, the judge. Maybe it's the prefect. The local sub-prefect? This idea gathered strength, for the judge began to perorate.

'You will recall, accordingly, that in giving you liberty to follow the threads of this enquiry I must impress upon you the necessity of remaining aware of political sensitivities.' Richard, or a carpenter, or anybody not a politician, would say 'Don't hit your own fingers with the hammer.'

'In other words, my friend,' going all lenient and humorous, 'tread warily. Do not fall foul of the raving lion that is Demos, who lurks as the Gospels tell us seeking whom he may devour.'

Castang, who had a vague notion it was Psalms, kept his mouth shut. The phrase had been insufficiently polished, but the chap could still nod his head in time to the music. And yet there were moments now and again when he could almost believe the man human.

'I don't want to be a source of complaint in any quarter,' he said humbly. 'Monsieur Richard wouldn't like that at all.'

'I cannot fail to give weight to your assurance,' with pomp. 'An emollient spirit, and no china gets broken. Splendid. Continue then with the verbal reports; put yourself in touch with me at once at any new turn. Emollient, Castang, rather than ebullient.' It was a joke.

What was all this bloop in aid of? Someone, presumably this tradesman's widow with the deputy-in-the-pocket, has been phoning somebody. A prefect to judge from the prose style. Who phoned the judge, telling him not to let the cops get out of hand, this being a marginal electoral district. The magistrature, being upper-class, is a bit hoity-toity, and refuses to tell the cops simply to go study breaking-and-entering statistics. That – roughly – was about it.

As Richard pointed out now and again, police work could be any colour you liked, from pastel pink to cumulonimbus violet, just depending on how close you were to an electoral year.

And Castang had twelve, nearly fifteen years as a cop. And this was the first independent enquiry, into anything serious like a homicide, he had ever been given. Richard would say too, Walk Carefully. Because the Public, known as Demos if you're a judge and have had a classical education, is base, craven and hypocritical, and needs a large array of scapegoats upon which to discharge vindictive terrors.

As goats go, policemen will do nicely.

CHAPTER EIGHTEEN

A soft autumn day. Castang found himself disliking it, wishing for harsh drying airs from the east, for thin acid sunshine of early springtime. Too soft, too moist.

Bustling little town, and bloody prosperous. A thousand shysters like Thonon running about selling illusions and doing well out of it. Everyone making money and parading it with a new bow-window, a bigger garage, a grander deep-freeze. Everywhere blatant, boisterous self-advertisement. And don't suggest there's anything wrong with that, or we'll lynch you and enjoy it. Every buzzing bluebottle loud, proud and gorged.

Castang regretted the Rue d'Aboukir. He had a hell of a nostalgia for it. There you were a professional. You knew where you stood. You were a cop, there was a man with a gun. Pick him up and take him away. That was clear; the gun on your own belt was supposed to mean something. You didn't just sit in bars being witty and picking your teeth with the foresight.

Whereas here you were hemmed in by a gang whose one idea was to suffocate you, because you were a nuisance, a piece of grit who for one second might interrupt the music, the thick golden tinkle of money pouring into the till.

At least he'd had one clear instruction. Anaesthetise Granny, this naughty old biddy who's come ramping down from Paris possessed of political influence.

He got rid of young Lucciani first, and felt better, more able to cope with Democracy. He was a functionary of the Ministry of the Interior, comforting himself with the phrase Vera was fond of from Stendhal. 'Really one would rather kiss the Minister of the Interior's arse than one's shoemaker's.' It came from *Lucien Leuwen*, that young man who set out to tackle Democracy after some years of 'making intensive warfare upon new boots and cigars'.

He hadn't yet been inside the 'little house' next door to Sabine's. For a cottage it was surprisingly big, and pleasant with a little paved yard and nasturtiums growing. These people were damned lucky not to be stuck in a miserable tiny flat, but they hankered after what was after all a fine and beautiful house, and he couldn't blame them.

A pleasant living-room with colour-washed walls, untidy, but with a peculiar discipline imposed upon it by the presence of Mum.

Now what had got into Mum, that she came racing down here from her good bourgeois royal town? It wasn't Paris. It was Versailles. Worse, if anything. Madame was very much 'La Versaillaise'.

She had her Sunday suit on. Neat, ungaudy, nothing out of place. A pale-grey suit, with a white batiste blouse, and a ruffle. The ruffle had a narrow black edge, and little black spots. One couldn't accuse her of wearing mourning, but neither of not wearing mourning; it was a nice touch. Mourning for somebody pretty distant, like one's daughter's mother-in-law. One is not incorrect, but one does not care to show ostentation. Versaillaise bourgeoisie!

She was sitting in a large armchair: it was the only armchair, which was why she was sitting in it. He got a place on a low sofa, tatty and a bit greasy, and decidedly uncomfortable until he felt about and found a plastic toy animal under the cushion.

Janet went through her doorpost-sidling act until dismissed by a wave of Mum's hand: I'll look after this, dear. Podgy and well-kept, this hand; polished nails and a lot of large diamonds. She sat upright, knees together, contained and concentrated. A strong calm face of a pale even shade owing nothing to make-up; the colour and texture of a petit-beurre biscuit.

'Well, young man?'

Castang took his time: coughing, blowing his nose, getting rid of paper hanky in hygienic fashion, fussing with cushion, laughing at emergence of giraffe. Madame Wilhems was worth study: she looked pretty formidable.

He didn't like her face much. It was built up of self-sufficiency and contempt, and a solid certainty that nothing would happen to interfere with Mum's well-entrenched comforts. Protruding boiled grey eye. The same long straight nose as the daughter, but larger and a lot fleshier. No chin, but she managed very well without.

'Well, young man?' In no hurry.

'I'm sorry. Bit of a sad occasion.'

'It will be distinctly sad, unless this rather silly matter is brought back into proportion. It is sad, for example, that one should not be safe from murderous vandals. I prefer to avoid pious clichés, because I dislike hypocrisies. Sabine Arthur was an old woman, and in shaky health. When such people die, it is sensible to temper natural sorrow with relief that things got no worse. Better a regret for a quick and painless death than the much greater regret for a drawn-out, aimless, miserable age. It is clear that very shortly she would have needed expert care. Specialised care. I trust I make myself plain.'

'She seemed pretty robust to me, reading the medical report.'

The eyebrows drew together.

'I do not care to be fenced with. Mental illness is a fact like another.'

'Yes. A person being elderly or tiresome or whatever does not alter the fact, in law, of a death by violence.'

'Let's understand each other, Inspector. You deal in facts; so do I. I have precious little time for suppositions. She was killed, and that is a fact I do not dispute or try to hide from myself. It is another fact that her mind was much decayed. Such persons do not behave in a rational manner. You will not dispute this: it is notorious that she was given to fantasies and babbled tales of fears and visions. I am even given to understand that she approached you with her hysterical imaginings which you were obliged to dismiss as groundless.'

Castang said nothing: if she were surprised at that she said nothing to show it.

'She sought the company of deranged persons, of the silly and weak-minded. Old women, with a belief in visions, apparitions of a religious nature. Some such may be kind-hearted and well-intentioned: others may be seekers after sensation, who stir up trouble. Some, even, abuse the credulity of the generous for financial gain.'

'Are you suggesting,' said Castang, sounding surprised, 'that some deranged person broke in and killed her?'

Mum dismissed this with a wave of the hand. She leaned forward a little.

'I do not know what gossip you may have listened to in the village. The opinion seems widespread that Sabine Arthur was a sort of saint. The local priest seems an innocent old man. But I have spoken to His Lordship the Bishop,' impressively. 'These superstitious cults are foolish and may be harmful.'

Castang, quite genuinely, was wondering what all this was about. A counter-attack upon anybody saying nasty things about her daughter; that much was evident. And perhaps Sabine had been charitable towards some faintly dotty pious cult. And the fraud squad had trouble frequently enough with fortune-tellers and phoney religious sects. That somebody of that sort might turn up with a claim wouldn't surprise him, but it was the first he'd heard of it.

'She bore the reputation of a charitable person: I'm aware,' he said. 'I'm only enquiring into a homicide.'

Mum didn't insist. The shrewd eyes were weighing him up. 'This thief, or vandal, who broke in – the judge seems confident of your laying hands upon him. I'm bound to say the hope seems extravagant.'

'The likelihood is that there have been, or will be, similar offences. We are examining the matter. The district is large. It may take some time.'

No chin, but a multiplicity of firm folds in flesh. A movement in these left him with small doubt of her opinion about this remark. But she was prudent and experienced. She did not know him, and he might not be such a fool as he looked.

'I'm not disputing your competence, young man.'

A lot of police work is like this. Some witnesses just tell lies. The bourgeoisie is more complicated. In the long run, money is what worries them, even more than what people will think. Mum seemed able in business matters. What was a cop after all? Just another tiresome functionary in the administration.

But what was Mum after? Just making sure that she knew all the ways he might choose to be an annoyance? Or was she screening something?

She cocked an eye at the daughter, who had sidled in again without being noticed, so as not to miss anything, and was sitting now plump and pussified in the corner on a pouffe, with wide kitten's eyes and a saucer of cream she felt too languid to sip at just now: it will still be there by and by. Nobody is going to take it away. They had better not try, either.

'Janet, it seems to me that you might offer a glass of port to the Inspector.' The kitten uncurled.

'Does that mean you'd like one?' Silky oblique insolence not aimed anywhere; left drifting like thistledown to stick to someone's coat.

'No, child.' As expertly ambiguous; anything from 'you know it doesn't agree with me at this time of day' to a phrase enjoyed by Vera – 'not that champagne, dear; it's what we keep for the police.'

The ball was in his court. The stout lady, not really stout; more well and expensively corseted, was studying him with pursed mouth.

'The hypothetical marauder,' he said pleasantly, 'doesn't seem to me to give the whole of the picture, necessarily.'

'Very well, Monsieur…?'

'Castang.'

'You have formed other conclusions. May we hear them?' Patient, courteous.

He got his port, put it on the extreme edge of a small table, where ten to one he'd knock it over and have to go on his knees mopping with a hanky. Not taking any bets he put it in the middle, got the drift of a half-suppressed smile from the daughter.

'I don't have any conclusions, Madame; that is the judge's role.'

Mum gave a short male laugh.

'Judges! If they ever knew anything there'd be no need for the police.'

'Quite so, Madame, but if I said that I'd be out of a job.'

'You and I will get along. You don't lack intelligence. Have you never thought of the magistracy yourself, as a career?'

Not bad and not very good either, like this port.

'Contented enough as I am, Madame.'

'Don't sip it man; drink it. I'm not taking any, so that there's no need to stand on ceremony. These children don't drink. Perhaps it's wise of them, but they miss some of the pleasures of existence. Give the Inspector some more, Janet.

'Now, Monsieur Castang, in confidence and without prejudice, wouldn't you agree that this examining magistrate is an ass?... Oh, I can see by the expression on your face,' merrily.

'I'm not making a foolish generalisation. I've known some able and intelligent judges, in Versailles and elsewhere. But these provincial corners... Now I'm not mistaken, you are from Paris, isn't it so?'

Half true. He nodded.

'Unmistakable; I'm myself. And just between us – really, Janet, haven't you a biscuit or something? Anybody would think you'd been badly brought up – you know and I know that this judge is an ass. Oh, you needn't bother to contradict just to keep yourself in countenance! He'd like to think of nothing but his marauder. It simplifies his existence. No little local difficulties then. In an election year, the good man knows he'd be ill-advised to permit any little scandals which might embarrass a government candidate. You're aware of this. The same applies to you. You're an intelligent person.'

So're you, dear lady.

'You won't compromise yourself; sensible of you. I applaud that. No more need be said, but I reassure you; no need to act the gaping country cousin with me. I want one thing; to ensure that a stop is put to malicious gossip.

'Poor Sabine! She had a mind, as a young woman, I'm told. I don't move in these artistic circles, and have small taste for such things, but I am assured she possessed talent.'

Who had assured her? Sounded like Barde talking.

'In Paris she might have made something of it. A name for herself... But out of timidity or provinciality she chose to marry a mediocre little man and spend her days in this dusty little corner. It was inevitable that she fell into the kind of company one finds in these places. A dowager or two with an interest in clerical matters, fingers in convents, meddling with the episcopate, a local canon – generally gaga – in their pocket. Some of these people, I repeat it, are harmful. They succeeded in poisoning poor Sabine's mind against her son, and against my daughter. You follow me, Monsieur Castang?'

'You'd make a good lawyer.'

Not altogether pleased by that, but she was thoroughly animated by now. A faint dusky flush appeared.

'Lawyers! I don't know a great deal about law, but I have experience in protecting my interests. I've employed lawyers upon occasion. They are sufficiently skilled at justifying their expense for one to be confident they can justify anything. But we need no lawyers here.'

He was beginning to have enough of Mum, but if she thought he was wax in her hands, so much the better. He finished the port; asked permission to light a cigarette. Graciously granted, and he was starting to need it.

The door opened and Gérard came in. Strong-minded old biddy: it had evidently been laid down that she would handle the police and the judge, because he said nothing, gave Castang a sour nod, went over to a drawer and hunted through a tangle of bits of string and electric flex, found a bit of wire for whatever he wanted and went off again without a word. It irritated Mum.

'Monsieur Castang, I don't wish to be indiscreet, but experience teaches me that where property is concerned it is unwise to leave loose ends.'

He quite agreed.

'This house next door – white elephant in my opinion, but classified, I understand: cultural-affairs people forbid knocking it down. Folklore, but even in disrepair the house has value. More important still is that large garden. I'm told that Sabine, poor soul, had been approached with a view to inducing her to part with some of this land – I daresay you've heard something about this?'

'The matter had been discussed, I believe.'

'My understanding from the local notary is that no contract was entered into.'

'Not that I'm aware of.' It looked as though Thonon had had a shot at 'the children' and been snubbed for his pains.

'I've taken pains to make sure that there is no dispute about this property. I'm glad to say that Sabine saw to it, at least, that the children's inheritance should be unquestioned. I mention it only because it would seem that malicious tongues have been at work, trying to raise doubts about her intentions.'

'I know of no obstacle.'

'Good. The judge seems to be shilly-shallying. I've spoken to him; I may go to see him.'

There weren't many people she hadn't spoken to. She'd been pretty energetic. He'd done nothing. Gossiping with the neighbours, stuffing himself with food and drink, having dirty daydreams about Martine. While she'd been a proper detective. He'd better turn all his operations over to Mum.

'I'm labouring the point, perhaps,' she said, nothing if not thorough. 'This house is in poor condition and needs care; there are leaks in the roof to mention no worse. Now it appears you have forbidden the children access to it.'

'Purely a formality.'

'Oh yes, due process. We can temper that with a little common sense, surely. I take advantage of an informal conversation to ask you to have this ban lifted. You have surely no further technical tests or whatnot to make, and that door and shutter need mending.'

'I'll see what I can do, Madame,' with warm enthusiasm. 'Not my decision, properly speaking – a civil matter. Monsieur le Commissaire – I'll tell you what; I'll have a word with him, shall I, and I'm sure he'll see your point. Leave it to me.'

Mum had her mouth pursed up, suspicious of too much sunny co-operation, but she couldn't well complain of it. He got up hastily to go, getting a lifeless hand to shake – bit grudgingly.

'You'll be staying some days, I imagine?' he asked.

'I may, Inspector; I may.'

The kitten stretched on its cushion and blinked torpidly. He thought there might be sparks flying off the fur shortly. Would 'the children' be altogether happy with the masterful way Mum handled the fuzz?

CHAPTER NINETEEN

Peyrefitte, still up to his neck in the Four Black Bastards, was cross at being led up the garden path. When, early that morning, Castang had grunted that all this was a feather in the cap of the constabulary, but nothing to do with Sabine, he'd been unwilling to admit it. Now he did admit it, and was angry with the judge, who'd let himself get persuaded by wishful thinking and an anonymous denunciation. He'd said as much – more tactfully – to the magistrate, who wasn't having that, naturally.

'Very well, Commissaire, you will direct your enquiries towards finding out, won't you. Who is sending phoney denunciations? Some disgruntled accomplice, no doubt.'

Renewed police work on these-damned-Spaniards was beginning to point to a butcher, a shady person, suspected of having trafficked in carcasses that had been condemned by the Health Department. Another fellow who had too many gold coins. Wouldn't be sorry to pin something on that whore, said Monsieur Peyrefitte, if it can be managed.

'Your phone been ringing?' asked Castang.

'Who, the judge?'

'Madame Wilhems.'

'Oh, the Granny down from Paris, I've heard about her. No, thank God.'

'Doesn't want to appear too eager. Agitated about her rights. Wants to clean up that shutter and door; says the house is wide open. Wanted me to change all that. I said I'd love to, naturally, but that it was your decision.'

'Why, when it's the judge's ruling, anyhow?'

'Judge wished her on me, and a damned tiresome morning she's given me. I wish her on you, but warn you first.'

'I'll send her back to the bloody judge.'

'Of course, but stall her a bit. An old cow: I don't want her upsetting him. If she blows in, perhaps you'd say you'd be delighted, of course, but it just needs his assent and you'll be seeing him by and by.'

'All right. Why so much fuss?'

'I've really no idea. I don't see that there can be anything odd about that shutter.'

'You're not thinking there was some kind of fiddle?'

'No evidence whatever. Probably just a question of property at stake. Isn't it always? She's bothered too about the house agent. I've seen Thonon, by the way. His story's reasonable enough. Didn't want to come out with having been there that night because he's still got hopes of swinging a property deal.'

'So you don't think it was him?'

'Of course not, unless the judge starts getting ideas.'

'Is there anything queer, about the property?'

'I don't suppose so. Sheer coincidence, and of course when money's involved they all start prevaricating... All terrified that something might interfere with their making a profit, and all cursing Sabine for getting herself killed. Nothing fishy about Thonon in your eyes, is there?'

'More honest than most, I'd have thought.'

'I had dinner last night in a place called the Bay Tree.'

'Place has been a brothel since Vauban's day.'

'I'm all for ancient traditions, too.'

'See no reason why it shouldn't stay that way,' said Peyrefitte comfortably. 'That young woman is sensible about it.'

'I ran into Thonon's daughter there. Student in Paris, as I gather. Friendly with the woman Sophie.'

'No drugs or stuff, if that's what you're thinking. Sophie's no fool; she'd tell me… I have her in to see me now and again. Thonon's okay as far as we're concerned. So far, that is. Never can tell, much, with these property dealers but hell, infringement of building legislation… one has more to worry about. I'm going to light a fire under this butcher,' contentedly.

A small town, where everybody gossiped. A place where nothing ever happened, where the scandal of the year was the mayor's trafficking in influence to get his parking-lot built! Where anonymous denunciations flew, where nobody could really live in peace. Poor old Barde couldn't even enjoy his maids in peace, an estate agent had to slip about furtively at night, and even Sabine, quiet, respectable widow of a cultural-affairs civil servant, spun strange webs and dark suspicions. Nothing happened but it could be blamed on the Black Brothers. And Sabine had been frightened, frightened enough to come all the way to the city and tell the Police Judiciaire about her worries, frowning nervously and polishing her glasses. And then she had been found dead. Violence. And violence belonged to the youth, to bored frustrated boys hanging about with nothing to do but go to a sex film, like Lucciani, or go fishing, like Gérard. While the elderly amused themselves with bridge parties. Or emotional religious outbursts. The only person he'd met so far who seemed to lead a normal existence was Sophie, who ran a little café-restaurant, with a little bit of quiet provincial prostitution on the side.

Had it really been no more than some wandering juvenile delinquent in search of excitement? Perfectly possible. Stay content with that, Castang told himself. The more you go poking at gossip and rumour the less you'll find out.

But you'd like to do something with your first independent homicide investigation. Find a dramatic development.

There'd never be anything of the sort. Nothing would ever happen, here.

But he had a little time. The judicial authorities were in a good mood: they would be pleasurably busy with the Black Brothers for the next forty-eight hours. Like the youth, they wanted a little excitement, something exotic. Basque villains provided it. He himself would just like to poke a bit further. This snug little town, tight and secure in its fortifications, prosperous and bland with its modern suburbs and industrial development, microcosm of provincial existence in today's Europe, bored him stiff, but Sabine didn't.

He wanted to find out more about Sabine, to get to know her, to understand her. She was the most interesting of all these people. But she was dead.

CHAPTER TWENTY

Mademoiselle Aubrienne, the noted sculptress, proved difficult to find. This was explained after diligent enquiry, when she turned out to be neither Aubrienne, nor a sculptress.

'O'Brien, my dear man. Irish – no you obviously don't know how much this benighted continent owes to poor old Ireland. Never had the curiosity to read history.'

'Nobody's telling me I lack curiosity,' said Castang. 'Takes different directions, that's all.'

'I forgive you. I'm so used to being Aubrienne I no longer notice, but I refuse to apologise for French incapacity. O'Briens were kings before police forces were invented, and it's not a sign of progress.'

A fierce little thing, sprightly and talkative. Intelligent, even if dotty. Castang would take the one with the other.

A tiny woman with a dried-up, Indian face, grey hair in an untidy bun, bifocal glasses giving her a peering look, a combative manner. One of those persons, often charming, to whom a day without a row, it doesn't matter much with whom, is a day without salt.

Drinking tea, strong and black-looking, from a round brown teapot with a crocheted cosy. She lived in a little cottage with polychrome painted furniture: birds and flowers in primitive motifs flitted over the panels. Vera would have felt at home: a Czech look. The walls were a jumble-sale of watercolours, cut-out silhouettes, collages of feathers. Real birds, in cages, occupied whatever space there was over.

Miss O'Brien was not in a cage, but a rocking-chair. She pulled a portfolio off another chair, for him to sit on. Instead of a shawl with bobbles, like the tea cosy, she was wearing a work-man's dungaree overall, on top of a scarlet sweater.

He looked for signs of sculptor's clay or stuff. There wasn't any.

'What're you gazing about for?'

'Oh, busts and things.'

'Oh dear; the police... Know anything about art?'

'No.'

'So much the better, and no need of that "I'm afraid" tone. And d'you want to know anything?'

'Not in the least.'

'God and His Saints be praised. Not a namby-pamby. So I don't have to explain about art. Gloria laus et honor, as we sang before we lapsed into heresy.'

Ah. One of the religious maniacs Mum had complained of: good.

'I'm not a sculptor. Work in stained glass. Difficult tech-nique. I've not the remotest intention of trying to explain, so don't bother thinking of intelligent questions to show how cultivated you are.'

'I'm not.'

'Be grateful. The French insist on being cultivated, and on everyone knowing it. Spiritual pride.'

It wasn't a blow: he got the same from Vera.

'It's that infernal being in the right all the time that's maddening about them.'

'Do you think I could have some tea?' he asked humbly.

'You may indeed. Irish tea, though, not tisane. Probably lay you on your back. So you're Police Judiciaire, oh oh. And you want information, oh oh.'

Sarcasm. She wasn't impressed, and she wasn't curious: the cops would have to do better.

'An officer is it, and judges of instruction, and enquiries into Madame Lipschitz and all: dies irae.' Sniggering, little black eye agleam, pecking at him as though he were a sunflower-seed.

'Were they kings of Ireland?'

'Thomond, man. Ancient province, like Maine or Anjou. Now distressed and dismembered.'

'You speak French very well.'

'Oh, stop bullshitting, man.'

He nearly said Ook, as though struck in the stomach by Bishop Odo's massive club, to be observed in the Bayeux Tapestry. All these Irish saints – the poor old French had indeed had a hard time of it in the ninth century!

'How d'you come to hear of me, anyhow?'

'Monsieur Barde, I think it was.'

'Barde, is it? No wonder you thought I was a sculptor! What would he know, outside his sad little nursery-maid existence? He gave you my name. A damnable liberty he took there. All right, I knew Sabine, and Vincent too. Good man, that. Silly woman, our poor Sabine. Merit in her verses. She will have died with God beside her.'

'That,' said Castang, 'must afford us all considerable comfort. My job is to find out who else was present.'

He'd succeeded in putting an end to the island of saints-and-scholars! Let the Irish civilise the rest of Europe by all means, but not stop him from working.

'Mademoiselle Aubrienne – don't bother correcting my

pronunciation – I've been told that Madame Lipschitz went in for pious works. I mean no mockery. Perhaps she exaggerated. I attach little importance to it, but there's a suggestion that she went in for fakirs and faith-healers and saw miracles. Gone all mystic, maybe. Maybe you're a good person to ask whether there's any truth in that.'

She was sober and serious at once.

'Ah. Yes, I am the right person. I think I can answer you. I think I might know too who implanted that suggestion, and why.'

'Yes?'

'The children, maybe? Always frightened, you see, that Sabine's credulity would be abused,' with fierce sarcasm.

'Go on, would you.'

'Give me a second to collect myself. I'll try and make a good witness for you. You might bear in mind that I don't tell lies. I don't steal, either, or read other people's letters. I suppose I'm talkative,' pathetically, 'but I'm not malicious.'

He sat stolid. The tea was very nasty, but it put blood into one. What was that stuff the Irish drank? – Guinness: what would that be like? She was thinking.

'That's not enough, is it? Look, I'm not a fool or a fanatic. I don't like miracle-workers any more than you do.

'I wasn't close friends with Sabine Lipschitz; never have been. But I knew her well. I was, for many years, close friends with Vincent.'

Wasn't this what he wanted? Somebody who would bring Sabine back to life? A chattery little body, perhaps. But if an artist, could she draw Sabine for him?

'He used to come in, sitting where you are. And in the work-shop. One of the few people I'd let in, because he sat still, said nothing.

'Here he talked. I was in his confidence. A man will confide in unlikely people. I imagine I need not tell you that.

'I was in the house, fairly often. He was fond of little dinner parties. Sabine was not an especially good cook, but there were things she did nicely; she made a good hostess, oddly enough.

'Bonds between us there were too. She was a craftsman in her profession, and so am I. We had no close intimacy, but we respected – trusted too – one another.

'A bond of affection too for Vincent. A good man. Led a sad and disappointed life; died with a sense of inadequacy, short-coming. Undeserved... No, I'll tell you no more of that; that's not your business. What perhaps is, though, Sabine was conscious that much of this sense of futility was her fault. She carried a bitter load of remorse. She was a tightly knit, obstinate woman. Fought battles with herself.

'You could say too we shared our faith in our religion. Meant much to both of us.

'In these years since Vincent's death I've seen much less of her. We drifted apart too for other reasons I'll come to. However, to finish with the religious maniacs.

'Simple people – like Sabine – who believe, fervently, show it in emotional gushing language, often. They have antiquated silly little traditions and observances. And one finds people who turn this simple faith to profit. It has always been so. Anyone with a scrap of wisdom takes that lightly.

'Sabine had no truck with charlatans. She had taste, brains, judgement. But the simple – the poor in heart – she felt kinship for.

'We'll leave the miracles and apparitions aside. Sabine was convinced of them. The Cardinal isn't. We owe him obedience. He doesn't like them, and neither do I, since they attract the silly, the credulous, and also the sharks. Is that enough?'

'Yes.'

'Sabine... Some years ago, twenty or thereabouts, Sabine had a deep movement of the heart. Guts. Nervous system. I don't know what the quack calls it. To make no bones about it she'd been married years and never had a child, despite prayers, pilgrimages, and charms, and astrologers – funny, deep, peasant woman. It ate deeply into her. Because of the notion that she had never come up to the husband, who thought himself, good silly man, such a long way below her. So she decided to adopt a child, and did. Poor foolish Sabine, and my bright sensitive Vincent – never saw what a dangerous thing they were doing.'

'Did anybody?' asked Castang. He was interested. Not so much professionally as personally. He'd no children either.

'Not me, in any case. Vincent spoke of all sorts of things, and when you knew him you could translate the code, but of this never. Superstition, no doubt. Never speak of what is close to the heart – very primitive. Like these Malayan peasants who think if you say "tiger" the dreadful beast will come for you.

'He didn't speak of it till much later, when it was too late, and too much to hold down. Convinced that he had failed in this as in all else. "What have I done?" – over and over. Killed him, of course,' said Miss O'Brien, briskly.

'But I'm rambling: Sabine – now to her dying breath she hadn't ever understood. A trap with hard teeth. Thought it a good and charitable action to take a child from an orphanage and bring it up as one's own. Lavishing every care and skill on it, pouring out all the love in one's heart.'

'Isn't it?' asked Castang, wondering whether he was a sentimentalist.

'The moment you tell yourself it is, it certainly is not,' tart. 'Do it unselfconsciously, then yes. One more won't cost much. From simple goodness. Not beastly charity. Or do it professionally, like a nun. For God, not for her. Everyday work, devotion, being trained for that. Loving them and mothering them then is all right.'

She'd given this thought. Castang felt respect for the ridiculous little woman.

'Taking them to fill a gap, and then expecting them to be grateful – hopeless; fatal.'

'That's clear enough.'

'Ought to be. In your profession how many horrors do you see caused by children who've had too little affection – or too much? Or the wrong sort?'

'You're a good witness,' he said, laughing.

'Garrulous,' said the old girl, bleakly. 'And now you'd like a drink. I've nothing much. The drop of paddy's fearfully dear here. I've no opinion of that stuff the supermarket calls Scotch.'

And so say all of us, and Monsieur Barde. We won't mention him though; he's supermarket-scotch in her eyes.

What was the old dear hunting for now, like an Aberdeen terrier halfway down a rabbit hole?

'Bottle of beer somewhere,' muffled, backing out of cupboards. 'The workshop can be hot and one hasn't the time for tea.'

Castang found it a nice change from Mum and her glass of port.

'Go on.'

'I've been wondering whether I should. There; nothing is ever gained by not trusting people. Your face, by the way, doesn't really do.'

'Doesn't it?' a bit dashed. He'd always thought you could buy a second-hand car from that face, without too many fears.

'Sorry; stupidly put. I have the habit of looking at faces in terms of models. Saints, you know. Nowadays one doesn't have Jeromes and Sebastians from Correggio – they have to be modern.'

A pity. He'd be quite flattered, to be a saint in a window. Peaceful existence, too.

'Joan of Arc in a tank with a beret?'

'No no, that's altogether bad and sentimental. You might do

in a Crucifixion. There's a look of someone who does his job. Roman soldier. Guard to protect unpopular tax-collectors.'

'I'm holding nails, and it doesn't matter whether or not I believe it's a false prophet?'

'That, yes, but I absolve you from holding nails. An executioner's assistant is a very low-grade sort of person. Condemned criminals, you know, who have purchased their freedom at an ignoble price. You're holding back morbid onlookers, the kind that flock to aeroplane crashes.'

'Not so bad,' said Castang. 'Prevention of conduct likely to occasion a breach of the peace.'

'But I'm also concerned with seeing justice done. Towards a dead woman.'

'In spite of the face, and in spite of the job, so am I. We don't go in for that much these days: it's out of fashion, like public executions. Justice being done might disturb public tranquillity.'

'When was it, the last one in public?'

'In 1939, in Versailles. The public behaved badly. There were breaches of the peace. It wasn't a very good year, taken all round.'

The bird hopped on the branch, pecking eagerly at fruit.

'I want you to do a little better, you know, than repressing idle gossip.'

'Miss Aubrienne,' said Castang, 'I'm not far advanced, in this enquiry. I feel pretty convinced of one thing. If I can understand this woman, and what went on in her mind, I'll get somewhere with it. So I listen to you. I hope on the whole, patiently.'

She looked at him for some time. The realisation was slowly dawning that she too was a curious onlooker, held back by his arm.

'Let's go on, shall we?' said Castang.

CHAPTER TWENTY-ONE

The child,' said Miss O'Brien soberly, 'came into the lives of two people, who were advancing into comfortable middle age, and stiffened in their little ways. The movement, the natural turbulence of a child, made for strain.

'Picture Vincent, a man accustomed to quiet and unbroken concentration. A pot, broken by medieval carelessness and vandalism, would not worry him. That people would empty their dustbins for a hundred years on top of a mosaic pavement seemed to him natural. But the breakage of today's mustard pot threw him into a frenzy.

'Sabine was not perturbed in the same way. She had small interest in housekeeping, and few precise notions of time and place. And she enjoyed playing Mama; this new fascinating game of torn trousers and toothbrushes. It was exciting and demanding: she could fuss about compensations and deprivations. I think myself she had a fine time. That's not meant to sound spiteful.

'I'm not myself much of a witness to those years. I saw relatively little of her, and she was so wrapped up in the child that she thought of little else. Much of this comes from a friend now dead.'

'François-Xavier Martigues, Poet of Our Region?'

'Yes. Who told you?'

'The notary. Sorry.'

'Dear old man. Responsible though for foolishness. He encouraged them. Thought it just the thing for Sabine; deepen and enrich. He was thinking, you see, of literature.

'I was foolish and tactless myself. I told them I disagreed, in a rigid, opinionated manner. I told them it was blah. Full of good sense and righteousness. I did harm: we had a foolish quarrel.

'It's that, now, which I have to try to repair. How silly intelligent women can be – myself and Sabine both. If I were foolish enough to try to apportion blame in percentages, like a magistrate, I would judge myself harshly.

'My sympathies were with Vincent. He was in poor health. He'd been imprisoned by Germans, in two wars. Coping with an adolescent boy takes youth and energy, and he had neither. And his character needed care and consolation, to be made much of by women. Try and see him, pottering among his little ethnographic studies, doing good work. Living in hope of making an important discovery, finding a really outstanding archaeological piece. A fine early statue, say.'

'And never finding it.'

'That's correct. Say that the child became the early statue. Into it went all his hopes. He was terribly proud of it, and continually disappointed.

'Tragic, perhaps, that the child showed much promise. Instead of being a stolid little peasant he was a bright, nervous boy, who did all sorts of bizarre things. And they hung, and doted. I've one or two old drawings.'

She darted over to a corner, pulled out an old portfolio, undid faded ribbons, pulled out a sheet.

'As a witness, it's passable. Not too bad a drawing, and shows a certain likeness too.'

Red chalk. Recognisable the half-starved look, hangdog and drowned-rat. Also the fine mouth, the high beautiful forehead. But already the suspicious glare.

'Judas as a teenager?' he suggested.

'Not bad. He's the most interesting, isn't he? Apostles are dull. But the traitor – it's a truism. A fatal intelligence, and perhaps a passion for politics. Perhaps he decided that Christ was a traitor.

'But poor Sabine saw only sentimentality. Infant Francis of Assisi collecting butterflies. I sketched what I saw. Much good, some bad. Character at war with itself. Much would depend,' with emphasis, 'on the hands he fell into.'

Sabine. And then Janet.

Don't let's have any imaginative reconstructions, thought the cop. As Vera says, pictures which tell little anecdotes aren't worth much. Stick to realities. Sabine hit on the head. The Rue d'Aboukir. A harsh smell of dust and rags. Shots fired, missing him by precious little.

It didn't take much to kill people. A momentary loss of reason. What's that? Exasperated nerves, a scrap of bad luck, a momentary failure of discipline. Or self-defence. Two cops had fired at the man in the Rue d'Aboukir. They'd hit no one. If they had, everybody would have been pleased. One less to cause trouble and extra work.

Who had killed Sabine? And had it been in self-defence? Had Sabine committed crimes or felonies 'against the person'?

There are only two crimes, against the person.

Killing. Subdivisions: mutilation, torture, rape, wounding.

And stealing. Subdivisions: taking as hostage, kidnapping, imprisoning, enslaving.

Everything else is just a misdemeanour.

To understand Sabine dead one had to see Sabine alive.

Anything else was a police photograph of a corpse, with a touch of glycerine on the eyes to make them shine.

Sabine as a saint. The police detested saints. Crucifixions were bad enough. Cross-examining disciples even worse.

'What d'you mean he went up in the sky? You on heroin or something? Roll your sleeves up; let's have a look at your forearms.'

Sabine as the dim-witted pious female, intoxicated by superstition. That might suit Mum's book: it was hardly the impression he'd received.

Sabine as a well-intentioned criminal. Well well, avoid literature.

'I shouldn't have shown you that,' said the old dear. 'This isn't the Rogues' Gallery: give it back, please.'

She thought the boy had killed Sabine. Not that she'd say so. And not that he'd ask!

A bit literary. A cop disliked that. A bit too much like the Massacre in the Rue Transnonain, Daumier's too-well-known political and literary picture, slanted and sentimental, of a piece of bad police work.

One of Vera's stories. The painter Renoir, sketching the actress Hortense Schneider. The writer Zola looking on, gassing away interminably about social justice. Renoir fed-up.

'This is all very boring. Show us your tits, Schneider.'

Example, said Castang, of good police work.

He lit a cigarette and finished his beer.

'We were talking about Vincent,' he said.

'Vincent... He looked forward to retiring. Had it all planned. No more dust, or smells of municipal cheeseparing. That's a nice house. Sabine's fault that it never became properly habitable. He was going to cultivate that lovely great garden. And there'd be a bottle of white wine down the well, to cool, and it would all be the Lake Isle of Innisfree.'

'The what?'

'Oh, literature. Never mind. A poem. Yeats – Irish poet. A poor thing. Nine bean-rows would he have there, and a hive for the honey-bee. You see? – stupid Vincent! And stupid Sabine. A toshy poem, in my opinion, and I go and quote it: that's the Irish for you!'

This old girl had seen the false, feeble self-indulgence.

'Left to themselves, you see, they understood art. Sabine was a good poet, Vincent a good archaeologist. But that damn boy there, like a bad imitation Renoir, playing in the garden, chasing butterflies, sunlight on the fair hair and blue eyes.

'Vincent there drinking it in, mapping out in his mind the brilliant career the boy would have, so much better than his own. First prize in Latin composition.

'Bright enough, of course. You've understood that by this time. But he didn't want to be a literary portrait or an archaeological discovery. Unconcentrated, impatient, uncoordinated – and of course, never forget it, basically an abandoned child. Wary and suspicious as all hell. So last in the class, and damn the Latin composition.

'And Vincent would come here, and drink weak tea, and mumble out a lot of tosh about how he'd read *Madame Bovary* for pleasure at the age of ten, while this horrible boy just read comics.

'I tried to dig him out of it, but no use. Groaning away there about how idle and spineless the boy was. Wasn't in the least spineless, but once they decided he was going to be, by God he would be.

'I've said too much already,' abruptly. 'Go on out of it, you,' shooing a cat. Yes and you too, Mister Inspector. You'll want your dinner anyhow. Think about it by all means. Don't go arresting people, though, on the grounds of what I tell you.'

A dear old woman. Wide awake. Full of homely wisdom. Art, too.

CHAPTER TWENTY-TWO

Castang sulked along, hands in his pockets, through dusty, autumn sunshine, hating himself and everybody else, finding himself wearisomely dim-witted. I'd like to go out, he thought, and take some stupid vagabond by the collar, and say 'You'll do'. And if he didn't admit it, then thump him till he did. Because anything else...

If this, then that, and there are witnesses to back it up. Lots of lovely witnesses. Recalcitrant or chatterbox, but all sure that the truth was what they saw and knew, simple and clear-cut, and if you didn't like it then you were a crooked cop.

Everything was very quiet. Lunchtime was well advanced. Nothing on the streets but sickly smells of stew and cabbage, other people's beastly meals.

Why didn't somebody commit an offence likely to lead to a breach of the peace? He'd draw his gun, and shoot the bugger to bits. Lake Isle indeed. Hive for honey-bee. Pool of sticky honey, and him up to the neck in it.

Need something to eat. Irish tea followed by beer, not to speak of bubbly old ladies, had made him hollow and over-buoyant, an empty bottle with no message inside tossing on choppy waters; eddying about at the mercy of the waves.

Waves brought him to the Bay Tree, where loudly laughing businessmen had reached the cheese, and Sophie was measuring with her eye along a knifeblade to get twelve equal pieces out of a tart. She cut and looked up.

'Another regular. All alone? No room for a few minutes: this lot are nearly finished.'

'When do you eat?'

'When I'm clear. Quarter of an hour.'

'Will you eat with me?'

'All right, lonely heart – yes, yes, coming.'

'I'll hold out that long.'

'Have a drink – help yourself; steal some cheese if you're starving.'

How many cafés were there left for heavens' sake where they let you help yourself! He took a crust of bread to stop his stomach rumbling. From an obscure corner of memory came the sarcastic voice of a police-school instructor.

'You think the decline in public honesty is something new! You can forget the nostalgic tales about the good old days, because you know when it was that the waiters stopped leaving the bottles on the table? The Paris Exhibition of 1900! And it was the rich visitors who thought it funny to steal the cafés blind.'

The degrading French mania for petty cheating was taught them by the bourgeois, not all of whom were French. You get rich by skinning five-cent pieces off your neighbour's back. So what would you do now to restore trust and self-respect, and slough off that crust of hard cold suspicion? Will the cops start by leaving the bottle out?

The lip twisted up into a sour little knot of smile. His neighbour at the bar, drinking a cup of coffee over a racing paper, looked at him and made a face. If anybody had nudged this good man's elbow and muttered 'PJ cop' he wouldn't have been surprised. Looked a right bastard, he would have thought.

'There,' said Sophie, finishing off a half-glass of vittel-cassis. 'Always like this; they come tumbling in together and then all rush off late after a long quarrel about whose turn it is.'

'You can't leave them the bottle.'

'Yes I do because they always empty it. They look at the bill and say they can't possibly have had that much, and I just point. But they come regularly, and that's the way Léonie and I live. Think everything is permitted them. They go in the kitchen and dip their fingers and suck them, and go yum-yum, and come out here to slap my bottom.'

The sour knot was untwisting.

'Everybody wants something for nothing.'

'Not quite everyone,' looking at him. 'Martine's father, for instance – you might think about that. Scrupulous. Doesn't say all astonished "Oh, I've forgotten my cheque-book." I'm sold right out of beef; can you eat fish?'

A thoroughly casual meal, much more so than at home. Vera had a taste for formality, and hated policemen in a hurry, gobbling. As it was they had too many hastily bolted hunks in greasy humid pubs, 'washed down' (as she said, one of the filthiest phrases in the language) with drinks from hastily swilled glasses 'with tuberculosis germs all over'. So that she tended to be school-marmish at table, telling one to sit up straight and not fidget.

Meals with Sophie were alarmingly domestic.

'Damn, I've no knife,' taking the butter knife and wiping it on the cloth, 'no matter; got to be changed anyhow.' It was more than doubtful whether Vera would approve of Sophie.

It suited him. The woman had been scurrying, and needed to unwind. And it was not only physical ballast, in his belly, that he needed. He had these vivid, splintered little pictures to digest. Scraps of bright-coloured glass set in lead, or concrete nowadays... Old Vincent in the garden, propping up pea-vines, muttering about *Madame Bovary*. Sabine as Mama, buttering fresh crusts and making huge cups of cocoa for a meagre little boy who would always look pale and haggard, no matter how much grub he absorbed. A house untidy and badly dusted, with bits of model ships and butterfly collections all mixed up with fragments of tesselated pavement and pottery shards. Vincent silent and irritable the whole evening because of a bad school report, snapping when the television got turned on. 'This cretinous trash – are you incapable of reading a book?'

A nice meal: raw ham with olives and radishes, grilled trout, fennel done with bone marrow, a piece of tart unsold 'because a bit burned underneath' and 'give me whatever you think fair', she said, making coffee. He helped clear away, thinking joyfully of the Hotel Central and hideous fried potatoes.

'I'm going to have a bit of a sit; you in a hurry?'

'No,' said Castang pleasurably. It was time to start work again, but this was as good a place as any to begin. She brought coffee.

'You were a bit naughty to Martine, you know.'

'Yes, a nice girl, but a bit too daft.'

'A bit too vulnerable! Means everything with all her heart. She might do the wrong thing, but she won't do it idly or negligently.'

'But stupidly. What could she hope to gain?'

'There you are – you think in terms of what can be gained! Not her style. She hoped that if you were approached transparently, with generosity, you might behave generously yourself. And so you did, I'm glad to say. Or you wouldn't be sitting here with me. She thinks that even a cop will be sincere given the chance.'

'Never altogether – as you know.'

'You want something from me,' said Sophie. 'I don't know what, yet, but I've experience of cops.'

161

'Nothing much. Sincerity, maybe.'

'And what do I get?'

'Nothing much either. I've no influence around here. A good word with Peyrefitte, which you might not even want.'

'Mm. Well, you were straight with Martine, at least. Not just jig jig and then good girl, that was fun. Try me.'

'All right; I will. An old lady gets killed. By some intruder, just like the paper said. Nothing to show it wasn't. But there are background circumstances which don't get told me. One of these is Thonon. There's nothing against him. He's reticent, all right, because of a bit of tax evasion or maybe a fiddle with building permits, some small stuff that wouldn't interest me. You know this place, and some at least of the people in it,' nodding towards the table where the businessmen had been sitting. 'Now why should Martine feel so bothered, running to get me to lay off? Lay off what?'

'I see. That's not too difficult. He has a dishonest sort of job, but he's a straight man. You can see from the girl. Good father-daughter relationship. Your old lady – I can't help you. Know nothing about her. That crowd I serve, yes, they can be very indiscreet, but I heard nothing. They were as surprised as you'd expect. Everyone accepted the vagabond theory: it can happen to anybody, nowadays. Why should there be anything else?'

'Most probably there isn't.'

'As for Martine getting worked up – oh foo: that's just young-girl romanticism. She sees you as a mystery story and gets a bit breathless. Saw you hanging about and started dramatising. She dramatises most things as you've surely realised. Including me. She sees me in kind of a pink light,' said Sophie. 'Damaged goods, poor her. Tart with a heart. Fix her up with a good man.' Castang laughed.

Sophie did not laugh.

'I was a girl like that myself. And now I've a boy of my own. He's eight. I don't see him at lunchtime; Léonie gives him dinner on the corner of the kitchen table. I'm rushed and sweaty, and I haven't time to show affection, and I don't want to show impatience. The waitress, bright and joky. Concentrate on that. So I get one hour in the evening, when he comes back and does homework. Five till six. So I've only learned one thing since I was eighteen myself. Keep your life in compartments.'

'By day and by night.'

'Ah,' she drawled, 'you mean does he know? Of course he does, and he doesn't say so, and I don't tell him. You want me to tell you, maybe, all about what I think when I'm in bed with a man? As he grows up he'll learn all about it, and what work there is with this piddling restaurant, and this scruffy little bar, and this squalid little town, and what I'd do without Léonie, and all about the paperwork and the regulations, the municipal hygiene and the running water, and what I may charge and may not charge, and how to bribe public officials – are you really interested?' viciously, 'would you like to learn all that too? Fucking well shut up, then. I don't tell Martine either. She's a nice little bourgeois girl, straight and good and sheltered, and I'd like to see her stay that way.'

'All right, understood.'

'You're not a bad bugger. Too soft to make a real skinflint cop.'

'I can be bastardly upon occasion.

'This isn't it. Leave Martine alone.'

'You made a nice speech. But it rings a little false, you know.'

'Huh?'

'Martine is romantic, and lives a sheltered existence. That could explain her ringing me up, acting the mysterious and secretive. She wouldn't offer to take me to bed. It doesn't cover her being frightened. I think of more than just a tax fiddle coming to light.

'There's more to it, as I think you know. And I think you know what it is. Or you wouldn't be trying to distract me with a long tear-brimming speech about you being driven into prostitution by the hard-hearted Minister of Finance.'

'Coo. Can be bastardly after all.'

'Just sincere. That's what you wanted, wasn't it? Cops aren't sincere much. People aren't with them either, on the whole. All these generous offers from lovely young girls.'

'I prefer sleeping alone in the afternoons, but I'll stretch a point.' He started to laugh, and after a moment so did she.

'All right,' he said at last. 'Now what has Daddy really done that has Martine in such a flap?'

She smashed out her cigarette end and took another.

'Now we understand each other, I'll say it again; I'd feel pretty sure, nothing criminal. He might be short of liquid, and that could be the source of Martine's worry. The wife's all right, but she likes money, and he likes to give it to her. Then there's that big house, and the girl's horse. The bills must come pretty high.'

'He gamble or anything?'

'No, but the competition is tough, and credit is tight. He had a deal set up with the old lady. Martine knew that, because she told me. And now the old lady's dead and that queered the deal. Then you come poking into it. Queers it further, screws it maybe right up. But I think he was counting on it. Martine had a boy-scout notion of smoothing you out and generally unscrewing. Without Daddy knowing. Being strapped for money, for those who aren't used to it, is humiliating. I truly don't think it has to be more complex than that.'

'If it was that simple why not tell me straight out before?'

Sophie studied him. He studied her. Nice girl. Pretty, too. Pale, thin, a bit anaemic-looking. Mouth cut beautifully, with unusual precision.

'You're a criminal-brigade cop, you know. And there was a murder. That's a bit intimidating. You're quite right, everyone has been wondering whether there wasn't more to it than the hippy blunt instrument. Everybody wondering where he stands, with you around. They feel uneasy. Now look, I don't want to throw you out, but I have to be at work again at five: go be a cop somewhere else.'

'I'm nearly through. Do you know a man called Barde?'

She looked startled.

'I do as a matter of fact. Very slightly: he's an occasional customer. But what's that, out of the blue?'

'Very little. Cop talk. I was talking to him. Nothing material: he knew the dead woman in bygone days. Martine saw me near her house, which is near his: thought I was spying on her.'

'Nice neighbourhood.'

'One just likes to know a little more about who one talks to.'

'I don't know him much. Don't particularly want to. As a waitress I sort them out crudely; the ones who are pleasant to serve or not. He's an aren't. That's all.'

'On what grounds?'

'Oh, patronising, condescending. Comes with the hundred franc note as though he were conferring a favour. Not so much that he's the type that gives trouble. More that he has the notion his beautiful personality more than makes up for trouble caused. Phoney manners. Upsets a glass and starts a song: "Oh, I *am* so sorry, *do* forgive me."'

Castang grinned, listening to Barde's voice.

'And likes to stay the night, perhaps?'

'Oh,' comically, 'he has very kindly offered to a few times. Somehow I haven't managed to be disengaged. He's a slug. No real dignity: it's all phoney standing, like apartment houses with marble entries. Blithers about his family and being at school with the Proc. But owes money everywhere – tradesmen can wait because what importance have their affairs. A phoney big squire in riding boots that aren't paid for.' He sniggered. 'That's it – village gossip from the village call girl – go on; buzz off.'

CHAPTER TWENTY-THREE

O h, the fine affair! He'd only been digesting his dinner, taking a pastoral stroll in the fresh air on his way to sort out Popaul Thonon. He'd been conscientious, making a detour by way of the Hotel Central to see if there were any messages. And look at him now! The place was in an uproar, and the Police Judiciaire highly unpopular.

Messages, grumbled the patronne – cow she was! Should just about think there were: all morning it's been going on, and through lunch time. As though one hadn't enough to do without that phone ringing. It hadn't stopped, and people haven't the right to be inconsiderate – there, it's ringing again. Not here to run errands for customers, police or no police, and tell them I said so.

Castang, jolted out of any post-prandial euphoria, cut the tirade off by blocking his hearing ostentatiously with both earpieces.

'What's it now?' he mumbled.

'Lucciani,' bleated that donkey.

'Is that who's creating all this uproar?' said Castang ominously.

'No, listen, look, Richard said to let you know, and I'm trying everywhere to get hold of you, and nobody knew where you were, and it's not my fault, but that old bag...'

'And you forgot your toothpaste in the bathroom and you'd like me to wrap it in a neat little parcel to send on?'

'No, wait, look, listen –' The accumulation of ums and ers was adding to exasperation.

'Where the hell are you, anyhow? You're supposed to be working.'

'Well, I am working. I'm in Longueville, Richard told me to stop off to see about that lab report and then –'

'Never mind: what the hell are all these calls in aid of?'

'I keep trying to tell you, the lab report, they sent it stupidly back here instead of on to us, the blood's human and it's the right group, the fellow what's disappeared, no not this one but the other.'

'What fellow?'

'Well, the gendarmerie, they think they'd like to ask that fisherman fellow some more questions, because making an affray, leastways that's a pretext, see.'

Castang wasn't in the least interested. The gendarmerie in Longueville might not all have doctorates of philosophy, but were perfectly competent. He didn't want to know anything at all about them and their affray. Unfortunately, he would be held responsible for any confusion caused by this mumbling boy.

'Talk sense. Who's stopping them?'

'Well listen, the fellow's done a bunk, see.'

'*Stop saying listen.* He's *what?*'

'He's nowhere to be found.'

'Look for him then; where's he gone to?'

'East Jesus for all I know,' obnoxiously jaunty.

'And you are standing there, all pleased with yourself, telling me about it?'

'Well, I knew you were in charge of the case and so I thought I better let you know.'

Castang held the phone away from his face, shook his head at it, sighed deeply, put it back again, adopted a deep bass voice like an operatic villain.

'Now *you* listen. You go find him, see. Or you'll be headed for East Jesus arse foremost, and what's *your* blood group?'

'Well, we're searching.'

'Search to more purpose,' banging the phone down. He hadn't walked more than two paces away from this dunderhead when the cretinous telephone rang again.

'Twenty pork chops for tomorrow, butcher, and how about a calf's head, and don't forget the brains.'

'What?' said Peyrefitte's voice bemused. 'This is the Comm **t** oh, is that you, Castang, at last?'

'But I've my hand held up. Please, miss, may I leave the room, miss, please?'

'All very well for you to be funny, but I'll have you know there's a fine flap going on and it's your work and not mine and I've quite enough with these black bastards.'

'What fine flap?'

'Some fellow that's wanted on an affray charge in Longueville and took to the woods.'

'Oh yes, of course. And you want him arrested, yes, is that right? Okay then, send me up a cop with a pair of handcuffs and I'll look into the matter.'

'No, no, no, no,' crossly. 'The gendarmerie were waiting at a crossroads and stopped his car.'

Castang was childishly determined to keep out of this.

'Oh fine, that's lovely then, deafening applause.'

'And I've got him right here for you.'

'No you haven't. You may have thought you did, for a few minutes, but that was just a small administrative error.'

'Now what the hell? You coming here to interrogate this man? The gendarmerie have just brought him in.'

'What should I want to interrogate him about? I don't know him from Martin Bormann.'

'But he's your case, damn it.'

'He most emphatically is not my case, and the gendarmerie can stick him straight back in their car if they've nowhere better. Take him back to Longueville where he belongs and not to be so goddam zealous another time. Everybody sees fugitives from justice and tries to stick me with them.'

'Now stop being silly, Castang,' in a most irritatingly patient and jolly way. 'Longueville is legally in the administrative sector here. He's got to be held for the Proc, but I gather there's a suspicion of homicide. Anyway this is your pigeon: Richard made that perfectly clear.'

Castang said things about Commissaire Richard.

'Yes yes, I know,' said Peyrefitte, 'but you're here and that means on the spot.'

'Where's the dossier anyhow?'

'They're sending it over by messenger. There's no need to make so much fuss. It's open and shut; the fellow admits everything, or did anyhow, in the car coming over. What's left but formalities?'

'Why didn't you say so in the first place?' grumbled Castang unreasonably. 'Oh, all right then, I'll try and get over this evening.'

He rang Richard, who was unanswerable as usual.

'There's nothing to it. Some dispute about fish, there on the river bank. The gendarmerie has done all the work. You've only to take the man's statement, and fill in a few forms, and you have it all wrapped up for your judge there, and it's something for the press. Make everybody happy; show them how efficient you are.' Quite as usual, no way of telling from his voice whether he was being sarcastic. 'How's your old lady coming along?'

'Everyone's got something to hide. I don't much believe in the vagabond. It'll serve to gain time, and it might even be of use.'

'Or I wouldn't waste Lucciani's time on it.'

'I'm not without hope of turning something up here.'

'Nor am I,' said Richard, and put his phone down. Castang didn't know whether this was supposed to be encouraging.

The fisherman's papers wouldn't be there anyhow before this evening. A session with Popaul was more urgent.

And after all that, Thonon wasn't even back from lunch.

CHAPTER TWENTY-FOUR

The secretary looked at the clock. Monsieur Thonon was showing a house to an important client whom he'd been lunching with. But he'd be back any moment. She wondered whether to show a little languorous coyness with the police, decided against it, frowned in concentration over her typing. They both sat and collected their thoughts, such as these were. The blue Peugeot came sailing along the Place d'Armes, found its habitual place occupied, tucked itself crossly in fifty metres further along. Steps came back, with a bit of crisp heel-tapping, a concentrated frown six feet higher. The door opened and closed rather hard. The girl looked up from her typing.

'He take it?'

'He's not sure he can afford it, meaning ten percent less but he'll try for twenty. Any calls?'

'Monsieur Castang is here.'

'Oh,' turning stiffly, restraining himself. 'Good day to you. I thought we'd finished with all that.'

'Some points to tidy up.'

'Have I anyone booked, Marianne?'

'Not till five.'

'Come on in then. But this is a bore, you know. I don't mind, I suppose. But it all seems very tortuous.'

'Not really. We looked at things in general. I made no notes, and I didn't press you. I could ask you to come to the commissariat to make a statement with a stenographer present.' Thonon shoved his pipe between his teeth and bit on it. 'You seem a little irritable.'

Thonon fiddled with his tobacco pouch before making his mind up.

'This death puts a spoke in my wheel. That's normal. Then you put another. It's difficult to do business in a normal way with the police knocking about. Your bread and butter, but you realise that people don't exactly find it an everyday occurrence. People – families concerned – feel under strain. You come blowing in, worrying at me. I suppose that's just scrutiny of these circumstances, uh, the coincidental connection, but you can't blame me if I feel you're leaning on me.'

'Mmhm,' said Castang. You're sensitive, you feel some strain, that's inhibiting – is that it?'

'In outline, I suppose that's more or less it.'

'Fill it in then. Anything I can do to help, I will.'

'Oh,' fiddling with his pipe and choosing words, 'I'm... I gather that the mother-in-law has appeared from Paris. Didn't come just for the funeral, I suspect. I hear in fact that she's an interfering old biddy, not likely to make things easier for me. Been ringing up all and sundry.'

'Oh yes,' said Castang amiably, 'I've met her. Businesslike, in fact pushing. Yes, I can see she'll make it tough for you. Especially since I've heard it suggested that you were exceptionally eager to do this stroke of business: is that right?'

Thonon's pale face, a natural pallor going with dark hair, flushed.

'What d'you mean, exceptionally? As I explained with some

care, I put a lot of work and trouble into this, and I don't want to see it go to waste.'

'That it was urgent to you – that the urgency might make you particularly anxious – would there be some truth in that?'

The flush got deeper, with an angry look.

'I'd like to know who makes that sort of insinuation, and on what grounds?'

'No need to be angry; this is in confidence, just between us. On the grounds that you are short of ready money. Nothing in that to be ashamed of. I can see readily enough that you have an expensive establishment, and that means a lot of outgoings.'

'Who made the suggestion?'

'I don't have to tell you, you know. I've interviewed a lot of people. The suggestion might be slightly malicious, which is why I put it to you.' Polite, deprecating, like a bank manager.

'Someone you've interviewed,' with sarcastic emphasis. 'Like I hear you had a nice tea-cosy chat with Barde.' Of course; from Martine.

'So I did: why fix on him?'

'It's just the sort of poisonous remark he tosses out lightly, with a laugh pretending it's not to be taken seriously. Barde, yes, I can see it. Quite typical. Now let me tell you I'll defend myself against this sort of insinuation. I can tell you why Monsieur Barde makes suggestions of that sort. Maybe it'll help open your eyes.'

'I ask nothing better,' blandly.

'Barde would like to get into the act, that's why. He has no professional standing or competence whatever, but he thinks it quite ethical to try real-estate deals, and extort a commission, without taking any pains, or giving the slightest guarantee. Because he's Monsieur Barde, and we're nobodies. And if anyone complained about unfair competition he couldn't care less, and if one made a legal complaint, say about false pretences, that's all right,' bitterly. 'When you've been to school with the proc you're okay, see.'

'Just to amuse himself?' sounding incredulous, feeling pleased, learning more.

'Heaven, man, you're being obtuse. You fall for Barde, the way he takes everyone in. Display of affluence, a drawling I-don't-need-to-work manner, and phoney talk about art. Owes money everywhere, including the bank. Strapped. Hasn't a penny, stoops to turn one.'

'I see. You suggest he'd like to swing a deal like this himself. And that by defaming you he diminishes your chances? To increase his own? Is that what you suggest?'

'Why d'you think,' teeth clenched on pipe, 'I wanted and tried to keep this quiet.'

'Did you know that Barde was an old friend of Madame Lipschitz? Before her death?'

'No.'

'Bit over-vehement, aren't you? Suppose Barde heard, which he won't from me, what you said, that would be defamation too, no? Small town gossip: he's strapped, you're strapped, we can go on conjugating a verb and it doesn't mean much.'

'He'd say that, would he? And you know what I'd do? I'd plead fair comment. I could find you three different agents in this town whose legitimate business was injured by Barde's meddling. And I could tell you to look at information available to anybody who takes the trouble, like land-registry records, and see what Barde owned, and what he has sold. That he's daisied through his inheritance. Bad debts are common knowledge. Complaints have been made. And headed off.'

'By the proc?'

'Saying that's asking for trouble,' with some humour, 'like accusing a cop of corruption.'

'But the complaints came to nothing.'

'Right. But spread gossip about me, that I was trying to put pressure on a client to get a deal through because I'm supposed to be living beyond my means, and I've the cops on my neck at all hours. Oh, nothing personal.'

'Perhaps you'd now be surprised to hear that Barde never mentioned your name.'

Thonon was deflated.

'It wouldn't have been the first time, that's all,' in an obstinate mutter. 'Who was it anyhow?'

'Never mind. I don't believe everything I hear. Don't reach any conclusions, either.'

'I don't care a damn what conclusions you reach.'

'Your mouth is robbing your ears. Listen to me now. You're anxious for this deal. You thought you could still do it with the inheritors. Mum is a tougher proposition. All right so far? And you need this deal, to dig you out of a hole. Still all right? Any comment?' There wasn't any comment.

'I'm learning about small towns,' said Castang equably. 'Suppose now that I ask you to think about something. The press, the local paper-hawk; there probably isn't more than one in a place this size. Correspondent for a bigger paper, maybe.

'Haven't seen him yet myself. He's been briefed, I dare say, by the Palais, about discreet enquiries and such. He knows I'd give him some flannel about an incomplete enquiry, stuff not worth listening to, let alone print. He may not be following me around, but nothing stops him noticing, to take an example, that I've come to see you twice in the thirty-six hours I've been here. I don't know what he might get in his head.

'Then, the judge. I trot about, collecting laborious scraps of information and fitting them together like a broken pot. But it's the judge who draws inferences, makes conclusions, decides what is or isn't relevant. Some judges will let a cop work, give him some rope. Some are fussy, like to hold you up very tight on a rein.

'This judge is fussy. And he's in a hurry. Nor is he entirely satisfied with the stuff about the vandal who broke in and got surprised and killed the old lady in a panic. It remains the basic theory. Perhaps it's not quite that straight-up-and-down.

'I have to give him an account of my doings. He might want to hear for himself about your dealings with Madame Lipschitz. That's just as a witness to this business of the house deal. No suspicions, no accusations.

'All the same, the press might make something of that. They get no news, they start fabricating it. Only innuendo, and pretty meaningless, but just when you want to make a deal it could be embarrassing, even damaging.'

Thonon sat still, elbows on the table, hands gripping his pipe, watching and listening.

'What's all the long speech for then?'

'To give you time to think.'

'And then?'

'I've a suggestion. You can think I'm trying to trick you into something; I don't care, I'm used to that. Or you can think I'm just being sensible, which would make me happier.'

'What is it?'

'I give you a bit of time. Think things over a bit more. Talk to your family maybe. And I might come up to see you, quietly, in your house perhaps, say this evening. You could give me a ring if you liked, about supper time, at the Hotel Central.'

'What's to be gained from that, for either of us?'

'You haven't perhaps been altogether open with me, so far. Suppose there was something you didn't want known, which showed you in a poor light – why, it might help you if you went yourself down to the Palais and talked it over with the judge, privately.'

Thonon was saying nothing still, smoking his pipe calmly enough, looking at Castang with a controlled expression, as though keeping himself from a loud burst of laughter, or a sudden gush of words.

'That wouldn't compromise you, you know,' went on Castang, with his air of being a sympathetic chap once you got to know him. 'You'd be safeguarding your liberties, instead of letting the judge, perhaps, draw the wrong conclusion. Decide, of course, as you think fit.'

Thonon laid the pipe in the ashtray.

'All this, of course, is simply your technique for putting leverage on me. Right?'

'It is and it isn't.'

'Threats and inducements. Make a clean breast and it'll save you trouble later. I suppose the cops are always like this. Same as asking when you're going to stop beating your wife. I'm either admitting guilt, according to this argument, or trying to conceal it.'

Castang spread his hands and laughed.

'Of course we're forbidden to make threats and inducements, and equally we often do: get no work done otherwise, half the time.'

Thonon gave a sour little laugh.

'So go to the judge, you say. So that he can be zealous. I can be innocent of anything at all, but he allows a cloud of suspicion to rest on me in order, if I'm to believe you, to please the proc, the press, and the public. Just to gain time he can charge me with homicide.'

'As to that,' said Castang calmly, 'it's not a bad thing. The system's quite good. If any presumption of guilt exists nobody can question you, because you can't be forced to incriminate yourself. Even the judge can't say boo to you without a lawyer present to protect and advise you, telling the judge politely please to rephrase that, because it sounds tendentious.'

'You're being cynical.'

'Not in the least.'

'And are you seriously telling me that I'm in this situation?'

'I don't know,' said Castang, 'and that's why I suggested a meeting this evening, to talk things over quietly.'

'You think me guilty of this crime,' said Thonon abruptly.

'I don't think anything at all, except that you might be in a position where the judge decided he had sufficient grounds for letting suspicion rest against you.'

'On the basis of hearsay gossip,' bitterly.

'I'll tell you about that tonight. With, if I may, your family present.'

'Being enigmatic again. This is simply outrageous.'

'Why? You aren't arrested or anything: I've no grounds. You may or may not be withholding information which the judge might think germane to a homicide investigation; that's the formal jargon. Oh, if you were to try running off to Tahiti I could have you pinched, sure. I can hold you in a cell for twenty-four hours. That's the limit. Then I must present you to the judge, who decides whether he can hold you. No habeas corpus, but comes to the same thing.'

'That rule gets bent.'

'And so does habeas corpus. You think the English are saints or something? Go before a magistrate there, within twenty-four hours, exactly the same, and when he asks why you shouldn't be set at liberty the cops say blandly they need a remand to complete their enquiries and yes, your worship, we do have an objection to bail.'

'And all this,' incredulous, 'because I was trying to talk that old girl into selling me her house and happened to drop in that evening.'

Castang said nothing.

'Very well. Half past seven. At my house.'

'Good,' said Castang, feeling for the doorhandle, 'and by the way – have a word with Martine.'

CHAPTER TWENTY-FIVE

The Place de la République was the seat of the municipal administration of a smallish French town; the 'mairie' or town hall; where you go to get born, married, or buried. During your life, many other things can happen to you, and to have permission for these, in a highly centralised state like the Republic, you must go to the regional apparatus of government. To pay taxes, say, or get a doctor's bill reimbursed by Social Security.

It was only five minutes' walk from the Place d'Armes, but a different world. A different century for a start: nineteenth instead of eighteenth. Instead of being light and simple in proportions, it was sombre and top-heavy: leaden architecture, which strove for dignity and succeeded in being ponderous. However big the windows they would always repel light, instead of admitting it. It was not a theatre for bugle calls and the click of accoutrements, but a setting for public executions, conducted with the utmost parsimony in the middle of a grudging and petty existence.

All these bureaux with ridiculous names are collectively termed the intendance, a contemptuous word. They are full of functionaries – another bad word. And these people are some-times alive and intelligent. They can be courteous and charm-ing. Even the police can be all four.

Not of course the Petty Functionary. He is a bastard anywhere, intoxicated by his petty authority. He is the Post-master from Przemysl, bawling out Turkish immigrants for daring to spell their names in Turkish. Inventing new sorts of rubber stamps. Atrophied both by his arrogance and his servil-ity, he is scarcely alive at all.

But there are superior functionaries too. They are some-times alive.

Castang had spent much of his life in these rabbit warrens, and tapped briskly down corridors.

Equipment; subdivision Environment. Parks and Open Spaces. Waters and Forests. A Departmental Director for Sani-tary and Social Action; he was getting warm. National Agency for Amelioration of Housing; chilly again. He turned a corner.

Ah. Building Permits. Commercial, Industrial. Public Works. Last, Persons. He was a Person. Members of the Public Apply Next Door, but he knocked smartly and entered. A spruce elderly man looked up from a crowded desk.

'You know,' mildly, 'this is a private office. It's even written there, in large letters.'

'Police,' said Castang, producing a card. 'I wanted it to be discreet.'

'Well. Police Judiciaire I see. Monsieur Castang. Well. My name is Delalande. Sit down. No, that's a bad chair; try this. I don't smoke, but please do. So: a breath of excitement. I am agog.' He didn't look in the least agog, but he never would.

The door to the communicating office opened and a fat man came in with papers, importance, a draught.

'I think you see that I have a visitor,' said Delalande. This mildness was more deadly than shouting: the fat person withdrew.

'In what way can I serve you?' Professional urbanity, and perhaps, too, a desire to be of service.

'Do you have a young man called Lipschitz working in your service?'

'Indeed I do. Today he is on a leave of absence. He lost his mother under tragic circumstances. Known as leave upon Family Affairs. I dare say that you know all about this.'

'That's right. I'm enquiring into this death, as you guess or already know. The family affairs; they're a bit complicated. So it occurred to me to come and see you, for a character reference, in a sense. No, better, a different viewpoint. We tend to see things from too narrow an angle.'

'It could hardly be narrower than mine,' mildly. 'I know nothing of his family affairs.'

'Piercing spotlights from all angles,' suggested Castang. 'Even upon the front shown in working hours.'

'I see. You might think of circulating a little memo, to point out the beauty of piercing spotlights. A means, for instance, of promoting broadened vision within the framework of interdepartmental intercourse. I'm thinking of the Sewerage people. Now they stand somewhat in need of broadened vision. However to your purpose: Monsieur Lipschitz: yes... He does me good, I dare say. He's an intelligent young man. He provides, aha, an astringent element. Gingers me up, you know. Most valuable... On the other hand, it could perhaps be said of him that his horizons too stood in need of a little broadening.'

'You're thinking perhaps of getting him transferred to the Sewerage?'

'Yes, they could do with an astringent element: there's much to be said for that. However, as Promoter of the Faith I am bound to wage a just war.'

'But a Holy War.'

'I must remain scrupulous,' said Monsieur Delalande, who had evidently a taste for mild civil-service jokes. 'An act such as you describe would be contrary to the Geneva Convention. Much like poison gas. Or perhaps explosive bullets.'

'An ultimate weapon.'

'Not a bad description; he is rather a violent young man. Suffers from excess thyroid, to judge by his eyes. Says astonishing things. He told me the other day that honesty was a ridiculous concept. He's all the plagues of Egypt – minus one if we admit the Sewerage. Well,' dropping into his normal voice, 'suppose we don't dramatise. He'd be quite interesting to a pathologist. He can turn a polished phrase; produces indeed the most ingenious sophisms. Witness the example I gave you: asked to explain himself, he said that honesty being contrary to all human nature he found it a dishonest concept. He has an extreme fear of deprivation, which leads to naked covetousness. A perfect Attila of anarchy. And no notion of property at all: there isn't a paperclip safe anywhere along the corridor. The entire office is plundered, and lives terrorised beneath his heel.'

'Bar yourself.'

'I have my methods,' agreed Monsieur Delalande, with the French attachment to the works of Sir Arthur Conan Doyle.

'Do you feel sorry for him?'

'It's astonishingly difficult to feel sorry for him,' ruefully. 'Very immature, of course. Is it a psychopathic element? I hesitate to use other jargons than my own. An accomplished actor.'

'That and the feeling of deprivation – you've quoted two classic symptoms.'

'True. And the skill at self-justification.'

'Would he commit a crime?'

'No, no,' smiling faintly, 'you musn't ask me that. I have no knowledge of anything beyond misdemeanour. But he's not a good person. He can see, you understand, no need to be. He's in the right, totally, at all times. Nothing will convince him of the contrary. An anarchist.'

'He sounds, in official language, a sore trial.'

'Family affairs,' remarked Delalande elliptically. 'Birthdays and boyfriends one leaves to the typists, in general, but I have gathered that he had a bad start. An orphan. And the elements, the metals and things in his composition: they're at war with each other. If the metaphor is not too lurid for you he's highly radioactive: he glows in the dark.'

Castang was liking his new witness.

'One would wish to be sorry for him, very much. Plainly he's very unhappy. Equally, he'll never get out of the...'

'Shit.'

'Quite. You see why the Sewerage couldn't cope. Too much of their own.'

'Can I seize on a few of the points you've made?'

'By all means.'

'The naked covetousness, honesty a ridiculous concept, anarchy, no notion of property – he doesn't exactly sound cut out for public service.'

'Just so. And of course I see where you are tending. I take precautions, naturally. I should in any case. No public service is ever altogether free of abuses and corruption. A fact one must always bear in mind when dealing with it.'

'As witness,' said Castang, 'the police.'

'The point is well taken. This particular service is vulnerable, building permits being a sought-after commodity. Let's say that I see his claws are kept cut. Naturally, any abuse would see the end of him at once. It would be a pity really. His abilities are great, whereas one is never short of competent mediocrities. He knows, of course, that I wouldn't give threepence for his future here. I don't want to prejudice another future, elsewhere. I've been hoping that he would anticipate me. I'd be rid of a scourge. What can I tell you? – it will come, one way or the other, shortly; within weeks. This bereavement may help me avoid the obligation by making it unnecessary: there was a murmur about coming into some money.'

'In confidence,' said Castang, 'can you tell me whether you have in fact had any small trouble?'

'Not yet...'

'Has there been any approach to your office for a permit to build on the Lipschitz property – from any quarter?'

'Yes, there was, but eight or nine months ago. A house agent asking whether, theoretically, permission would be forthcoming.'

'Monsieur Thonon?'

'That's correct. Nothing unreasonable – an informal approach. I told him naturally that if a technical dossier was presented with the usual architectural plans it would be considered in the normal way. There is no objection *a priori,* from the urbanisation angle.'

'He was just checking up in a prudent way?'

'No doubt, with a view to making an offer presumably. If you're wondering whether there was or is any collusion with our young man – set that thought at rest.'

'And – if you'll forgive me – no effort at putting pressure on yourself?'

'Such efforts are frequent,' smiling thinly, 'but not in this instance.'

'Any personal opinion about Thonon that you'd feel able to give me? Hints have been made that he sails close to the law occasionally, and you might be well placed to judge of that.'

'Not in specific terms. Most house agents dabble in building promotion if they see an opportunity to turn it to advantage. You know as well as I do that the profits are considerable. There's evidently a temptation to small dishonesties in various shades of grey: that's inevitable. Most promoters as a consequence get a reputation for being sharks. I do not need, I imagine, to say that I don't go clapping telescopes to my blind eye, but I don't hold their mouths open to look at their teeth, either.

It's the difference between a bit of wire and a bit of string. Some people are born bent; others have bentness thrust upon them.'

'I'm obliged to you,' said Castang.

'I'm an experienced official,' said Delalande mildly. 'Where building permits are concerned, the skulduggery is a bottomless pit. I don't make a parade of my skill in detecting it. That young man keeps me on my toes, but I'm accustomed to that.'

'I don't suppose I'm likely to create any troubles for you,' said Castang. 'If I see any likelihood I'll give you a phone-call. I don't like scandals any more than you do. And the judge has a holy horror of them.'

The two shook hands, with polite, civil-service laughs.

CHAPTER TWENTY-SIX

Castang was feeling the need for a short jolt at the pub, but the Place de la République didn't have a pub. He had to go sneaking past the Commissariat of Police with a guilty conscience, frightened lest Monsieur Peyrefitte come bouncing out to take him by the collar. He got back feeling a bit better equipped to interrogate his fisherman.

Stupid damn fisherman! Dim-witted crime, dim-witted behaviour. Trying to make sense of him, Castang found himself growing denser every second. The sharp-witted civil servant indeed! With a horrid rapidity he turned into the sort of cop to be found in all police stations, belching when he sat down (he'd had two beers) and making an unnatural number of typing errors, cursing and plying the rubber laboriously. One of those animals skilful at adopting the colours and patterns of their background.

The fisherman was indeed unusually clueless about absolutely everything – he was quite willing to say whatever anybody wanted him to say, or whatever he thought that was at any given moment. Thought is not quite the right word. The dialogue jolted along on a cat-sat-on-the-mat level.

'Trapping fish, see, that's not right. Dynamite and that.' Illegal methods, typed Castang. It didn't look right. He'd spelt it with one l and two gs.

'What d'you mean you were standing behind him? He was facing you, you said, a moment ago.'

'That's right.'

'Well, which was it?'

'I don't know.'

'Now look,' patiently, 'try and reconstruct it. You had this knife in your hand, right?'

'That was for my fish.'

'Never mind that. You push the button and it opens. Now that's an offensive weapon and classed as such.'

'With the locking blade, see, doesn't close back on your own finger.'

'Listen, man, you had a go at him, not at your finger.'

'Well, he's bigger than me.'

Castang wished either that he'd had no beer at all, or that he'd had two more.

It wasn't fair. One got muddled up with people like Sabine. One should stick to people like this. After all, most crimes were like this. Meaningless in the sense that there wasn't any why, or at least the why didn't play any part. As well ask why an eighteen-year-old boy arrived drunk in a café near closing time (Castang's last homicide case, just three weeks before). Why had the owner refused to serve him? Why had the boy got all aggressive with a knife? – enormous German hunting knife, inconvenient and cumbersome object. So the owner, a big tough fellow who wasn't taking cheek from snot-boys, went to put the little bugger out the door. And died six hours later as a result. All these stupid 'why' questions simply didn't enter into it.

He really did wish like hell that Peyrefitte had been right all along and that Sabine had been clonked by a yobbo who'd simply thought the house was empty and would be easy to break into. Not specially to steal anything: just for excitement. Day by day life was so boring. No reason at all for killing her. I mean, these old women started yelling and you gave them a tap, like, to keep them quiet and they just fell down. Didn't even know she was dead. No reason why she should be dead. Most unreasonable of her. You went away then. It wasn't interesting and exciting any more. You were bored again.

Don't know why. All the sociologists, all the industrial psychologists, all the educational authorities say you're bored. Why?

Boring existence, boring job. Dim-witted at the start. Born bored. Even your own mother was bored with you.

The trouble with this scenario was that nobody had seen the yobbo. He could perfectly well be a figment of the imagination. A product of wishful thinking. He simplified policemen's lives. Or would, if the judge wasn't so tiresome, and if that blasted mayor hadn't been on the fiddle with building permits, and Thonon on the fiddle with his income tax, and everybody, quite as usual, in this stupid little town on the fiddle in some small way with some small thing. Even Sophie was on the fiddle with Commissaire Peyrefitte. To make ends meet; that was all they wanted, just to make ends meet. Bits of string, and bits of wire.

The fisherman signed everything he was asked to. It could have been written that he thought he was the reincarnation of John Wilkes Booth and this other fellow looked like Abraham Lincoln (who as everyone knew had a bad habit of fishing with dynamite in the intervals of building log cabins and making speeches) – he'd still have signed it.

His job finished, Castang went to see Commissaire Peyrefitte.

Monsieur Peyrefitte was in a good mood. Castang had tidied up all that fish nonsense. He himself was in fine fettle. He'd tied the four black bastards to all sorts of weird things. What was more he'd found out who had written the anonymous letter denouncing them for the Sabine do. A butcher, another bastard, a fat white one this time, a French bastard. He'd had his eye on that one for some time. Suspicion of trafficking in animal carcasses condemned by the Health Department as unfit for human consumption. He had too many gold coins too. There wasn't much else you could pin on him, and the pains and penalties prescribed by law for these misdemeanours were notoriously inadequate. Didn't matter. Fellow had no notions of honour, by Spanish standards. Monsieur Peyrefitte didn't have to make a fool of himself writing out a lot of bullshit charge-sheets. He would just tell the fellow the Spaniards would turn him into shepherd's pie, and watch him shake like a jelly, and he, Peyrefitte, would laugh, yes, laugh.

He was, thus, sympathetic to Monsieur Castang's worries about this tiresome boy Gérard, whose name was legally Lipschitz but who didn't want to be Lipschitz. Not that one blamed him really: silly sort of name, I mean, say it slowly, several times.

'I like this. You, butcher, you're hamburger.'

'Petburger,' suggested Castang.

'What's petburger?'

'American for dogfood.'

'Good, good, I like that. Butcher, you're a carcass unfit for human consumption, and you've been condemned by the Health Department from Bilbao. And don't come to me saying you're being threatened, because I'll laugh.'

'Lovely,' said Castang. 'Now this horrible boy – I don't want to twist his tail without your advice and consent, since you're the senator round here.'

'Senator for Petburgville,' Mr Peyrefitte, much refreshed by his blinding wit.

'Problem is that the judge wants something cut and dried. Little point in handing him an inconclusive sort of situation that's liable to go dragging on for months. And those two terrible women; he doesn't want them to bother him.'

'Just so.'

'Can't see much point in reopening the technical dossier. I'm not very happy about that woodshed door, but nothing to make of it the technical end.'

'That would be my opinion too.'

'But the time might be ripe to look at the boy's teeth a bit, close to,' in another vague echo of Monsieur Delalande.

'Don't see that as much of a problem.'

'Got to get him away from those two women.'

'Well, he's at home. We get him down here.'

'Would you like to question him?' asked Castang tactfully.

'No no, don't want to hamper you.'

'As long then as it's in your presence.'

The long and the short of all this was a piece of paper delivered at home by a cop. Printed form: Monsieur such-and-such is urgently requested to present himself with all possible speed at the local commissariat. Motive: Affair Concerning Him. From curiosity or from fear, this piece of paper works like a dose of salts.

Gérard came tramping in with assurance. Peyrefitte had become a familiar figure, the man in charge of the pompous formalities in cases of violent and unexplained death. Lots of bits of paper, culminating in that civil-service masterpiece known as the Permission to Bury. This was just another of those. And as for that idiot PJ cop, who thought himself sophisticated, that was just a busybody. Running about pretending to be active, giving himself a countenance by assumed airs of importance (quite an accurate diagnosis: Castang would have quite agreed).

This was all nonsense: the judge had admitted as much to Ma. An enquiry into vagabondage and violence, a matter of statistics, worked up by the computer at the PJ regional office, back in the city.

This fellow Castang was just a clerk in an administration. Gérard was one himself: he knew all about them. One had to give the fellow rope enough to satisfy that mania for interference. And hope he'd hang his stupid self while at it.

They were all so damned dense! (Castang, after his fish orgy, would have agreed there, too.) None of them understood or ever would. His relationship with Sabine, for instance. He had loved her, in a special way. But one had to be objective, and avoid hypocrisies. It didn't stop him loving her to understand that she was a tedious old loony. And so cunning, and so tortuous. So typical of her to get hit on the head in a complicated fashion. I mean, face it. Not very nice, or pleasant, that she was hit on the head, or to think about that. But one mustn't get involved with her being hit on the head.

So like her; so exactly what one would expect – if that were possible, I mean… I mean creating a drama, causing trouble and delay. Trailing a long scarf with a fringe, that way of hers, getting it caught in the motor.

So that now the fuzz (just another pest exactly like the Sewerage) had to convince itself it was earning a living. Dragging him down here. As for the extreme urgency, he knew that line: meant you'd been riding a bicycle with a defective rear light.

One thing: he'd answered the bell, taken the message. Janet knew nothing about it: he'd handle this without interference from her. She had sometimes, especially when Ma was around, that blasted managerial manner inherited from Mumsiewums that really did send him flaming frenzied.

Just as he'd thought, there were the two clowns, heads together over some jackanapes paper, making faces at it. Just like that old clown Delalande. Wads of stuff in triplicate about a proposed chimney on top of a proposed garage next door to some peasant's piddling cottage.

'Sit down then,' said Castang, all friendly and cheery. 'Want to get this sorted out, since we've got to a stage where all this business can be explained and understood. There're one or two little things before I pass the dossier to the judge for his signature, that I'd like to have filled in.'

'Yes, I know. Since you haven't a hope of finding whoever broke in; so a lot more paperwork to explain why not.'

'That's about it,' amiably, 'and I see that you're a connoisseur of procedure. Good, then: to begin at the beginning, you recall that Madame Lipschitz came to see us some weeks ago. Felt uneasy: fears of funny noises or whatnot. She came to Monsieur Peyrefitte, who gave her some sound advice, and she came to us, and I paid her a call, just to see if there was anything I could add to that advice. You happened to drop in, as you remember.'

'A fine piece of hypocrisy,' said Gérard, 'and misleading. You posed as a dealer, and that gave me a notion this break-in was the work of a gang.'

'Very true. However, shortly afterwards Madame Lipschitz was indeed attacked, so there might have been something in her fears after all, however irrational we all thought them.'

'We've been over all this,' shrugging, impatient. 'Nothing in it, not even coincidence. She saw bogies everywhere. Does that mean she knew of a break-in, or suspected it? That's nonsensical.'

'Just setting it down in order. There's one point though which really is a coincidence. I recall your saying, when I met you on that occasion, that you'd dropped in because you couldn't find the key to the woodshed. I suppose you did find it? Where did it turn up finally?'

'Somewhere or other – I don't remember where. Sabine hid it and forgot the place: she was always doing things like that. What earthly importance has it?'

'Very little, I dare say. Now this is a photograph of a mark upon the wood of the door, showing that the shutter was forced with something like a crowbar; sort of thing one opens crates with. Now such an implement was actually in the woodshed. Which was locked. The point was thought unimportant. House-breakers carry these things sometimes, and householders often possess them, and so what all round. However, it's now an open question, since I observed that the key was sometimes in your mother's possession, sometimes in yours. The door might even have been open?'

'I suppose so,' sulkily enough. 'Nothing much in the shed to pinch. Sabine had a mania for going about locking things.'

'On this occasion,' writing, 'the shed was found locked. We now know that it was sometimes open, and that the key was left lying about. You agree?'

'What importance could it have?'

'A point inadequately cleared up; no more. Now your wife's statement – here it is. "I was actually on my way to the shed when I saw the broken shutter." She found the shed door locked – do you recall?'

'I never asked her,' blankly. 'She'd have said "Oh, Sabine again" and gone back for the key. And so what? – I don't get it.'

'A bar of this sort – mostly used to break up crates for kindling. Might it have been left outside?'

'Doesn't sound likely.'

'But possible, you'd agree. It now seems likely that this bar was used to force entry.'

The boy just went on looking blank. Castang veered away from it.

'We turn to another aspect.'

An expression now of patience, maintained with difficulty.

'It doesn't take long,' said Castang. 'You're aware that I've made a few brief enquiries around the town. Led me naturally enough to an agent who was negotiating with Madame

Lipschitz over the sale of some ground. This Monsieur Thonon was in fact there earlier in the evening. He tells me perfectly openly that he hoped to make a deal. You knew about this?'

'Vaguely. Sabine was always threatening to sell, or dickering with the idea.'

'Monsieur Thonon's version is that since your mother was elderly, albeit in good health, he had some verbal assurance from you as the heir that if you decided to sell the property you would employ him as agent – could you confirm that?'

'I don't know about confirm. Like I say, she had fantasies. I didn't take it seriously and wasn't interested.'

'No? It seems to me that you had a legitimate interest.'

'You don't understand. She changed her mind from one minute to the next, and used the idea as a sort of leverage on me when she wanted to pick a quarrel. He did approach me once with a sort of mutter about would I sell if it were up to me. I didn't give him any assurance – oh well, I might have said vaguely I'd consider it. It was all remote. Sabine wasn't ill or anything. She'd hinted at selling so often I was bored with the subject. Anyway, why should I commit myself?'

'That's reasonable,' said Castang, writing. 'To be quite fair to Monsieur Thonon, it would be a good thing to establish that he had no financial interest in your mother's death. So no promise or commitment from yourself?'

'Certainly not. Does he claim he has?'

'One wouldn't expect him to,' smiling.

'I don't know what Sabine may have told him,' said Gérard tartly. 'I'm not a lawyer, but I imagine that any agreement she might have come to would be cancelled by her death.'

'Doubtless,' bland. 'Well, that seems to dispose of the question of interest – you'd agree, Monsieur Peyrefitte? No point in pursuing that further.

'Good. One thing still. Remote, but an investigation could not neglect the possibility altogether. That of a quarrel or argument which might have turned to violence, on the night in question. The point was made formally, of course, at the beginning of the enquiry. Let's see,' shuffling through typed reports. 'Here we are. Had you perhaps had a quarrel? Negative. Or known of such? Negative. Had any reason to suppose such would be possible? Equally negative. And you'll confirm that now, of course, to myself, won't you?'

'Absolutely. I know of no quarrel. Sabine knew a lot of dotty people. I don't know whether any of them were dotty enough to break into the house,' sarcastically.

'Ah, wait now a sec. I thought we'd established that the house might never have been broken into at all.'

'What?' sounding astonished.

'The woodshed, while found locked, might have been open. One door open, so might another. Eh, Commissaire?'

'Puts a new complexion on things,' said that gentleman.

'But the marks... the broken shutter.' The boy didn't believe his ears.

'Oh, that's the easiest thing in the world to fake,' as though Castang had done it himself. 'Lock the door and pretend to reopen it by breaking. Woman is already dead. Object,' primly, 'is to mislead.'

'But my mother never left doors open, and always hooked the shutters at night.'

No longer 'Sabine'.

'Makes no difference. If we accept the possibility of one stratagem, another follows. Suppose somebody knocked, or made any noise that might awake her or induce her to open a door. Someone she knew, of course. She'd open without thinking. Now that brings up a few interesting hypotheses, am I wrong, Commissaire?'

'Absolutely right,' portentously.

'The first persons she'd open to, of course, would be the members of her own family.'

'You gone off your bloody rocker?' asked Gérard incredulously.

'Have I, Commissaire?'

'The prudent officer,' such as himself, say, 'could not neglect these possibilities.'

'But we... I – I could walk in at any time. You yourself saw that. I wouldn't go sneaking around in the middle of the night.'

'I did observe that your mother was troubled by what she described as a habit of lurking.'

'Oh,' contemptuous, 'that again. She saw eavesdroppers everywhere. She was one herself; that's why.'

'The point remains open, Monsieur Lipschitz. It is not hard to think of reasons, even innocent reasons, why you should walk around at night.'

'Look, I was in bed, asleep.'

'It may well be so. Just consider this. We suppose, say, that your mother decided, finally, to sell her property, a hypothesis born out by Monsieur Thonon's activities. He states, by the way, that she asked him to call upon her at night, and the implication is that she wished to talk with him unobserved. Let us assume that in fact you noticed this slightly surreptitious meeting. You could have thought this contrary to your interests. At that stage, a quarrel could break out. Terminating in violence. Such things have been known.'

The boy's lips had gone pale, throwing into relief the red-rimmed eyes and hanging limp hair.

'I don't give a damn what you hypothesise, or whatever name you give it. I just deny it. A lot of crap about where the wood-shed key was or wasn't. It's no evidence of anything. You're just trying to intimidate me.'

'That will be for Monsieur le Commissaire to decide.'

'Stop talking nonsense, my boy,' said Peyrefitte. 'It's being explained to you that you'd do well to think carefully whether there's anything to add to your previous statements. Concealment of relevant information from a judicial enquiry is a grave breach of the code. So's conspiracy.'

'A further point to keep in mind,' remarked Castang, 'is that even passive acquiescence in a criminal act disbars from inheritance. By the way, Commissaire, point of law there, what do you say? Even if it be deemed that insufficient proof exists to proceed against a person in the criminal court – now how does that go?'

'Redress may be sought in the civil court, or by constituting oneself as a civil party before the tribunal in case of criminal proceedings taken against a third party.' Loving it.

'What stands out a mile,' said Castang, 'is that the judge won't be satisfied. Not satisfied at all. He'll ask for further information. This is going to take months.'

And the two wiseacres nodded at one another.

'You'd better go home, Monsieur Lipschitz,' said Peyrefitte, 'and take counsel with yourself. I must request you to hold yourself at the judge's disposal, should he find questions to put to you. And let's see, you're an employee in public service: you'd better consider yourself suspended for the moment. No stigma on you: that can be called sick leave. I'll notify your superior.'

The boy sat like a bit of wet string. Castang shuffled his papers.

'Would you step into the next room, where your statement can be typed for your signature?'

'What's your opinion of all that?' asked Castang.

'Do no harm,' said Monsieur Peyrefitte. 'Make a fine hullabaloo at home around now. Puts a stop on the granny too: she was a thought too overbearing in her manner.'

'She'll be ringing up lawyers,' said Castang frivolously.

'Do you think there's anything in it at all?'

'I shouldn't think so. He was so utterly taken aback. But he's a pipsqueak. And the girl's a sly little bitch. And they bedevilled the old lady. Petty meannesses. I'll give you an example. She told me this one herself, not angrily, but infinitely saddened, and certainly embittered. Child needed a winter coat. The girl came sidling and whining to Sabine about being poor. Sabine took her to the town, sweet as peaches the whole way, and bought an expensive coat. Next week was the child's birthday, and Sabine wasn't invited for as much as a cup of coffee.

'That's typical. There's no doubt but that the old lady was seriously beginning to think of selling it all up. Maybe go off and live in a flat somewhere.'

'Wouldn't alter the inheritance.'

'No, but deprive them of a big profit, perhaps. There could well have been a row.'

'We can't establish that.'

'No. On present knowledge, can't establish a damn thing.'

'I wouldn't believe much in any conspiracy to do away with Sabine just to stop her selling the house,' said Peyrefitte sensibly.

'No more would I. I might believe though in some knowledge or suspicion, which they're afraid would compromise them. A conspiracy to keep quiet, to steer clear of trouble. And the old lady was a bit dotty. She might have promised money to someone, and they got to know. What the hell am I to tell the judge? Might not have too much trouble – old Mother Wilhems put his back up proper, telling him how much better things got arranged in Versailles. I wish I had something definite.'

'What about this Thonon?' asked Peyrefitte. 'He's not out in the sunshine either, seems to me. He might have been a party to some conspiracy.'

'It's what I've been thinking. He's a sympathetic fellow, but a weakish character. He's short of money. He could have been tempted into a fraud of some sort. Tried to enlist, maybe, the boy, into a fiddle over building permits.'

'The boy worked there, you mean. Some conspiracy which, maybe, Sabine got wind of?'

'I haven't a notion. But I'm seeing Thonon this evening. I gave him a shaking up. Told him I'd allow him a chance to tell me informally whatever he knows. Adopt the heavy menace if need be.'

'What was all that about the woodshed key?' a bit foggily.

'Nothing at all, very likely. When I was there last month, the boy was disagreeable to Sabine about it. Drew my attention. Oh well, at least we've got the affray-making fisherman. Something for the judge.'

'And for the press.'

'If only they were all that simple.'

Tired, not very happy, not contented about anything much, Castang had a shower, phoned his wife to say he still didn't know how long he would be away: she was not best pleased. He had supper in the Hotel Central. Soup, some fish, salad, fruit, all as tired and faded as he felt himself. The dank dining-room was silent, with a dozen commercial gentlemen assuaging appetite with sweaty cheese. A clatter of revelry from the café in front, souring him. Everybody having fun. Even the salesmen chalking up successes. Just him, mucking up everything, sitting there all clueless. Commissaire Peyrefitte might not be too worried, but Commissaire Richard would not be pleased at all. He had just succeeded in making everybody hostile, and hadn't done any useful work at all. No positive results.

Bugger. Bugger. Bugger.

CHAPTER TWENTY-SEVEN

'Green Gables' was to his mind a horrible house; a big shapeless suburban villa pretending to be a Norman manor house, with phoney pigeon-cotes all over the shop. But it was much pleasanter within. Thonon in a smoking-jacket thing, Martine looking joyless, Mamma, met for the first time, with blonde hair looking a bit tinted, who had been pretty when young, now faded and lined with anxiety. But putting on face, which he liked. Making this 'a social occasion'.

'Do come in. Let me take your coat. The nights are beginning to turn chilly now, aren't they? Do please make yourself comfortable. Pierrot, see to drinks, dear, won't you.'

A bourgeois interior: one or two signs of affluence, a few of simplicity. A piano for Martine to practise at as a child: some photographs. Children as sweet baby, chubby toddler, gawky adolescent. Some shelves of books which had been read, some records listened to, some pictures looked at. A nice interior, comfortable, a feeling of home, of loyalty and trust and a family square, proof against adversity. He was glad he'd come.

Was it a lake isle? Well, perhaps it was. Thonon and the wife both gave a feeling of coming from bourgeois backgrounds and not liking it much. Money was nice, but there were other things too. One ran after money, and got it too. Perhaps a bit of corner-cutting along the way. A bit dishonest. In face of an avaricious society, and a voracious government, who wasn't? Was he himself? They'd wanted, at least, to give the children something better than a set of bourgeois attitudes. Succeeded, too. Martine might be a silly girl, but she was poles away from that ghastly Janet.

No need to feel ashamed. He was a cop doing a job. Even very nice people committed crimes. Not necessarily homicide.

They sat waiting for him. Thonon pretending to be very casual and relaxed with his pipe. Mamma stiff and tense on the edge of a cushion. Martine fat and stodgy with the spot still threatening at the corner of her nose. Hair lustreless. Sadly less pretty than last night. He had to make a speech, damn it.

'When all this happened,' lamely, 'everybody thought it one of those sordid crimes. They often aren't solved at all. A trail of violence and destruction, which sometimes links up. A purse disappeared but there wasn't much in it. Not a real housebreaker. We look for other petty hold-ups and the like. Someone, on drugs maybe, looking for easy finance. We still are doing just this, in fact, but I'm not confident it'll yield much.

'It happened that Madame Lipschitz recently came to see us with a vague tale of disaster, and I tried to see what lay behind it: seemed banal enough. Neurotic fears of a sensitive elderly woman living alone, and a certain amount of unhappy family squabbling.

'And then she got killed, and I was left wondering whether something needed more explaining. An atmosphere of tension, and trouble. There were a good few things that seemed wrong, some pretty complex, psychological stuff going back in history, but I'm not a doctor, I'm a cop, and a cop tends to see things in a material sort of light. People squabble, and the root of it is generally money. I was interested, inevitably, to hear of a question of Madame Lipschitz selling her house.

'I come down to personalities now. Your account, Monsieur Thonon, sounded straightforward. I don't believe you killed anyone. It's too improbable, fundamentally idiotic.'

There was a melodramatic sigh, rather loud, from Martine, and Mamma was twisting her handkerchief in an agitated fashion, but she kept quiet.

'There's a possibility though of a conspiracy,' Castang went on. 'Raises two hypotheses, both tenable. That she was killed because she was an obstacle to some plot. Or, perhaps, she became aware of a plot, and tried or threatened to expose it.

'One thing stands out. If a conspiracy exists Monsieur Thonon appears a likely go-between, even if not an active party. Nobody denies that this property, carefully handled, could prove pretty valuable.

'A bit of fraudulent dealing, maybe involving corruption of a few officials, doesn't interest me much. I'm here for a homicide. That's not just Plonk hitting Plouc with a spanner: it's anyone sharing or possessing guilty knowledge about that spanner.

'I'm finished, pretty near. I'm saying that one can make a deal, shifty maybe, but nothing very bad. Then something horrible happens. One resolves to say nothing. Through fear of disgrace; for family reasons; a threat to income and professional position; fear maybe of financial loss. Possible threat of blackmail finally, aimed at any or all of these fears.

'I want to say that bargains are possible. Even with a judge. He'll often agree to close an eye to a racket, for the sake of solid evidence in a major case. I shouldn't say so, but one can make this bargain with a homicide cop. He doesn't have to be crooked.

'But withhold information from a cop, and he'll bear down all the harder. I can ask the judge for a warrant against some fellow, even without direct evidence, on what is called intimate conviction. I leave the arguments to lawyers. I can go home. I'd like that. And now what about it?'

Martine opened her mouth, angrily, but Thonon put a stop to her.

'Just let me. You give us all a refill.

All right, Castang, that's a sales pitch. I appreciate your fairness. I can see that you could have come down on me. You didn't try to make yourself publicity: I'm grateful.

'So you set up this meeting, and plainly you're waiting for a disclosure. And you offer me a large opportunity to minimise my role in some racket, grasp at all the means of protecting my family, and so on. Twist events to look as good as possible, blacken everyone else, finally admit the smallest possible part in what you call a conspiracy. Throw myself finally on your mercy, reckoning that you're a nice enough man, cop or no cop. Since you were nice, as I hear, to this big silly girl Martine.'

Who was now crying and gulping. Everybody looked at her kindly: no one said sharply to stop the snivel and go wash her face.

'She thought – like you – that I had guilty knowledge, and was stuck with it by trying to shield her mother and herself. And goes off to play detective. Please do try to forget about that, anyway. Her innocence is obvious.' Thonon sighed, and made a face at his pipe, which was tasting bitter: he threw it aside.

'The hell of it is that you're going to be disappointed and angry. I've nothing for you at all. No crime, no conspiracy, no go-between, no knowledge of anything whatever. I was working on the deal I told you of, with Madame Lipschitz and nobody else, and by an unlucky bit of timing I was there that evening.

'So now I'm vulnerable, and I feel pretty helpless. I wanted that deal, because as you guessed I need it. I don't know what I'd have done if anybody had proposed a scheme to me for making it easier. I can only say that nobody did. So there I am: hammer me. I've no credit with the judge, no protection, no nothing.

'All I can say is,' finishing his drink, looking around him, 'is that I'm indifferent to losing all this and even my livelihood, as long as my family believes me.'

Under stress, people wishing to be simple and natural have an unhappy knack of sounding false and melodramatic when they wish most to sound truthful.

'They do,' said the wife quietly from the corner, where she was sitting quietly with her legs tucked under her.

Martine blew her nose loudly.

'So says this soppy great idiot cow who started all this.'

'Moo,' said her mother. 'From one cow to another.'

Touching scene, thought Castang crossly. He'd like to take a stick to the whole pack. Lit a cigarette, instead.

'Well… Sisyphus and his stone… I'm not clever either. All right. Assume I accept what you say. I can't guarantee you the judge. The most I can do is ask for a bit more time. But help me then,' viciously. 'Christ upon a bicycle, do something. Don't confuse things any further.' He finished his drink, put the glass down softly, ragingly, longing to throw it at somebody.

'Listen,' said Thonon. 'If I may say so, you've been certain that if there was a deal I was in on it. Can't you try to establish whether there mightn't have been another deal, parallel, which I knew nothing about?'

Castang looked sour, and then grinned a bit.

'If you could establish that, you'd be off the hook. Can you?'

'No,' ruefully.

'Develop it a bit, just the same.'

'Nobody knew about that deal but me. I mean I worked it out bit by bit. Place hasn't been on the market in a hundred years. No architect or anything. Made a plan myself, and then went to see if there'd be planning permission; fellow in the local office called Delalande. Idea was mine and no one else's.'

'Tell me,' asked Castang. 'Since Sabine was in active health, and could easily last twenty years, why did you ever mention the deal to the son?'

'Well, to try and acquire an ally; I mean he'd benefit too, eventually. And in the end one couldn't keep it dark. He works in that planning office; hear all about it, sooner or later.'

'Yes, I see.'

'I think he did it himself.' The irrepressible Martine. 'Killed her, I mean.'

Castang smiled a little.

Tempting theory. Nothing to back it up, unfortunately. I'll be saying goodnight. I'll let you know what the judge decides – should that concern you,' dryly. 'We'll hope – is that the word? Leave it at that, yes?'

A funny thing happened, that evening.

The Hotel Central was full of people drinking, getting boastful, telling big stories. They'd told the boss off! Cut him down to size. If that's the way it is I just walk out, see? You should have seen his face! Climbed down smartish. And I got the rise, and I got it backdated three months, see?

Castang got his key, was walking up the stairs with a dull idea that bed would be welcome. He felt his jacket pulled. He was tired enough to be irritable; turned round with a snap.

Janet! Janet mad and out for blood.

'I want to talk to you!' Loud sharp voice making people turn round. She really was going to tell the boss off!

'Tomorrow. Commissaire's office.' This was no place for 'words' or even words.

'No!' Loudly. If he hadn't been jaded he might have made an effort. Been conciliatory, like the book says one always should.

'I've nothing to hear and less to say. Let go of my jacket.'

'Nothing to say!' in a yell. Damn these women. Shopkeepers, generations of experience at yelling in the street at yacking housewives. The whole damned pub had turned around now, licking its lips.

'Spends the day acting the Gestapo, making wild accusations against people, and now he's nothing to say, and now just listen to me, and I'll tell you and these people what you are, that's a bribed-up cop and a stupid little moron.'

One cop, stunned. Heard it all often, but wasn't expecting it from this quarter. The public was enjoying this. Not just the fuzz getting ripped off: facile and fickle sympathies could easily accumulate. He didn't feel happy, and was taking too much time wondering how to cope. And there came the landlord, a person sensitive to scandals on licensed premises, and wishful to keep on equable terms with cops.

'Now miss, quieten down.' And at Castang, 'Put a stop to it, then.'

Yes yes, put a stop. Call a cop, give her a slap, shout louder than she did. An idea, that… He was stuck on this stupid stairway, like a dancer at the Casino de Paris wiggling her ostrich-feather. She'd tackle him round the knees any second like a rugby-player.

He managed to step down. Better.

'Right! That's obstruction and resisting arrest. Probably drunk. Your mother will be more than pleased.' It would be quite easy to get into a rage too. Hardly any need to pretend. He didn't like this young woman, never had, small prospect that he would.

'Don't dare try and lay a finger on me,' standing her ground and glaring. An opening he was grateful for.

'Quick enough to lay hands on me though, aren't you. Making a scandal in public, stupid little girl. Out of here, or I'll call the wagon and have you flung in it.'

Didn't impress her as it should. Accustomed to the boy Gérard, who roared at her doubtless, and doubtless regretted it, rapidly.

'Out,' bellowed Castang. 'Finger on you – thrash your bottom for twopence.' A completely wrong and bad thing to say, but the crowd was not impressed by her. It was rather taken by this last suggestion: there was a snigger; a bold spirit cried, 'Turn her over then, copper.'

She felt she had lost ground, and lost her head with it. She swung a hand to slap him. Mistake: it effaced his stupidity. Screaming females are a problem: slappers aren't. He caught her wrist, turned her round, marched her to the door and slung her on to the pavement. Too humiliated for an immediate comeback.

Castang, one dignified re-entry.

'Any further disturbance,' with pompous chill, 'and there'll be an official complaint.' He looked for his key and found it in his hand.

Unwelcome publicity, and he hadn't come too well out of it. But why?… It was disturbing.

Was there reasoning behind it? Or none? Female going to bat for oppressed male? Or a manoeuvre? An effort to make him lose face? More than that? She was, he had thought, a cold little thing; a mechanical, clicking, efficient little mind like the tumblers of a lock.

He fell into bed. For the life of him he couldn't tell what she was up to.

CHAPTER TWENTY-EIGHT

Slept like a baby. Despite glug-glug noises, a bathtap vibrating like the *Great Eastern* under full steam, a lavatory-flush three inches from his bedhead. Shaved with a new blade, sailed into his coffee ready for anything, even a displeased judge of instruction.

Resolution was to be tried at once, because the press was on to him at last. On at him too: here it came, up horribly early, stumping over full of zeal, sitting down at his table.

Oh well, last night had been the brimming drop in the over-flowing cup: couldn't blame him.

'Inspector, you'll admit: I've been patient.'

'So have I. Keeping things that way, I hope.'

'Some things stand out, don't they? More coffee? Like your staying on, for instance. Abandoned the vagabond theory?'

'No. My associate can do that better in the city. Centralised services.'

'We'll leave that then, shall we? – not very interesting. I've got to do better today than the usual handout: that's fair, isn't it?'

'I'm going to the Palais. Nothing to get excited about.'

'What about last night?'

'Nothing about last night,' bald enough and bleak enough for the journalist to drop that one.

'Ready to make an arrest?'

'No.'

'You've been in and out of Thonon's office a few times.'

'No mystery. He was working on a real-estate deal. Late, because he works late. So an important witness in place and time.'

'A connection with your visit to the planning office?'

'That's right. Confirmed.'

'But he's a suspect?'

'Not at present, and that's all about him.'

'Okay. Staying much longer, you think?'

'Researches here and in the city should give results soon.'

'Oh come, not the old enigmatic line.'

'This kind of enquiry starts by looking simple, goes sometimes through a stage of appearing complex, generally ends up simple.'

'You're arousing curiosity. The public has the right to be informed.'

'I don't question it. But it's boring. Some details which aren't immediately verifiable, that's all.'

'The word is that you questioned the son at the commissariat yesterday, and were a bit rough.' Castang cursed the talkative clown in Peyrefitte's office. Tell him about that... 'There's a rumour of a lawyer flying down from Paris.' The fellow had seen Granny.

'People get excited about simple things. Question of how closely the house was really protected against a break-in.'

'The family seem to think you're treating them in a hostile manner.'

'The mere fact of PJ enquiry in a country district leads people to dramatise.'

'Oh all right, all right, the lips are sealed. A few personal questions, Inspector – you're from Paris, aren't you? How long have you been in the brigade, are you married, that sort of thing.'

'Yes and yes, seven years, I am as you see me.'

'I see what they mean about hostility.'

'I'd give you facts if I had any. Indiscretions would be against the public interest and I can't allow personalities. I'm sorry, but those are the judge's express orders.'

'An anecdote then – something comic for the readers.'

'I don't know any jokes, I'm feeble-minded. Tell me one and I'll see it an hour later in the bathroom.'

It wasn't good at all: the press would be vengeful. 'Plainly bewildered by the turn of events, Inspector Castang could find no words to express his discouragement. We are not alone, we believe, in voicing the opinion that a less tactless officer might achieve more positive results.' The judge wouldn't think him funny either.

The magistrate kept him waiting, and when Castang got in had his nose down in a pile of paper: burdens of office. Still, when he did look up the glance was more brisk than curt.

'You hear from your commissaire?'

'No sir,' hoping that Richard had not been traitorous.

'Well, I have, on the telephone this morning. He says that likely vagabonds are in short supply.'

'With respect, sir, the hypothesis hasn't got us very far.'

'Well now,' throwing his pen down after signing his name three times in rapid fire, 'you've been bending your mind elsewhere as it appears. I trust that you have respected my injunctions regarding tact with the local population?' Old bastard.

'I've done some questioning, yes.'

'You're going to ask me for an arrest warrant?' picking up the pen as though to sign it then and there.

'I doubt if you'd find sufficient grounds for that yet, sir.'

The judge assumed a disappointed air.

'After examining the witnesses you might decide that there was a case to answer. I'm not convinced, myself.'

'That is exactly what I told you to avoid: unsubstantiated suggestions about local people.'

Castang decided to nail his trousers to the mast.

'Madame Wilhems been making trouble?'

'She forced her way into my house last night. Really, Castang, what were you and Peyrefitte thinking of?'

'She hasn't anything to complain of. I don't suppose the boy killed anyone, and if he did we've no evidence. But there's something there they don't want known, and that's why the old dame is kicking up.'

'She certainly was obstreperous,' with feeling. The judge didn't know any jokes this morning either.

'I was only an ignorant provincial cop – a Paris lawyer would make hay of me. Bluff. She'd have to pay him; she'd hate that.'

'That the boy has guilty knowledge and she's aware of it – is that your line?'

'If she knew for sure we'd never have seen her. Interest brought her down, I feel sure. Financial interest. Thonon's been building an elaborate scheme for months. The boy certainly knew.'

'There are grounds against this boy, all right. Unstable, greedy, discontented with a life that is a dead end. Doesn't want just to be richer, but to be more important, acquire standing, be a success. He doesn't forgive Sabine for pulling him out of an orphanage; he feels cheated, and he's full of grievances. I don't see him as an assassin though. Nor his wife. I might be wrong.'

The judge brought his fingers down sharply with a crack upon the wood.

'Won't do. Floundering about in tendentious suppositions. If old lady Wilhems knew or even guessed at this she wouldn't act so confidently.'

'Greatest living expert in having her cake and eating it too,' said Castang disgustedly. 'She could probably persuade herself she didn't know. A great justifier. Filthy old woman.'

'Shopkeeper class,' said the judge indifferently. It was the remark, thought Castang, of a man who has inherited a secure income. A Barde-like remark.

'The girl and the granny could be Lady Macbeth, but I don't think we'd get anywhere with them either, in our present state of knowledge.'

'Now the man Thonon,' said the judge. 'I'm not far from supposing that an adequate case could be made out, there.'

'Thought as much myself, for a time.'

'But now?' frowning.

'He doesn't give a brilliant account of himself. He was over-anxious to conclude this housing deal, and he's probably guilty of technical offences. But killing anybody – I can't make it rhyme.'

The judge took his glasses off and arranged them nicely, parallel with the blotter; put his elbows on either side. Preliminary to a discourse.

'You know, Castang,' unexpectedly mildly, 'I'm aware that you're a competent officer. I can see that for myself, even without Richard's faith in you. You've done some homework, and you feel sure you've located a complicated affair, which you'd like to call a conspiracy. It may be so. But who killed this woman? We're no nearer to that. The crux of the affair is not who was arranging a property deal nor seeking to defraud the fiscal authority. You know this, but you shy away from it. We feel reasonably certain that she was killed in a panic and without real intent. None of your findings contradict that supposition. They confirm it. Whether there was housebreaking, or whether a conspiracy went wrong in some way – no one is likely to have planned deliberately to kill. That, as you put it, contains fundamental improbabilities.

'So we should be looking for a pattern of psychological collapse. This family group is greedy and selfish, as you suggest, but that is insufficient. There is ground, it appears to me, for hearing this Thonon, if only to get to the bottom of his manoeuvres.

'No doubt I was myself at fault; a little too hasty and superficial in my view at the start. I must act with prudence.

'Now you're anxious, plainly, to conclude this enquiry, and make a show of your undoubted talents, but that would be a wrong attitude, wouldn't it.

'I think in consequence, my dear Castang, that your role in this affair may be finished. Do not misunderstand me. I shall give you due and proper credit in whatever summary I make of my conclusions. I am in no sense seeking to minimise the value of your work.'

Castang said nothing: what was there to say? It was a polite enough way of being given the sack. He didn't suppose that it was the function of a judge of instruction to minister to policemen's self-esteem.

It was his first independent enquiry. First time he'd been out of Richard's shadow. He'd wanted to make a go of it. Alone.

It had made him over-anxious, yes. And a bit cocksure also. Been too quick to believe he could show the sleepy hicks a thing or two. No experience of small towns.

Not for the first time, he thought of the Rue d'Aboukir. Just a job, dirty and dangerous, but clear-cut. Castang quite an athletic boy, and fairly alert still in the reflexes, which were useful things when getting shot at. A mistake, though, to confuse them with grey matter.

From that to the sly little sorceries of backwoods property dealing – that Sabine's father had got rich at, and poor at – was a long way. Too long. Islands in lakes were expensive commodities, and sought-after. People would go a long way to get them.

His vanity had got a bit swollen, no doubt. The ambitions a bit too bounding. Richard, perhaps, had quite deliberately set a trap for him. Puncture Castang a little. Quite gently. Say to the judge, a bit obliquely, that perhaps there was no urgent need to clonk him over the ear with a crowbar. Nobody'd really wanted to clonk Sabine either. Not that hard, at least.

The judge wasn't a fool. A great mistake, a basic mistake, to have thought him a pompous, swollen ass in a piddling sub-prefecture town. Himself had been the ass.

Castang was wondering drearily how to acknowledge dismissal with grace when they were interrupted. The judge's clerk, an elderly effaced person with fuzz growing out of his ears, came in with flat-footed but silent movements – it was more than he himself had been able to manage – and whispered something to the magistrate.

'Very good.' He looked at Castang, and seemed to make his mind up. 'The good Madame Wilhems! She begins, I find, to exaggerate. Where are you going to, man?' as Castang got on his feet.

'I thought you'd finished with me, sir.'

'By no means. Change chairs – that's it. No, I want you present. We shall see. This is not an interrogation. We may get somewhere.'

He sat himself on the hard chair, kept for escorting cops, in the corner. The judge stood, practised in the look of insincere pleasure kept for boring guests at formal parties, people invited to discharge some small social obligation.

'Do come in, Madame. Be pleased to sit down.'

Granny had a social air too. Sub-prefect attending the annual banquet of the golf club. This vanished on seeing Castang. Really!

'I had thought that a conversation would be in confidence.'

'Assuredly.'

'In the presence of the police?'

The judge was armoured in blandness.

'Your visit, Madame, concerns the Lipschitz affair?'

'Among other things.'

'Inspector Castang is the investigating officer, duly appointed. His presence is proper. I need not add that he enjoys my confidence'

Even a formal, meaningless expression of loyalty can raise the flagging heart.

'I came to you last night with a private protest,' said Granny, biting it off between the strong brownish teeth as a housewife bites off a thread she is sewing with. 'I come this morning to ensure that my protest is officially registered.'

'I acknowledge your protest. I fear I cannot register it in the terms of our informal conversation.'

'What does this mean?'

'That I am bound, naturally, to take note of any complaint you see fit to lodge with me. I am bound, equally, to maintain a certain caution.'

'Monsieur le Juge! Are you telling me – seriously – that you entertain for a moment the ludicrous suspicions which this person has been good enough to voice?'

'I entertain no suspicions, nor suppositions. My duty is to probe, to weigh, to analyse.'

'This is not the tone,' vexed, 'of our last meeting.'

'As a private person receiving a lady,' glacial at the notion that he had not been properly brought up, 'I hope I observe all courtesies. The magistrate in his office is invested with public responsibilities.'

'Let us understand one another.'

'I am in possession, Madame, of the summary statement made by your son-in-law, made before Monsieur Castang here and in the presence of the Commissaire, as is perfectly proper.'

'Those insinuations are nothing short of an outrage and so I tell him to his face.'

'Natural that you should be a little upset. It can never be pleasant to have a homicide in the family.' Well-brought-up people didn't. Castang's jaw-muscles twitched a little.

'Nobody,' said Granny, 'could deplore this death more than myself and my family. I have every right to ask why these interrogations should be thought necessary.'

'That is simply answered. A house agent hoped to persuade Madame Lipschitz to part with a piece of ground. With the consent of the planning authorities this would prove a valuable speculation. It was necessary to him to establish whether obstacles to his plan existed, or whether an official voice might oppose the scheme. Your son-in-law worked in the bureau concerned. This young gentleman might be a stumbling-block, on personal grounds, to the man's scheme. And on the official level he might prove a valuable ally. At the least, a useful source of information, well in advance of any official decisions.'

It takes the high bourgeoisie, thought Castang still and small in his ringside seat, to sound so damned insulting in a polite voice.

'Furthermore,' in the magistrate's best furthermore tone, 'this agent by his admission did not possess the capital for a venture of this importance. He was unwilling to take a promoter into his confidence, being unwilling to share the spoils. Greed has been the undoing of many a bold plan. He relied upon his bank, but bankers require guarantees.'

Granny's face was stone. Knew all about property deals, and a great deal about banks.

'Alliances would be sought,' as bland as ever. 'Naturally, the parties tend to deny any agreement. The agent would be reticent, disclosing as little as possible of his profit in order to keep the price down. There is also the house itself. Being classified, it acquired added value, but by the same token it could not be demolished, altered, nor encroached upon. Technically, no doubt, it is all quite a ticklish piece of business. Involving tortuous schemes. Monsieur Castang properly restrains himself from suggesting that these have direct bearing upon the unhappy death of Madame Lipschitz. He is nonetheless right to find them relevant.'

'All this,' said Granny, flicking the podgy hard hand with its many rings, 'is in no sense established to my satisfaction. The machinations of an agent do not concern me. That any member of my family is involved is an unjustifiable conclusion. This man's tales may not be true. Let him be interrogated, as I strongly urged upon you last night. And let him be cross-examined. Then we shall see.'

'The contrary holds good as well,' said the judge curtly. 'As and when I decide may be necessary, I shall myself examine the parties. Including your daughter, should I see fit.'

Castang had heard of people going livid. He had never quite known what it meant. Now he thought he did. Nasty asphyxiated colour Granny had gone.

'And by what reasoning, Monsieur le Juge, can you show that my daughter could be concerned by these airy suppositions?'

'My dear lady, the wife is deemed in law to share her husband's fortunes. Even in a marriage contract stipulating separate holdings. This young man possesses great expectations, as our friend Dickens aptly puts it.'

'Piffle,' said Granny.

The judge was fond of the word himself, but not used to having it thrown at him. And Granny... a little too much in the habit of treating provincial notabilities with contempt.

'If that is the attitude you take,' she went on, 'I will instruct my solicitor to remind you of other examples where magistrates exceeded their powers.'

Castang feeling glee, but also alarm. A judge would now lose his temper.

'Even in the privacy of my office I will tolerate no innuendo against the serenity of justice.'

'I'll seek civil redress against defamation and attempt to defraud.'

'The Court will appraise, Madame, the Court will appraise.'

Was it this familiar, banal phrase that caused Granny to go too far?

'The Court would doubtless appraise also the spectacle of a judge of instruction using official powers to persecute tax-paying citizens while offering comfort and protection to his friends.'

Turkeycocks of both sexes stood and glared, Castang remaining invisible.

'Any further words you see fit to use,' said the judge ominously, 'will be taken down in writing. Insult towards a magistrate is sanctioned by the penal code.'

'From now on, Monsieur, my solicitor will speak for me.' And, with hauteur, stormed out.

The judge had a mildish, baldish, tufted sort of face, now dark red.

'You hear that, Castang, you hear that. In my own office. Is the daughter like this too?'

'Soft and quiet. She can yell too, if she sees any advantage in it.'

'They've a lot of money. One wonders what she saw in this obscure young man. Expectations even then, I dare say. We shall see. Damn it, I've never been spoken to like that.'

'Well sir, it remains for me to type my official report to you.'

'One moment, Castang, one moment... Suppose I were to leave you another twenty-four hours in which to conduct this matter as you see fit... Leaving you freedom of movement.'

'To pursue Thonon?'

'I'll leave your Thonon quiet for that period. You'll realise that I can't make it longer than that.'

'Yes sir,' said Castang.

'After all, Castang, to be frank with you... If Thonon persists in his attitude I'm not likely to get far. I confront him with this Lipschitz boy; naturally they deny association. I need something concrete, Castang. Now this man Delalande at the planning office... Got to be very careful there.'

'Yes sir,' stolidly.

'Witnesses as recalcitrant as these... I'll go this far to help you. Improper, naturally, to offer inducements. If this Thonon – I can say this much on behalf of the Procureur. If he's innocent of a crime, then a liberal view would be taken of plots and peccadilloes. He might even avoid getting charged as an accessory – if he coughs up. The proof is that I'm prepared to leave him in peace for another day. He might even succeed in remaining at liberty... That's not a small matter: make him realise that. Once he was in custody I would resist a legal application for bail, and the instruction would in likelihood be prolonged.'

'Yes sir.'

'I'm not having any nonsense from that horrible old woman... Very well, Castang.'

'Yes sir.'

Food for thought he'd got there, as the saying went. And a couple of things heard to make his ears prick.

As the saying went.

But he still wished he were back in the Rue d'Aboukir. There in that filthy back room, behind a courtyard full of rag-traders, for a few days, a petty gangster had had a lake isle. Peace had come dropping slow on to bales of rag snippets from the sweatshops, arranged in an oriental divan.

It had smelt good to him, of bean-flowers and sun on rain-moistened earth. The cops outside were far away. He had trusted a rag man who had sold him, in exchange for being himself left quiet.

Sabine refused to sell her house. She wanted to. She wanted to do that little bit more, to make the final sacrifice for that poor wretched boy who would always feel deprived, cheated, defrauded. And she just couldn't. The house was her lake isle and always had been.

And Thonon. He had his own house at last. He'd fought his way up from a nasty cramped little apartment to a bourgeois 'villa' that was grand. Everybody could see it was grand. Take a look; stables and everything. A horse for my daughter to ride. A hive for the honey-bee.

To hang on to that, Thonon would go pretty far. As far, maybe, as losing his head over a tiresome cranky old woman and banging her over hers?

It would be possible. Criminals had dreams, just like policemen. The small criminal like the small policeman dreamed of a country house, Vera's dearest wish.

The big criminal dreamed a rich man's dreams. A seafront place with a mooring for the boat. Sardinia maybe. The Florida Keys. Mexico.

Got it, too, as often as not.

But the little criminal, in the Rue d'Aboukir or a small country town, had the same pathetic lake isle as a policeman's retirement; humble, unambitious.

Rare enough for either to get there. Never enough money, finally. The breaker had to keep breaking: the cop thought hopelessly of being offered a really big bribe. Not just a free suit or a go at the girls, or cheap car repairs.

Something solid. What Thonon had, but which was so difficult to keep up: inflation, dear boy... What the Lipschitz boy saw under his hand, if only that tedious old Sabine would hurry up and die.

What Vincent had actually realised, only to see it poisoned slowly.

That little plot of land, to the man in a rented urban flat. But the owners were so greedy. Wanted cash, not promises. They had dreams too.

Wasn't that the whole trouble? Every little body in all Europe dreaming of the quiet, sleepy, bee-loud glade. Millions and millions of them. Some with a municipal caravan site. Some with a suburban quarter-acre and a barbecue set.

In Portugal, say? Take a look, my boy. Golf courses for the English, club-house and gin-and-tonic. Ex-army officer despising the ex-petty functionary; 'Bretherton the Sanitary Wallah,' who worked in a municipal sewerage department. Like Delalande.

Or a chateau in the Dordogne. All right, my boy, go try. You've saved up a few thousand there. You'll get a hut with no roof, but the water's not far away. You can install a bathroom. Just a question of bribing the local plumber. And the local building permits official.

Quiet is not in the market place, said Vera when in moods of Czech melancholic romanticism: rare, but they happened.

Quiet is in the heart. Ask Vera. Ask Sophie. Who, for a lake isle for her child, does a bit of quiet whoring on the side.

CHAPTER TWENTY-NINE

Nice big quiet sunny morning. Early still. The judge hadn't kept him long, whatever it seemed. And to finish his enquiry, he had twenty-four great big huge hours, like those big clouds, fluffy and a bit off-white, sheep needing washing. Be grateful for the sun; it won't last long. Windows and doors open everywhere, smells of eau-de-javel and furniture polish, house-wives snapping dusters as though they had a cage of tigers back there.

Smell of coffee. Sophie in a disreputable dressing-gown, and peculiar slippers with pink candyfloss pompoms. Coping with a dishevelled Martine, who had been crying and would start again when she'd finished the present tirade.

Sophie's greeting of Castang: a bit summary.

'You're not too popular in some quarters. But as I keep telling this girl, more to it than meets the eye. Politics, no doubt. We'd like now to hear a bit of news, before the midday television bulletin. Want some coffee?'

'Yes. Hardened up.'

She brought him a big cup, black with a slosh of calva added. He drank it straight off: it helped that sideways-drifting feeling.

'Better. I got a bumpy ride this morning from the judge. That's one calculated indiscretion. And all right, Mademoiselle Martine, nobody's getting arrested just yet. That's two.

'And I've done a bit of horsetrading, that's three. And that's all: professional etiquette forbids further.'

'And that leaves you where?' asked Sophie sarcastically.

'I've got to do better. I've little time. Start now.' Where, he wondered?

'Do better?' The girls stared at one another.

'But we've told you absolutely everything,' began Martine.

'I suppose you have. All you knew or thought, anyhow. Have to find something now that hasn't been thought of. Known of, maybe, but was thought unimportant.'

'There's not a single thing concealed, not a single thing. Like Papa told you last night, and I know he's telling the truth.'

'Look, Martine. I didn't know I'd find you here, but it's perhaps a good thing I did. I can say a few things to you in confidence – such as every time you open your mouth you put your foot in it. Have you learned that by now?'

'Yes.'

'Stop yapping and behave normally. That way you can help. You want to help? Well, when you can I'll let you know, okay?'

'You're a foul fucker.'

'Yes. I'll explain something. As a man, and understand, I don't myself think your father has committed crimes. It's surely obvious: if I thought it I'd have pulled him in. I had grounds enough. As a cop I have areas of doubt. If the doubt persists it will weigh against him. So buzz off now: I want to talk to Sophie. I want you to go to the office, quite normally and not all red-eyed, and tell your father to come and join me here for lunch. I don't want to go to the Place d'Armes: press is hanging about there. And go home then and read a book. I'm doing what I can.'

'Very well,' icily, being adult. Left all dignified: the two others had to grin.

'And what in God's name do you want from me?' asked Sophie.

'Lunch for me and Popaul all discreet in the corner there.'

'Very well. What else?'

'Gossip. Pillow talk.'

'So?' guarded.

'I'll be very frank.'

'I ask nothing better.'

'I'm in a hell of a difficult position. I heard a scrap of gossip, let's call it, at the Palais this morning. Can't verify it with the judge, or his pals: or the local cops much: compromising. Nor Thonon, though he said something that matches it. Tampering with a witness. His version of events is unreliable: I needn't explain.'

'He'd seize on anything to take pressure off him?'

'Right, my girl.'

'So you come to me. For pillow talk.'

'Right, my girl.'

'And you trust me not to give you away. If it could compromise others it could compromise you too.'

'Right, girl.'

'How much trouble is Thonon in? Really in?'

'You're asking something you know a cop won't tell you.'

'All right. You're discreet. I am too; I bloody well have to be. You mean pillow talk from the judge or the commissaire. No. I don't know them. Have they...? – no, they haven't. Peyrefitte is straight enough with me. He leaves me alone. In return, as you guess without too much bother, I inform, on occasion. But anything shady about him? – no, I don't know. Fair enough?'

'The judge?'

'No. Nor his friends. They don't... frequent me.'

'All right,' said Castang. 'Thonon's in trouble as long as his affair's not cleared up. Not big legal trouble – there's no proof against him, and small chance of getting any. More like golf club trouble. Everybody will believe him guilty. And the typical mentality: you do a few shady tricks, and nobody minds. But get caught, and the whole club starts saying they knew all along that there was something fishy about that fellow.'

'So as long as it's unproved it's him.'

'Correct.'

'I'll do what I can.'

'A suggestion got made that a local notable did something outside the law, and that the judge, to oblige a pal, kind of took no notice.'

'But that's an old story – you mean the mayor's parking lot.'

'No no. That was public like you say. Even in the Paris papers. This would be something private. A favour done. Not generally known. Known to you, maybe, but thought part of the usual small-town act, and shrugged at; half-forgotten.'

'This notable of yours got a name?'

'No – a guess. The judge is quoting Dickens, but hasn't ever read him. Our pal Barde, maybe.'

'You asked about him before.'

'Just that I'd met him and was interested in a separate opinion. Now I want to look closer.'

'I told you my opinion. Not high. I haven't anything to add to it. I think he's a stinker, but that's not evidence.'

'You got any ideas about where I could learn more?'

'A cop wanting information goes to another cop.'

'I told you – that's liable to embarrass two cops.'

'I don't think so. I think Peyrefitte's straight enough. I think maybe if he'd been mixed up in some dirty deal like that – well, I think I'd have heard about it.'

'Thanks,' said Castang.

* * *

Monsieur Peyrefitte, not one of these damn zealous cops who run about the shop, was sitting placid in his office. Seemed happy.

'Oho,' just jovially enough, 'what pigeons have you been fluttering?'

'Well, I lost a lot of feathers.'

'He was on the phone. Wants the technical dossier reopened and checked. Don't know what you've been up to but I hope,' a little too casually, 'that we'll get let in on it.'

'What I came for,' said Castang innocently. 'Nothing to worry about for a start; that's just a show of zeal.'

'He's worried though. Too many presumptions and none of them any good.'

'He's not a bit pleased with me,' making a face, 'but he's given me a bit more time. What I'm to do with it is something else again. Fancy a drink? I've got a bit of gossip.'

Whetted, Monsieur Peyrefitte led the way to the pub.

'Morning Ernest. Two pastis then; make them good and firm... Well, what's your gossip?'

'You know a man called Barde? Like officially, I was thinking of, more than socially.'

'You're interested?'

'Tangentially. There was a thing which puzzled me, and I wondered whether we owed him any favours – for instance. After all, I don't live here.'

'No... on the whole, no... Personally, that is. If you were thinking, might he be a friend of mine and might that be a bother to you, no need to worry.'

'You know how it sometimes happens. Like Ernest might be making his own pastis, but one wouldn't really want to drop on him, because his is better than most.'

'I wish I did,' said the barman. 'A bit more ice?'

'I've enough to skate on.' Monsieur Peyrefitte rattled his blocks and Ernest withdrew, tactfully.

'He has enough to skate on,' said Peyrefitte. 'We had him once on a morals charge.'

'Ah?'

'Oh, nothing much. He beat a girl up. Just a bar-girl, you understand. Poor moral character. Not a local. We moved her on – she didn't really feel at home here. It didn't amount to much. But the girl complained.

'I asked Monsieur Barde to come and see me, you know? Give him a chance to explain, so to speak? Walked into the office like I was the poste restante. A gentleman, you see. Shakes hands with the tips of his fingers. I wasn't all that happy, because the girl needed a bit of treatment in the hospital, and the doctor put a report in. But Monsieur Barde didn't think it very important. He's been to the right school, you see. And sure enough, the Proc didn't think it worth a fuss. Said the girl was asking for trouble, and was lucky not to have charges laid against her. So he thought he wouldn't press it either way. But he'd be happier not to hear of her any further.'

'That's more or less what I expected,' said Castang slowly.

'One scrap of gossip deserves another.'

'Thonon, these two Lipschitz kids, what have we on any of them? The whole central problem's not touched. We're bouncing off it all the time.

'My gossip – oh, just a thing Thonon said. About Barde dabbling in estate deals. Turn himself a penny, under the commission a professional would charge. "I'm just an honest broker". A kickback on the price, and nobody knows anything about it.'

'It's pretty difficult to prove.'

'Yes. Thonon felt a bit bitter about that. And no estate agent would make a complaint. Even if he did, it would be liable not to stick. Unless one had irrefutable evidence.'

'Are you thinking...? Man – that's pretty tenuous.'

'Yes, but it would fit. Thonon had his little personal scheme, and kept quiet about it. Slipping over to see old lady Lipschitz late at night, and so on. Possibly in collusion with the children. Now we get this scrap of information that Barde liked to get into that sort of act. It's admitted that he knew the house, knew Sabine in the old days. It isn't impossible that he should have cooked up a scheme of his own.'

'No,' said Peyrefitte, 'but do you see yourself going to the judge with a rambling supposition like that?'

'He'd quote Dickens at me.'

'And as for finding any evidence...'

'I'm quite interested in this morals charge of yours,' said Castang. 'Ernest... Two more of the same.'

CHAPTER THIRTY

Martine had run her errand; Thonon came to lunch. Little help, though. The man was limp and apathetic, and what juice there was soon squeezed. Oh, all right, he might have suborned the Lipschitz boy a little bit. To make sure there was no trouble with the building permit office. Nothing illegal: just keeping the dossier at the top of the heap and ensuring that all old Delalande's scruples were respected. His plan had been quite straightforward and plain-sailing. Get a road run in at the back of that big garden. Water, electricity, drains, were at the corner. You could get four nice houses there. He would pay the boy a commission, and in return he would get the exclusive agency on the house after Sabine's death. But there was nothing on paper. Granny's gang could deny everything.

Well, yes, he had been trying to get Sabine to agree to sell the house earlier. He supposed it did look bad. Maybe there was a motive there for suppressing her. But he hadn't killed anyone. Not that it made any odds; he could see that he was cast for the part.

What was that? Barde? He wouldn't make a deal with Barde not if he were down to his last penny. Hadn't known anyhow that Barde was in any degree friendly with old Sabine. They could charge him now with anything they liked. He just didn't give a damn any more.

To satisfy Martine's appetite for intrigue was not difficult. She made him a cup of coffee at 'Green Gables' and kept an obedient lookout by the stables. When she reported that Monsieur Barde – thank heaven for a man of habit – had sallied out upon his afternoon digestive promenade, it was not too difficult to slip across. None of this was all that difficult. Important that the press know nothing about it. Important to get some official cover, and Commissaire Peyrefitte hadn't been very keen, but... As for Sophie, she was safe enough.

It was dubious whether Commissaire Richard would have allowed such goings on. A sophisticated person, he would have asked what Castang thought this was – a Mozart opera?

Castang had a notion that the maid was the key to the intrigue. All right. He knew nothing about Mozart operas. If anybody had enlightened him he would have said horrified that witty, intelligent girls like Susanna or Despina wouldn't do at all. What he wanted was a thoroughly silly and tiresome girl, whose own liking for intrigue creates trouble for everyone. Zerlina, at a pinch. Richard just might have been sufficiently entertained to let him try. Monsieur Peyrefitte had not been so much shocked as sceptical.

'And if it doesn't work?'

'Then nobody will ever hear anything about it,' with a confidence Castang wasn't feeling. 'She'll keep quiet, that's for sure.'

He didn't have trouble with his own role. Winked at the pretty parlour-maid: coarse fellow.

'His nibs in?'

'Touring the domain – be back in an hour.'

'Not that important – just a gossip. Just as soon chat to you. Where's your old biddy?'

'Having her siesta,' giggling. 'Is that all you do – gossip?'

'Gets a bit dull sometimes – you know: all work, no play. You're much in the same boat, no? Get bored sometimes?'

'Oh, I play too, from time to time.'

'Get out in the evenings?'

'What d'you think – that I'm a slave or something? Whenever I want.'

'It's a dull town, this. What about a drink, after hours? Bite to eat, maybe?'

She shook her head.

'Town full of peekers and gabby mouths. People gossip!'

'No sweat. I know a little place, on the ramparts. Nobody there, and the woman there knows how to keep quiet. I have to be careful too!'

'I might.'

'This evening?'

'Well… I've a transport problem.'

'Pick you up. Not here, of course. Bit along the road. Eight be all right? – when does his nibs have supper?'

'He ought to be fixed with his coffee by then,' giggling.

'Give him my love – or no, on second thoughts, not.'

There you are! And the fuss Peyrefitte had made! He sloped off, mighty jaunty. There'd been a time when policemen only approached bourgeois houses by the tradesmen's entrance… And they still should!

Peyrefitte had wanted to bring her down to the commissariat on some stupid pretext, but that, he had said, would only make her obstinate. She'd tell Barde! This was worth trying, surely.

And Peyrefitte had started to laugh. He was a reasonable man. A bit staggered by the obscene ideas the PJ got in its head. Castang had been airy, as though he did such things all the time.

The parallel police, you know. Come with a tale to the concierge that the electric wiring needs fixing, and slap microphones behind the skirting board.

Sophie had been rehearsed. She wasn't worried. Not with two policemen to cover her. And as Monsieur Peyrefitte said soothingly, in small towns there were things too, to which one learned to turn a blind eye. Lord Nelson. 'I can't see any signals.'

Castang didn't feel like Lord Nelson. He was a little smelly copper, doing a smelly little job. But he did want to make a success of his first independent enquiry.

CHAPTER THIRTY-ONE

Parked along the road at night, very much the suburban adulterer, he had time to feel frightened, despondent and ashamed of himself. But at only twenty past eight she popped along, smelling very strongly of Balmain. A scent for bourgeois young girls, that, like Martine. Not inappropriate; it had been Martine's youthful romanticism that gave him this idea in the first place.

'Told his nibs I was going to the movie.'

'That what you generally do?'

'What I generally tell him!' For a moment, Castang felt sorry for Barde. He was genuinely attached to this girl.

'Is he jealous?'

'He pretends to be, sometimes.'

'What's your name?'

'Clotilde.'

'No, the real name.'

'Odile.'

Really the chief worry was the expense account. Police comptrollers always thought you should do this kind of thing

233

fuelled by Coca-Cola. Whereas plainly only champagne would do the job. Damn the girl though; she'd hollow bones!

She wasn't, whatever Vera might have thought, unsympathetic. Neither as stupid nor as cold-blooded as one might imagine, superficially. Castang thought her rather nice.

Perhaps she'd learned a lot from Barde. Why not? He wasn't a stupid person. In fact the more he heard the more he liked Barde!

It was as though she knew perfectly that this was just another role given her to play. She could play it well. When they gave her more like it she wouldn't object to being typecast. It was a good living. She had a comfortable life, but she'd grown a bit tired of it. Here she was being given variety, champagne, a good laugh, and a pleasant sense of slightly illegal adventure.

She'd heard the cops were crooked bastards. Didn't care! But beneath a hardish surface she was not a horrid little girl. She had an honest loyalty to Barde that he liked. She would be capable of kindness, spontaneity, generosity. She stayed with Barde, perhaps, because the man gave her lavish presents. But she stuck up for him. Castang felt sorry for her, and not only because she was an instrument of treachery.

'Must be boring.'

'What work isn't? He's not mean, you know. And he's not dull. We play lots of games – not what you think! But chess, and "Go" – I've got quite good. And we've got a film projector, and lots of old films, and we turn the sound down, and he does Bogart and I do Bacall. We act bits of plays, too. It's just that it's nice to have a change.'

He had to stop himself finding it pathetic.

'How long d'you think you can keep it up?'

'I've been thinking of a job in the city, but I'm not a prostitute, you know.'

'I'm not pushing you.'

'Got that gleam in your eye. I'm not a complete fool. His nibs at the start didn't understand – started telling crackly stories and showing me photos. I'm wise to people who tell one they can get you a spot on the television.'

Get her another drink you fool.

'It's all right here,' with approval at Sophie whisking around in her quick impersonal shuffle. 'She's all right too. Doesn't come all smarmy over you trying to push her old oysters or whatever... You aren't mean either,' as he filled her glass from the second bottle. So much for Coca-Cola seductions!

'You get the geezer yet?' suddenly, '– the old dear who got broke in on? That stuff in the paper is all balls, isn't it? I knew you were a cop d'rectly I laid eyes on you... His nibs has burglar alarms up to here. He's got nice things. A Modigliani – don't see anything in it myself. Worth a lot though.'

'It's all a bit of a tangle.'

'I know – some fiddle over the property! Fishy deal fried by that agent – he lives along the road from us. Thinks himself grand. Got a toffee-nosed daughter on a horse. Thinks she doesn't have to earn a living. Students! They all think they're wonderful.'

'I want to get off duty – not back on.'

'All right, I get it; no questions no lies. Oh well, I couldn't care less. All the same to me.'

Castang poured himself another glass and drank to this not being true. Any more red herrings, and he would find himself saying it to Richard in brave tones over a farewell drink.

'No, I don't want soufflé – get them at home too often. Old Mother Hubbard's a terrific cook, say that for her. Sour old cow though – won't ever show me how. As though I cared – chocolate profiteroles, please.'

'And with your coffee?' asked Sophie blandly.

'A cointreau,' largely. Didn't really want it, but it was nice having it served one. She wouldn't be allowed to sit at the table with Barde. The old housekeeper wasn't interested in beds, but was fussy about who put their knees under the table. Not the girl's place!

'I've got to be in by midnight,' she said suddenly. 'I've a key but after then the safety bar goes up and there'd be a right fuss.'

'Let's go upstairs then.'

'Here? So!'

'She has a couple of rooms.'

'I get it. Trust the cops!' She downed the cointreau and patted her stomach in a childish way. 'Good. I enjoyed that. You're not cheap, anyhow.'

Castang did feel cheap. Back in the pub over a pastis or three it had seemed like a big greasy laugh. A matter of pillow talk! And if necessary Mr Peyrefitte making a stern Victorian entrance like Mr Barrett of Wimpole Street.

Despite plenty of champagne he felt a lot less confident now.

'Yippee!' bouncing playfully on the bed, kicking her well-shaped legs in the air, bicycling in a carefree way.

'You share the room with him, or what?'

'You're interested in him, aren't you! Jealous?'

'Just finishing my cigar.'

She didn't mind chatterboxing. It wasn't hard to get out of her what he wanted. Basically, that she couldn't give Barde an alibi, and nor could anyone else.

She had got undressed by this time, and was all round-eyed in bed, much like Miss Carmen Sternwood in similar circumstances. One half expected her to suck her thumb and say, 'Clotilde likes you a lot.'

He had got as far as undoing his tie and looking dissipated. He grinned at her, put his cigar out in the ashtray, went to the door and said, 'Commissaire,' in a quiet voice. She gave a yell and disappeared under the bedclothes.

'Now my girl,' said Peyrefitte in his official voice, 'no need to get in a state. Not going to hammer you if you're sensible.'

'Work before play, that's all,' said Castang amiably.

'Cheating whore.'

'Not that bad. We're after a gang of burglars, you know. And what you've told me,' in a deep impressive voice, 'leads us to believe they'll try to break into your house. So no time to lose. You can hop out and get dressed.'

'Ooh – you mean tonight?'

'So we are led to believe,' said Peyrefitte portentously. 'Oh all right, you can take your things and dress in the bathroom. And no nonsense. Don't worry – we'll say nothing to Monsieur Barde – as long as you behave yourself.'

'And as long as you go on telling the truth. Make sure of that. Go on, hop it. We'll take you back in the car And you needn't worry – we won't tell him about your adventures.'

In the little room, there was a short police conference.

'As long as he lets us in,' said Peyrefitte dubiously. 'You've still nothing on him. Just that he could have been out that night – proves nothing.'

'He'll let us in,' said Castang. 'Curiosity.'

'He'd better.' Policemen cannot just stroll in, after sunset, upon private premises.

'At all costs, Castang, we mustn't give cause for complaint.'

'Oh, she won't talk. That was the whole point, no?'

'But he'll know at once we've questioned this girl.'

'All the more reason to do it now. Give him time to sleep on it and he'll have a tale.'

'I'll back you up as far as I can,' gloomily.

Sophie let them out, wooden-faced. The girl was snivelling slightly, but only to show everyone that she felt hard done-by.

CHAPTER THIRTY-TWO

They left the car outside. The girl had a key to the wicket-gate in the wall. Monsieur Barde, as they had learned, liked to see to security at night, and it was he who opened the door in a dressing-gown, a book in his hand. He looked taken aback, but so would anybody, finding cops at the door, at midnight.

'Why, Commissaire. And Monsieur Er, too.' He shook a finger, playfully, at the girl. 'What have you been up to then, you little rascal? Getting picked up by the cops? Off with you, then. But to what, gentlemen, do I owe this pleasure?'

'My fault, I'm afraid,' said Castang apologetically. 'As you might recall, I've been a bit bothered about housebreakers here in the district.' The girl had gone running up the stairs, only too pleased to put off the awkward questions.

'At this hour of the night?' humorously.

'We thought we'd better slip along for a word to the wise, you know. I'm not quite sure whether your girl there may not have been a bit indiscreet – oh, quite unwittingly – about your security arrangements. And knowing you've some valuable stuff here...'

'Mm, good of you. But it can wait till morning, surely?'

The two policemen put on important, compressed-lip expressions.

'What's this girl been doing then? There's some threat against my property?'

'There could be a threat. I notice you stay up to let her in, which is wise. And she tells me you've a safety bar. But the windows?'

'Alarms on them all... Good heavens... I suppose you'd better come in, then... I'm sorry if I appear hesitant. It is rather late though. Seeing however that you've taken this trouble. And brought back that silly child – what has she been up to?'

Ouf. They were in.

'Been getting into bad company?' Castang appreciated this description of himself.

'That might be the opinion of some. Er – could anybody bribe her, perhaps, to turn the alarms off?'

'Improbable. They'd have to know, hm, about my domestic affairs.'

'Er – quite.'

'Well... we're men of the world, I hope.'

'We haven't questioned her in detail. Preferred to come to you. More discreet.'

'Speak out then, man. I won't be offended.'

'We confirm that you always lock up yourself.'

'My housekeeper grows old, and more than a little deaf.'

'So you wait up for the girl on her evenings out? Quite. And you are sometimes yourself out at night. Sorry to appear inquisitive. But if someone tried to take advantage of your absences?'

'An occasional bridge-party. I'm rarely later than one. What, if I may ask, is your question based upon?'

'Not at all. On the night, you see, that a housebreaker, with fatal consequences to Madame Lipschitz –'

'I understood,' cutting in, 'that this theory had been abandoned. The man Thonon...'

'As you probably know, we sometimes encourage publication of information with a certain purpose. Not necessarily false, you do see, but with perhaps undue emphasis. To give a malefactor a sense of confidence.'

'I see, I see. And now are you telling me that somebody has been tampering with my parlour-maid? To learn how my house is protected?'

'Trying, perhaps, to check up on your movements.' Peyrefitte, Castang had time to notice, was looking a bit less guilty.

'For instance, Monsieur Barde, on the night in question – you weren't out that evening?'

'No.'

'Sorry to appear so inquisitive. But it might help us to identify a malefactor. You do see?'

'Quite. I think, since we're chatting, I'll have a nightcap. Care for one?'

'Not just now.'

'So you think after all that this burglar, or is it a gang, comes from round here?' Barde was at the drinks table, his back to them.

'We think that possible,' said Monsieur Peyrefitte.

Barde took a generous swallow.

'I wonder why,' turning round.

'Oh,' said Castang, lighting a match for Barde's cigar, waving it gently to get a good even flame, 'someone with local knowledge... Very boring for you, all these questions. But we have to confirm it. Can I go on?' humbly.

'If it can serve justice, Inspector,' handsomely, 'by all means – I'm a man of the world. A little amorous adventure...'

'You've never been married, Monsieur Barde?'

'Once,' merrily. ' "It was not ecstasy but it was comfort" as Flora Finching puts it – *Little Dorrit*.' Oh dear, Dickens again.

'You're a sensible man, Monsieur Barde.'

'Splendid,' merrily. 'The very words of Inspector Bucket.'

'Do you engage in business at all?'

'I've no gift for it. The fluctuations of the Bourse,' waving a hand. How vulgar the Bourse did sound. 'I prefer art.'

'And you're a landed proprietor, of course. Sounds a bit old-fashioned: riding round your land, collecting rents and such. I ought to say independent means.'

'Come now,' indulgent to these clumsinesses, 'plenty of people invest in property.'

'Oh yes, quite. I meant only it sounds sort of feudal, with servants and all.'

'My housekeeper has been with me many years. As for the girl who excites your curiosity – what difference is there to a businessman's secretary?'

'Oh, quite.'

'I should be interested in how you came to make her acquaintance. If I understand, she was offered some sort of bribe?'

'I rather think she was pumped, concerning your way of life.'

'Deplorable. By whom?'

'Someone I've had an eye on for some time,' at which Monsieur Peyrefitte lowered his nose into a handkerchief.

'Thonon, doubtless. I hope you've got him in custody. Been sailing close to the law, that fellow. History of malpractice there.'

'We were talking about land – or revenues from land.'

'I didn't grasp the relevance. Not sure I do now.'

'Oh, we think it might even be crucial.'

'In what way?' helping himself to another drink. 'Sure you won't change your mind?'

'No thanks. Thonon, you see. He tells me you've sold quite large amounts of land – some through his agency.'

'That goes back quite a few years. I still don't see…'

'You mentioned malpractice: I'm curious to discover the grounds for your suggestion.'

'You don't I hope hint that I was concerned?'

'By no means. But as a citizen, if you were aware of malpractice – shouldn't you have drawn Monsieur le Commissaire's attention?'

Peyrefitte who had adopted wooden immobility permitted himself a slight nod, like royalty acknowledging a curtsey.

'Well, I hadn't grounds for formal complaint. But if you've this man on a criminal charge there's no need to look at minor misdeeds in the past.'

'But I have to correct you, I'm afraid. We have no criminal charge at present against Monsieur Thonon.'

'Yes yes, very correct. But if I'm to believe what I hear...' Indulgently.

'If we hypothesise a criminal proceeding, the judge would certainly enquire into the background.'

'I hardly think the judge will consider my property transactions are relative to his enquiry.'

'We think though that Monsieur Thonon's dealings are central to the enquiry,' said Castang, courteously.

'You mean that he was trying to buy that house? And keeping it dark, hoping to make an illegal profit?'

'Ah, that's the trick he tried with you, is it?' sounding sympathetic.

'Well – since we've had the point raised, and to lay it at rest, yes, to be exact. He was careful not to go outside the law there – or I should have complained, naturally. But speculation – flagrant. I was stupid, I'm afraid. No building round here much in those days. Then the town ramparts got classified: no further building allowed inside them. Thonon got wind of it in advance. Bought land here as agricultural, and chopped it up for building. Got a permit to develop. That I call malpractice, even if legal.'

'Sharp perhaps. Yes, I understand. Naturally, now you are aware, you wouldn't sell without precautions.'

'I don't actually have much further interest round here. My father sold a lot. Farmers… it didn't bring much in.'

'So you don't actually own any land now?'

'You seem curious about my affairs. I realise, I mean, that you're investigating these deals of Thonon's, but this is unnecessarily exhaustive, no?'

'Oh, I must explain,' said Castang, all apology. 'I'm being indiscreet really, but after all, you being a friend of the judge's, that's not so terrible. You see, if there's any case against this man Thonon, it would rest upon his anxiety to conclude the affair. And that he might have been infuriated, do you follow, by the obstinacy or suspicion of an old woman. Your local knowledge is invaluable to us. Well, yes, if you're having another, then yes, if I may.'

'I suppose that by and large… that all right?… there might be something in that.'

'Just between us, Monsieur Barde, it's not evidence – of course – but would you say Thonon had been living beyond his means?'

Barde took a whack at his third. Castang at his first. Same marvellous whisky as before. Drink that stuff all night, and you'd just get a generous glow. Never become rancorous, would you?

Rhetorical question, that.

'Well, since you ask… Jumped-up fellow. Nouveau-riche villa. Green Gables!' with contempt. 'What could sound more suburban? Fellow must be mortgaged up to here! And the daughter on a horse! – what do people like that want with a horse? Social climbers!

'Must be pushed to keep it up. A scrap more? – come on, man, can't walk on one leg. But the fellow's a petty tradesman – Pumblechook. *Great Expectations*, you know.'

'To round it off – you'd have a pretty shrewd idea about what business he could do, around here?'

'Well, it's a fact; there is a shortage of good building land. Out in the villages the peasants hang on, to get better prices. Or from sheer damned obstinacy.'

'Ah, yes. And this Lipschitz property?'

'Well, say this for Thonon: he had a good eye. Damned great garden right there on the village square: been there hundreds of years, so nobody thought of it.'

'Improper to speak of personalities,' said Castang with official primness. 'To do so is the examining magistrate's function, as I'm sure you'll agree.'

'Oh, quite. I don't wish to appear malicious.'

'So we hypothesise – don't we, Commissaire?'

'We suppose the existence of a certain nameless person.'

'That's right.' Castang delighted with this priggish formula. 'A person whose habits are extravagant, not matched by his income. Resources limited to a house which may be mortgaged, and he may be in trouble with the fiscal authorities. What he has is local knowledge, skill as a dealer, an eye for good ground. So much seems clear enough.

'We don't speculate about dealings with the Lipschitz boy, because that's not established. He has, though, cultivated Madame Lipschitz, with an eye to a fruitful deal, which will restore his fortunes. So he may be getting pushed by creditors. He might too have had trouble with Madame. Perhaps she saw through his scheme. And, perhaps, there was a quarrel. Wounding words, or a threat of disclosure; we don't know. But a blow was struck which killed her.'

'I don't altogether follow,' said Barde, looking puzzled. 'What about these bandits you're on the track of?'

'To be sure,' said Castang, who had forgotten all about the bandits. 'But we run some danger of being misled here.' The Four Black Bastards came to his rescue. 'The Commissaire had unearthed a group concerned in several acts of violence, but they turned out innocent of this one. We must satisfy ourselves that the bandits aren't obscuring the possible criminal responsibility of our friend Mr X.

'If X struck this blow – he decides to mask the affair as a sordid crime. It's not difficult. Keys lie about here and there. It's a simple matter to lock the door and the shutter, to break them open from the outside, using the instrument found in the woodshed. Relock if need be the kitchen door, push the broken shutter to, and decamp.

'Well now, Commissaire, if we find someone fulfilling the conditions of this hypothesis, have we grounds for an arrest? Monsieur Barde, I must beg your pardon. We're keeping you up late, being indiscreet about police business.'

'No no; it's fascinating.'

'What would your opinion be, Monsieur Peyrefitte?'

'It could so be argued. Not an arrest, but grounds for detaining your hypothetical man and presenting him to the judge in the morning for interrogation. Fulfilling the legal requirements.'

'We'd better be going,' said Castang, licking a trickle from his glass. 'Just one observation. Looking at all this, one does rather conclude that our friend Thonon fits the bill – just between us here. Doesn't one?'

'Well, objectively,' said Barde, 'I suppose it does look rather overwhelming.'

'So that logically, if one found another person to fit the same set of conditions, the same would apply, wouldn't it?'

'I don't think I follow.'

'Well; yourself, for instance.'

There was a silence.

'I still don't follow,' stiffly.

'Put briefly, you fill the hypothetical outline determined. Which as you agree was reasonable and unexaggerated.'

'Monsieur le Commissaire, this is distasteful, but I must ask you to call your subordinate to order. The suggestion, however frivolous, is unpardonable.'

'Why?' asked Peyrefitte simply.

He had been an onlooker, sitting awkwardly in a chair too low and too soft, taking off his glasses to wipe them rather frequently. Castang understood that he was going to drive the engine from now on.

Barde remained standing, bulky and Roman in his Paisley silk dressing-gown. He took another cigar, plainly determined to keep his self-control.

'Because it is so patently ridiculous.'

'Monsieur Barde,' courteously, 'I have left the conduct of this interview to Monsieur Castang, because he is the officer charged with the enquiry. He's only technically my subordinate. But as you remind me I am an officer of law, with judicial powers and responsibilities.

'So far, this has been an informal conversation. Monsieur Castang has put it to you that logically you can be asked – and no, it's not ridiculous – to account for your actions on the night in question. I've just one further query. I'm obliged to say to you that it is not the continuation of a casual discussion, but may be the beginning of an interrogation in formal terms. Where were you that night, and can it be confirmed?'

'Now look, man,' irritably, 'I'm telling you that where I was is my affair and needs no confirming.'

'It would be a help if the parlour-maid could, and unfortunately she confirms that she can't.'

'How would you expect a silly little slut like that to remember a date weeks ago?'

A pity, thought Castang, that he can't show her the same loyalty that she had towards him.

'It isn't every day,' dryly, 'that we have a murder around here.'

'This is preposterous.'

'We have questioned her. She was not with you at the time. She remembers clearly that you left the house earlier. She is unable to state the hour of your return, since you yourself lock up. It is now for me to ask formally where you were between the hours of say twelve and two in the morning.'

'But you can't suggest that my movements have any bearing on the – on whatever happened over there.'

'I suggest nothing. I ask whether you can provide confirmation.'

'Let me get this straight. What idiotic suspicions do you two owls imagine you entertain?'

'Let's remain polite, shall we?'

'Surely you can see how exasperating this is. I was with her, of course. In bed if you want to labour the point.'

'There is then no point in pursuing this, since it is one word against another.'

'Are you putting this girl's tale forward as of equal value to my word?'

'Has she a motive for lying?'

'Very probably.'

'That may be the function of a court to determine.'

'I should like you to remember something, Peyrefitte, which is that the judge of instruction decides about courts. He might,' in a humorous, tolerant tone, 'have opinions which don't alto-gether coincide with your own about the credibility of witnesses.'

The policeman's features twitched into a very small smile. It might have translated as 'I thought it would come to that.'

Barde took a different view of the twitch. He had regained his self-possession.

'While I respect your zealous endeavours, too much zeal is sometimes the prelude to a fall from grace, shall I say?'

'Mmhm. The judge might take a dim view. Or the Procureur might feel that there were insufficient grounds?'

'That,' tipping the ash neatly off his cigar, 'seems to me worth consideration.'

'Such a situation,' colourless, 'is foreseen by the code of criminal procedure. A magistrate with personal acquaintance is bound to step down in favour of a colleague. There being no other judge of instruction attached to this tribunal, the affair will doubtless be transferred to the city.'

'But this is deplorable. You have no evidence whatsoever. This one point of doubt.'

'I am not satisfied, Monsieur Barde,' bleakly. 'I would like you to dress. I wish you to accompany us to the Commissariat, where Monsieur Castang will ask you to make a statement in the form of an interrogation.'

With an air of immense fatigue, he leaned back and put his glasses on.

'With the Commissaire's approval,' said Castang formally, 'I'm holding you overnight.'

Barde's large face sought to maintain a Roman calm. The large navy blue eyes stared stupidly. The hand came up and brushed vaguely at his moustache. The massive forehead under the thick hair – still more fair than grey – had a puzzled frown. The jaw twitched like a horse's flank when a fly settles on it.

'You startle me.'

They watched and said nothing. Looking guilty is no proof whatever that one is guilty. There was a long way to go.

'You take me aback.'

'We'd like to examine all this in closer detail. That's all.'

'I protest. This is late at night. I am tired. Your mixture of trickery and intimidation might succeed in showing me in a poor light, temporarily. It is meaningless. I warn you, I shall repudiate any admission wrung from me by such dubious methods.'

They both knew, then, that there was no mistake.

'There won't be any dubious methods, Monsieur Barde.'

Of course he'd repudiate it all, five times. Much good might it do him.

'You'd like to get dressed now. We'll accompany you, if you don't mind.'

'It won't stand up in law, I tell you.'

'All in good time,' said Castang. The very words and voice of Commissaire Richard.

CHAPTER THIRTY-THREE

At about four, yawning uncontrollably, he got a few hours' sleep. At eight-thirty, sunken but shaved, he drank some bitter coffee and told the press that the judge would give them all they needed for their next day's edition in his own good time.

At a quarter to nine he was walking jerkily up the steps of the Palace of Justice. His skin felt dry and harsh. Eyes watery. He had smoked too much. At five to nine he was using officialese. At nine the judge dropped his pen on his blotter and said, 'Shocking,' like an English governess in a Feydeau farce.

'He collapsed completely.'

'I am dismayed.'

'Peyrefitte was present throughout. The rules were strictly observed. He's sleeping now; we didn't finish till half past three. This is the basic statement, signed by him. Peyrefitte will interrogate him formally at midday, and have it typed up. But this is it, in essence. He was quite docile. Later, no doubt, with a lawyer, he'll repudiate. But it will all be confirmed, by interrogation of the girl.'

'You mean this maid?'

'No no, she played no part in any of this, save to abolish his alibi, which by the way she was quite formal about. No, the Lipschitz girl. Janet.'

'Barde was playing bridge with me earlier that evening. I'll be called upon to say at what time he left my house. I withdraw, thank God.'

'I think it will be found that she was the moving spirit in all this. She saw Barde's weaknesses, perhaps instinctively. She wouldn't have slept with him or anything. She might well have hinted that she would,' dryly. 'I ought to have guessed as soon as she made such a terrific row at my poking at the boy's teeth, which so outraged her virtue.'

'But her motive…'

'Simple plain money-hunger, I've no doubt. She'd go to any length just to squeeze the last drop from the inheritance. She must have heard something of Thonon's plan from her husband. Barde claims she approached him. More likely she noticed him hanging around Sabine, and thought she'd get a better deal than through Thonon.'

'And the boy?'

'The enquiry will show, but I'd guess he knew nothing. He did I think have a genuine love for the old lady.'

'Since Barde – good God! – accuses this girl of inciting him – I suppose I can give you a warrant for her. They'll go to the city under escort. I suppose there'll have to be a press conference.'

'It's only fair that Thonon should be cleared. His misfortune was in trying the same trick. For technical reasons, meaning the building permit, he chose the boy as auxiliary. Barde, more astutely, chose the girl – or she chose him. Who actually hit the old lady is for a jury to decide; can't say I envy them. Sabine must have seen through it and tried to chuck them both out, and threatened to make it all public. "I'll tell the PJ inspector" – all my fault really. I'll take a little bet that it was the girl who arranged things to look like a break-in. Barde wouldn't have known about the crowbar in the woodshed, and anyway he had lost his head completely.'

'But Castang...' It sounded a little pathetic.

'How the hell should I know? Sorry sir, that's just fatigue; I beg your pardon. But Barde was a soft touch. I don't mean just liking girls, but hard up. Self-indulgent person. His standing, prestige, comforts. A well-lined nest, and he couldn't bear to lose it. The girl I don't pretend to understand. But you've seen Mum! Girl was brought up accustomed to her own way, and having few scruples about how to get it. The boy is a feeble impressionable object. That attracted her perhaps. A violent turbulent personality, easy to manipulate. When anything went wrong, that was Sabine's fault. When she married him, at a guess, she saw the potential in that property. But the novelty wore off. Stuck in boring countryside, two small children; precious little fun. The boy not earning much, and she must have known or guessed that sooner or later he'd be out of a job. Delalande was looking for a pretext to let him go. But Sabine stayed in obstinate good health, and pathetically unwilling to let her beloved house go. Unaccountably awkward about allowing herself to be plundered. The boy shilly-shallied, but the girl determined to head off Thonon, and get her fingers on a nice lump of capital. So she brought Barde into play. Putty in those capable little hands. I'm only theorising, of course. Haven't talked to her. Don't much wish to.'

The judge nodded, bleakly.

'Very well, Castang. I understand, I suppose. You, at least. You were over-anxious. I understand from Richard that this is your first independent enquiry. You wanted too to get your hands on it quickly – am I right? And you've done some questionable things too. Well, I won't reproach you too much.'

'Barde! Mm: it'll shake the Proc.' A bit maliciously? 'They were at school together. All right; I'll see to the press.'

* * *

Money-hunger? Was that all? Surely lake isles entered into it too. What wouldn't people do, to acquire them, defend them, fight for their dreams of peace and security!

Everybody was after one, starting with a small professional hold-up artist in the Rue d'Aboukir, who went after his with a gun.

These lake isles; they glowed in the mind. Long years painfully worked for. Persistent mirage needing money, money, money. Always slipping out of reach. What would one not do, to grab and hold the magic dream? Clutch it tight, hanging on, tooth and nail.

Anything. Yes. Murder.

Go back home. Quick as you can. To Richard and the job. To Vera and the flat. And be contented with both. Don't get led astray.

People have offered you some cosy little arrangements in the past. And you'd always wondered, if somebody offered a big enough bribe, how you'd handle it.

Well, now you know. The lake isle doesn't exist.

ABOUT THE AUTHOR

Nicolas Freeling (1927–2003) was a British crime novelist best known for the Van Der Valk detective series. After serving in the military and working as a hotel and restaurant cook throughout Europe, he began writing his first novel, *Love in Amsterdam*. Freeling's novel *King of the Rainy Country* received the Edgar Allan Poe Award from the Mystery Writers of America. Among his other literary awards are the Gold Dagger from the British Crime Writers Association and France's Grand Prix de Roman Policier.

THE HENRI CASTANG MYSTERIES

FROM OPEN ROAD MEDIA